The Corn
Whispers

Debbie Viggiano

ISBN 978-1542454414

www.debbieviggiano.com
http://debbieviggiano.blogspot.com/

Acknowledgements

There are a few people I'd like to thank for helping me with this book.

Firstly, my thanks to the lovely Jacqueline Steele Walkden for coming up with the fictitious village name of Lower Amblegate.

To the fabulous Rebecca Emin at Gingersnap Books who always assists so brilliantly with producing both kindle and paperback versions.

To Cathy Helms of Avalon Graphics for yet another terrific cover design.

To my family for putting up with me dropping out of the real world and retreating into one of fiction for hours at a time.

And finally, you, my wonderful reader, for buying this novel. I hope you enjoy!

For my family

Chapter One

My husband flung his arms around me. Suddenly I was being whirled round and round the kitchen. I gasped and gave a nervous giggle. There can't be many married couples who engage in a spot of Strictly Come Dancing early on a Tuesday morning in late April. But then again there aren't many married couples like us. Only yesterday my immediate neighbour, Alison, had caught Marcus and me on our doorstep. She'd been hurrying out of Number 3 about to embark on the school run just as I was waving Marcus off to work – or, rather, my husband was kissing me good-bye. Except his cursory brush against the edge of my mouth had swiftly slid to my lips and turned into a lingering kiss which almost immediately had become a full-blown hungry devouring of my mouth.

'Mmm, mmm. Oh, Florrie. Mmm, mmm. I need you. I need you so much. Mmm, mmm. I'll miss the eight oh-seven and catch the eight thirty-two. Mmm, mmm. Get back in the house, Florrie. I can't help it. Mmm, mmm. I simply have to have my wicked way with you and–'

'Oh for goodness sake, Marcus!' Alison's cut-glass accent had sliced through the air instantly putting a stop to things. 'What sort of message are you conveying to Tiffany?'

Marcus had promptly released me. We'd gazed at Alison's bespectacled daughter. Plugged into her iPod, Tiffany had been oblivious of her surroundings. The little girl had been neatly dressed in the uniform of Darwin Prep, the local private school. She was the most hot-housed child we'd ever met. The likelihood that Tiffany had been listening to iTunes was improbable, but there was every chance she'd been absorbing French vocabulary specifically downloaded for her by Alison. My neighbour had given her daughter a little prod in the back.

'Get in the car, Tiffany. Mummy will be with you in two minutes.' She'd turned back to glare at Marcus. 'It's high time you stopped this exhibitionist behaviour on your doorstep every morning. Do you really think the residents of The Cul-de-Sac want to witness borderline soft porn?'

Marcus had smiled at Alison disarmingly. 'There are only three houses in The Cul-de-Sac, Ali. It's hardly the world and his wife watching. Do I detect a touch of jealousy?'

Alison had pursed her lips and given Marcus a frosty look. 'Most certainly not. However, behaving lecherously in a public place is a big no-no. It's beyond uncouth.'

'Uncouth, eh? You don't fool me, Ali,' Marcus had playfully retorted. 'I don't think old Henry is giving you enough attention. C'mon, admit it. We've seen the sweep of your hubby's headlights along The Cul-de-Sac at midnight. What sort of time is that to

2

be coming home from the office? Your Henry is so burnt out from City trading he's not stoking your fire.'

Alison had immediately looked like she'd swallowed a gobstopper. 'My *fire*,' she'd spluttered, 'does not need *stoking*, thank you very much. And if Henry chooses to work long hours, that's his business. At least we know Christmas will be in the Caribbean as usual.'

And with that my neighbour had stuck her nose in the air and stalked off to her brand new four by four. Any onlooker would have been forgiven for thinking Alison, a vision in full make-up and high heels, had been heading off to a smart London office instead of simply keeping up with all the other high-maintenance mothers and their spoilt offspring at the gates of Darwin Prep.

At that precise moment, Daisy, our other immediate neighbour at Number 1, had opened the door to her house. Husband Tom had stepped out, three children scampering around his legs. The kids had been wearing mismatched overcoats suitable for St Mildred's Primary, the local school where Tom was headmaster. The children had also been arguing furiously. Tom had looked both henpecked and harassed as he shepherded his clamouring brood over to the family vehicle.

'Morning, Florrie. Morning, Marcus,' he'd called over his shoulder. 'I saw you both through the window, by the way. Nice

3

to see romance is alive and kicking, even if it is at Number 2, and not my house.'

'I heard that,' Daisy had called after her husband. She'd scowled at Tom's back. 'I'm ready, willing and available – just as long as it's before nine in the evening.' She'd shrugged and turned to Marcus and me. 'After that I'm out cold. The kids are exhausting.'

Tom had shut the car's rear door on the still noisy children. Walking back to Daisy, he'd plonked a dutiful kiss on her cheek. 'I have a pile of pastoral work to catch up on with the vicar this evening. I'll grab a sandwich while I'm out, so don't wait up.'

Daisy had given an exaggerated sigh. 'Story of my life,' she'd grumbled. 'No rumpy-pumpy for me this evening.'

'When are you ever awake for rumpy-pumpy?' Tom had countered.

'I'm awake now, aren't I?' Daisy had said belligerently. With her bed-head hair and crumpled pyjamas splattered with that morning's egg and baked beans, it was fair to say she hadn't looked her most alluring.

'You two should have a date night with each other,' I'd suggested.

'Ah, but you don't have children,' Tom had sighed. His expression had been one of long-suffering. 'They change your life. Wear you down. Pretty much wear you out too. I can't remember the last time Daisy and I managed to eat a meal peacefully together without one of the kids emitting a blood-curdling scream and all hell breaking out.'

'Take no notice of him,' Daisy had added hastily. She was fully up to date on my many attempts to get pregnant. And the many failures too.

'All I'm saying,' Tom had sighed, 'is that the days of being a loved-up couple like Florrie and Marcus here are a thing of the past for us.' He'd turned back to us with a deprecatory shrug. 'I take my hat off to you both. Honestly. I don't know any husbands and wives who have been married for five years still enjoying the honeymoon period.'

He'd given a warm smile and for a moment his whole face had transformed. He was actually a very good looking guy. Seconds later he'd morphed back into put-upon Tom complete with drooping mouth and matching posture.

'Forgive me for holding you both up. I must get the children to school and then,' he'd perked up slightly, 'have a coffee in the staff room for ten minutes. It's the one place where there is peace, quiet, and grown-up conversation.'

He'd inclined his head by way of farewell and, like a man going off to his execution, opened the driver's door. The Cul-de-Sac had briefly been filled with the din of still arguing children before Tom had pulled the door shut after him. From behind the steering wheel he'd raised a tired arm by way of farewell. Moments later he'd driven off in a cloud of exhaust.

Daisy had turned to us and suddenly

given a cheerful grin. 'Hurrah! Peace until I collect the mini mob at half past three. I'm going to put the kettle on and watch a bit of Jeremy Kyle. Fancy joining me, Florrie?'

'Are you trying to persuade my perfect wife to be a lazy good-for-nothing woman?' Marcus had teased.

'Excuse me?' Daisy had instantly bristled. 'The moment Jeremy has finished telling some poor cow that the father of her unborn child is an unfaithful lying bastard, I'll be off the sofa and cleaning this house from top to bottom. I shall then tackle an overflowing laundry bin, work my way through a mountain of ironing, and finally head off to the supermarket for a mammoth shop that will leave my arms like stretched spaghetti for the rest of the week. My days are full to bursting, Marcus. Make no mistake about it.'

'I'll consider myself told off,' Marcus had said graciously.

'And *I'm* busy too,' I'd reminded Marcus.

Despite not having a litter of kids making demands upon my time, I did have a huge canvas awaiting my attention in the loft room. Whilst I'd yet to strike it big and be represented by an art gallery, nonetheless I'd recently started to make a decent living producing colourful works for a local restaurant.

But all of that had happened yesterday. Sometimes things can change dramatically in the space of just twenty-four hours, which Marcus and I discovered on this particular Tuesday morning resulting in him dancing me around our kitchen. You see, after five barren years of marriage, I was pregnant. We gazed again at the double blue lines on the pregnancy tester before my husband squashed me into another hug.

'I can't believe it,' he murmured into my hair. 'It's nothing short of a miracle.'

Suddenly I couldn't think of anything to say. Already the enormity of the situation was starting to make itself felt. My heart quickened. Anxiety? *No, Florrie*, I told myself, *just shock*. Mentally, I took a deep breath. It would be fine. Everything would be fine. To the outsider my life was perfect. Enviably so. I lived in a desirable house in The Cul-de-Sac in the popular village of Lower Amblegate. I had fab neighbours and was married to a respectable man who was earning nicely thank you very much as a property surveyor. A little baby was the icing on the marital cake. I was the luckiest woman in the world. Wasn't I?

Chapter Two

I spent the next couple of hours brushing oils onto a vast rectangular canvas. But as colour and form grew, my mind continuously wandered elsewhere. My brain was whirling. Thoughts of babies, conception, the gestation period, trying to work out exactly how pregnant I was, all kept tumbling over and over like an old-fashioned video tape stuck on a loop. This pregnancy was indeed a miracle. As soon as we'd shaken the confetti from our hair, Marcus had wanted to get down to the business of starting a family.

'I want us to have ten children,' he'd grinned. 'Five boys and five girls.'

I'd laughed and suggested we let Mother Nature take her course and that two children would be perfect. As twenty-five-year-olds we had no real qualms about money. We both did the daily commute to London. Marcus had an escalating salary, and I was a stressed PA. Together, we earned good money. Not long after becoming engaged, we'd driven through Lower Amblegate and spotted The Cul-de-Sac. Investigating, we'd noted the For Sale board outside Number 2. We'd wasted no time making an appointment to view. Walking through the front door, we'd fallen in love with the larger than average rooms and huge windows letting in streams of lemony sunbeams. We'd felt as though the house had embraced us. Even the branches of the fruit trees dotted around the paddock-like garden had seemingly wrapped their leafy boughs around our shoulders, hugging us, urging us to stay. In the misty recesses of my mind I saw a little boy hanging off a tyre that swung from one of the sturdy branches, while a little girl played tea parties with her dollies in a home-made treehouse.

Buying it was, admittedly, a bit of a push. You don't see many twenty-five-year-olds starting out in a four-bedroomed detached, but we opted for living on baked beans and toast in order to get the deposit monies together. It was more than a dream home. It was our dream *family* home. A year after moving in, the initial room we'd set aside as a nursery remained empty. Eventually I'd mentioned my pregnancy concerns to my doctor during a routine smear test.

'You're young and a busy working lady,' he'd smiled reassuringly. 'I suspect you're living life in the fast lane, skipping meals and staying late at the office.' The doctor had been more precise than Mystic Meg. 'It's time to slow down. Make some changes. Eat properly – no missing breakfast. Take your lunch hour in full and go *out* of the office. Stretch those legs. Do some walking and fill those lungs with gallons of fresh air.' The "fresh air" bit hadn't been quite so accurate. At the time I'd been working near Fleet Street. The air had always been thick with the diesel fumes of a hundred buses and honking black cabs, while a haze of exhaust belched from scores of immobile cars stuck in congested lanes. In fact, the pollution was so bad that one of my colleagues regularly used to have an asthma attack on the walk to Blackfriars Station. But I didn't tell my doctor all that. Instead I hoovered up his words of hope. 'Some women simply need to prepare their bodies for pregnancy. I would bet my stethoscope that you're simply one of them.'

After two years I went back to the same doctor, who also summoned Marcus for examination. That's when the tests began. Apparently I had lazy ovaries causing an irregular menstrual cycle. This made it tricky to plot the most fertile time of the month. But, even trickier, Marcus's tests revealed a very low sperm count. There were no obvious reasons as to why. It was just one of those things.

'Try not to worry about it,' the doctor had said kindly. 'I've had many a man in my surgery with the same problem. They've all gone on to become fathers. I'm sure it will happen for both of you. One day. Meanwhile, try not to stress about it. Stress makes things much worse and, indeed, could even be the cause.'

Marcus immediately suggested I give up work. Certainly my job was full-on and incredibly demanding, but initially I'd been reluctant to walk away from my work. It wasn't simply a case of saying good-bye to the rat race; it meant saying good-bye to a lot of friends. No more gossip about who the married senior partner had secretly snogged at the Christmas party. No more jostling into the tiny rest room with the girls on a Friday night, fighting over the dingy mirror as we excitedly re-applied lipstick before setting off for an end-of-week drink at the hip local wine bar. But even more crucially, no more enjoyment of financial independence. Marcus, however, had been adamant.

'I'm earning enough now to cover the mortgage and bills. Give up the commute, Florrie. I want you to relax at home. If you're worried about being bored, take up a new hobby. Maybe knitting.' He'd looked pleased at that idea. 'Perhaps if you get those needles clicking away and churn out a few of those old-fashioned matinee jackets, it will get your body in homemaker mode. A baby is bound to follow.'

Within a month I'd gone on to fully bond with Daisy and Alison, my immediate stay-at-home neighbours. Alison, despite being a roaring snob, was a good sort with her heart in the right place. Daisy, Alison's complete antithesis, was scruffy and scatty but equally lovely. However, even their welcome friendship couldn't stop the moments of downright monotony. My neighbours had children to keep them busy, and their social lives flourished through the school mum network. It didn't matter how many times I was invited to join their respective coffee mornings with other school mums, my face didn't fit. I didn't have the right badge you see. I wasn't a parent. The only time I felt truly able to be myself with Alison and Daisy was when there weren't any other school mums around.

As for the home-making attempts, my foray into the world of matinee jackets had produced a single garment with so many holes from dropped stitches it had looked more like a dwarf's string vest. And there is only so long one can make a house gleam before feeling utterly fed up. I'd always played with paint and charcoal, producing sketches and colourful canvases. With so much time on my hands I'd returned to my old passion, tinkering about with oils and water colours under the rafters of the loft room which had been turned into a working studio. Occasionally, through word of mouth, I'd sell a painting which would leave me glowing for weeks.

Another year went by. We had a few attempts at IVF with no success. It was at this point I realised Marcus wasn't happy. Outwardly he was the same. Jovial. Cheerful. Caring. Loving. But inwardly it was another story. Privately I suspected he was wrestling with turmoil that his inability to father a child was making him feel emasculated. This was confirmed when, about three months ago, I'd received a surprise letter in the post.

The letter had been addressed just to me

in bold flowing handwriting. I'd stood in my immaculate kitchen surveying the envelope, wondering who it was from. The writing wasn't familiar. Eventually I'd tugged at the seal. And instantly recoiled in shock.

The written contents had never been discussed with anybody. Not Marcus, nor my parents, and most certainly not my dearest friends, Alison and Daisy. Nobody. I suppose my reasoning was that if I didn't discuss the letter, it didn't exist. No doubt some clever counsellor with umpteen certificates on their study walls would declare such a tactic to be a coping mechanism. And perhaps they'd be right. I still had the letter. It was hidden in a shoebox, tucked away in the depths of my wardrobe. Sometimes I'd forage within the wardrobe and withdraw the note, studying the style of writing, trying to analyse the character of the author, looking for clues as to who had put pen to paper. But then I'd hide it away again and try and forget all about it.

I put down my paintbrush, suddenly drawn to read the letter again, even though I knew what it said word for word. It was at that precise moment my mobile chirruped the arrival of a text. It was from Daisy.

Fancy a coffee?

I sighed. I was pleased her text had distracted me from digging out the letter. However, much as I loved Daisy, I knew I really should crack on with the current work in progress. The local Italian restaurant had already bought paintings off me and were after yet another. I stared at my easel, observing the riot of colour before me. It was coming together, but nonetheless not complete. I dithered. If I ignored Daisy's text, she'd take to the doorbell. If I stalled for time and asked for two hours' grace she'd only be chasing me later this afternoon. Wiping a blob of Prussian blue from my iPhone, I decided to reply. After all, I had amazing news to share. In fact, most newly pregnant women in my shoes would by now have employed a town crier to scream out an announcement. "O'yez! Gather round and know that Florence Milligan's ovaries have finally popped an egg and partied with a single exhausted sperm. God bless the fruit of Marcus Milligan's loins." I wasn't exactly behaving in a euphoric manner, was I? I began to tap the mobile screen with a paint-stained index finger.

Sounds good. As it happens, I have something wonderful to tell you!

Daisy's response was immediate.

In that case, I'll see if Alison is available too. We can't exclude her or neither of us will ever hear the end of it.

I mentally nodded. Too true.

Sure. I'll be over in a jiffy. Just give me a few moments to clean up.

I was just locking the front door when Alison emerged from Number 3. Her expensive perfume wafted on a little gust of spring air invading my senses. I sniffed appreciatively. It was a familiar smell, quite masculine with its musky overtones, although I couldn't place it, or remember where I'd smelt it before.

'Not bogged down with PTA meetings this morning then?' I grinned.

Alison shuddered dramatically, but we both knew she loved being involved with fund raising. No day was complete for Alison without sucking up to the School Governors at Darwin Prep. There wasn't a cake sale or a second-hand-uniform jamboree that Alison wasn't behind.

'There *is* a PTA meeting but thankfully much later this afternoon.' We stepped over the strips of grass separating the three houses she, Daisy and I lived in. 'However, I can't stay too long for coffee at Daisy's.' She placed a perfectly manicured nail over the doorbell and gave it a couple of sharp rings. 'I have to go to Harriet Montgomery's place in an hour or so. We're finalising the arrangements for the May Ball. It's also going to provide some fund-raising for Darwin Prep. With only a week to go there's still lots to do. Harriet absolutely insisted I was involved from the start. You know Harriet, don't you?'

Alison knew perfectly well I didn't personally know Harriet, but everybody in Lower Amblegate knew who Harriet Montgomery was. A beautiful ex-movie star, she'd dominated the big screen for ten years before dramatically announcing she was getting hitched and "taking a rest". Harriet Montgomery had gone on to marry famous business tycoon Martin Murray-Wells who was old enough to be her grandfather. As Daisy had sardonically said, "It must be love." They'd managed to produce one daughter, Piper, who also went to Darwin Prep. It went without saying that Alison was very keen for little Tiffany to be Piper's bestie. Meanwhile Alison was doing sterling work cosying up to Harriet at every given opportunity.

Daisy answered the door, eyes shining. She had managed to brush her hair since I'd last seen her but was still wearing the crumpled pyjamas covered in egg yolk and baked bean sauce. Alison clocked the grubby nightwear with distaste, but arched an eyebrow at Daisy's evident happiness.

'Why are you looking so perky?'

Together we stepped over the threshold into Daisy's hallway.

'Because I've just watched the best bit of breakfast telly ever!' Daisy clapped her hands together. 'There was this gorgeous bouncer pinning down this mouthy woman who was trying to knock seven bells out of this really chavvy female, and they were arguing over this ancient bloke. I mean, *really* ancient. He had to be at least fifty.'

Alison looked affronted. 'Can I remind you, Daisy, that Henry is fifty. He is *not*, as you so eloquently put it, *ancient*.'

'Oh, yeah,' Daisy flapped a hand dismissively, 'I forgot you like oldies. Still, at least Henry isn't as ancient as your mate's hubby.' Daisy nodded at the hall window. We followed her gaze and looked into the distance at a huge mansion perched high on a hill and overlooking the North Downs. It was Harriet Montgomery's pile. Alison didn't know whether to be peeved at Daisy's insult of being attracted to old men, or flattered that Daisy thought Alison and Harriet were "mates". Alison's ego got the better of her and the latter comment won.

'Harriet's hubby is delightful,' she cooed. 'Naturally I've met Martin several times. Martin is an absolute sweetheart.'

'Good to know.' Daisy shrugged as we followed her into the lounge. 'I still wouldn't want to bonk him though.'

'I personally think Martin is extremely debonair,' Alison said defensively as we carefully negotiated the floor. It was covered in discarded toys, colouring pads and breakfast detritus.

'Someone's got mentionitis,' said Daisy. 'You've just said "Martin" three times in as many seconds.'

Alison ignored the dig and carried on talking.

'I was just telling Florrie, I'm helping Harriet put the finishing touches to the village May Ball. It's a fundraising affair obviously. I fully expect you both to attend, even if you have to drag your husbands along kicking and screaming.'

'I'm not sure I want to rub shoulders with all your toffee-nosed friends,' Daisy grumbled.

'They are perfectly normal people,' said Alison irritably as she flopped down onto a sofa, 'and anyway, it's not just the Darwin Prep parents who will be there. Everyone in Lower Amblegate is invited.'

I sat down next to her, narrowly avoiding stepping on some congealed plates. Alison stared at them distastefully.

'You allow your children to eat on the floor?'

'Of course,' said Daisy. She gave Alison a strange look. 'It's near the telly.'

Alison looked appalled. 'Don't you *ever* sit up at the dining table as a family and make intelligent conversation about how to resolve world peace or debate whether Donald Trump will be a good president for America?'

'What the heck would we want to do that for?' Daisy asked in bewilderment. 'I'd miss Jeremy Kyle or Coronation Street.'

Alison's brow furrowed. 'But if you don't ever sit around a dining table, where do you entertain?'

'Entertain?' Now it was Daisy's turn to frown.

'Yes! As in hosting a soirée.'

'A what?'

Alison rolled her eyes. 'A dinner party, Daisy.'

'Ah,' Daisy looked enlightened. 'Where you're sitting, Ali. There's nothing like fish and chips out of newspaper on your lap.'

Alison looked stunned. The day she

offered the likes of Harriet Montgomery a take-out whilst sitting on a sofa or floor would be the day Hugh Heffner became a monk.

Daisy cleared her throat. 'Now then, ladies, coffee or tea?'

'I'll have coffee, please,' I said to Daisy.

'Do you have any Earl Grey?' asked Alison.

Daisy placed her hands on her hips. 'Honestly, Ali, I do wish you'd drop the airs and graces. You're not at Mrs La-de-da's house now. You're at mine, complete with chaos and mess. You'll have the supermarket special and love it.'

Alison looked pained. 'Well at least give me a porcelain cup and saucer rather than a cracked workman's mug.'

Daisy tutted, and stomped off. From out in the kitchen we could hear her huffing and puffing as she searched through cupboards for the elusive china. Five minutes later she returned with a tray bearing steaming drinks and a plate of biscuits.

'Have you thought about getting a cleaner?' Alison asked.

Daisy bit into a chocolate biscuit. 'Why would I want one of those?' she asked, dropping crumbs everywhere.

'To make this place ship-shape of course,' said Alison in exasperation. 'You have such a lovely house, Daisy, but inside it looks like it belongs to Mr and Mrs Slob. Doesn't Tom ever get annoyed?'

'Sure. But I just tell him I've done the

housework and the kids simply messed it all up again.'

'Doesn't he ever suss that you only do the minimum?'

'Nah,' Daisy shrugged and took another bite from the biscuit. 'I just squirt a bit of furniture polish in the air before he comes home and he says, "Wow, I can tell you've been working your socks off today." That's when he's home, anyway. After school, he's catching up on pastoral chit-chat with the vicar. These days he seems to be perpetually busy.'

Alison nodded. 'Your husband too, eh?' She rattled her cup into the saucer making Daisy and I jump slightly.

'I don't mind,' Daisy said helping herself to another chocolate biscuit. 'At least it gets me off the hook in the bedroom.'

'Don't you like,' Alison paused, '*sex*?' She mouthed the last word.

'Yeah,' Daisy nodded. 'Well, I did.' She chomped away, thoughtful for a moment. 'I guess it's just all a bit predictable though. And boring. Do I really want a late-night grapple which no longer makes the earth move for me? Especially when I've just washed the sheets. It just makes another job. I guess, like housework, sex for me is a chore.' She grinned, revealing a chocolate crumb lodged between her front teeth. 'We can't all be like our Florrie here. What's it like still fancying the pants off your hubby and having mad passionate sex morning, noon and night?'

I laughed, but couldn't quite meet Daisy's gaze and took a hasty swig of coffee so I wasn't able to reply.

'Anyway,' Daisy shifted in her chair. A regrouping gesture. She looked at me expectantly. 'What's this fab news you have for us both?'

Alison straightened up, giving me her full attention. 'Fab news?' She turned two wide eyes towards me. For the first time I noticed exactly how wide Alison's eyes actually were. Surely she hadn't had a lift? After all, she was only thirty-seven. I stared at her forehead. It was as smooth as polished marble. That had to be the work of botox. And, good heavens, her mouth was looking incredibly pouty. Was that a touch of filler around the upper lip? 'What fab news?' she repeated.

I blinked and, suddenly shy, gave a tiny smile. 'I'm expecting a baby.'

Daisy immediately stood up and punched the air, slopping coffee down herself in the process. 'Fan-flaming-tastic,' she whooped.

Alison's response was more reserved. 'That's wonderful news, Florrie,' she said quietly. 'I'm very pleased for you.'

I allowed my smile to turn into a full-on grin. Inside I was still quaking somewhat. Still trying to digest it all. But now I'd told my two dearest friends, it was as if an internal light switch had been flicked on so that I immediately began to feel like I was glowing radiantly.

'To be honest, Marcus and I are shell-shocked. But happy,' I added, nodding emphatically as some butterflies took off in my stomach. Nerves. I brushed the feeling away. Surely every expectant mother felt nervous. The fact that expectant mothers were more likely to feel nervous nearer to the time of their due date as opposed to the day of finding out they were pregnant was surely neither here nor there. Everyone was different, I firmly told myself. I looked from Daisy to Alison, and my megawatt smile instantly faded. Alison seemed to be struggling with her emotions. The duck-pout was wobbling alarmingly, and the wide-apart eyes were now swimming with unshed tears. Alarmed, I leant forward and touched her arm. 'Ali? Whatever's the matter?'

'N-nothing,' Alison sniffed. 'E-everything.'

'Eh?' Daisy hunkered down in front of Alison. 'You're not fretting about this chuffing May Ball, are you?' she asked. 'Of course we'll come. Even if I'm so tired that I collapse head first into the asparagus velouté and start snoring. I absolutely promise to be there for you.'

Alison sniffed and dabbed at her eyes. She gave a watery smile. 'Sorry. I'm just a bit out of sorts.'

'Why?' I put an arm around her cashmere-clad shoulder. 'You can tell us, Ali.'

The tears were threatening again. Her face worked. She was clearly wrestling with her emotions, unsure whether to confide in Daisy and me, or not. 'It's Henry,' she eventually said, almost choking on her husband's name.

Daisy and I looked at each other and paled.

'Is something wrong with him, Ali?' Daisy asked. 'I'm sorry I said he was old. He's not old really. Well, not old enough to die anyway.'

Alison gave an imperceptible shake of the head. 'He's not ill.' Foraging up one sleeve, she removed a tissue and noisily blew her nose. 'It's nothing like that.'

'What is it then?' I urged.

She gulped a few times, still not quite sure whether to divest a secret. Taking a deep breath, the need to unburden won.

'Henry's having an affair.'

Chapter Three

For a moment, Daisy and I simply stared at our weeping neighbour. Henry was having an affair? *Henry*? Was this the same Henry who spent his Saturdays taking Tiffany to London trekking around museums or art galleries, and his Sundays dutifully manicuring the lawn and flowerbeds under Alison's watchful eye? Boring Henry? Impossible! Daisy was the first to speak. From her position on the floor at Alison's feet, she leant forward and touched Alison's arm.

'Ali,' she said gently. 'Is there any chance you might be a teensy-weensy bit wrong?'

'I don't think so,' Alison sniffed. She trumpeted into the already overworked tissue.

'So you're not one-hundred percent sure?' I asked hopefully.

'I'm ninety-nine percent sure,' Alison said flatly. There was a moment's silence while we contemplated this. Alison stared blankly at the soggy paper hanky balled up in her hands.

Daisy was the first to speak. 'Sorry, Ali, but I think you're mistaken. After all, let's not beat about the bush. Henry's fifty.'

'What's that supposed to mean?' Alison's voice was suddenly sharp.

'Well, without sounding insulting...' Daisy hesitated, 'surely he's past it.'

Alison's cheeks flushed red. 'What *are* you talking about, Daisy? Are you suggesting that at the end of Henry's forty-ninth year and on the stroke of midnight, he was suddenly struck impotent?' Alison straightened up on the sofa, indignant now. 'Is that what you think? That the moment a male embraces the Big Five-Oh all his teeth fall out, he loses his hair and bits of his body stop working?'

Daisy frowned. 'Well...yeah. I mean Henry's teeth are whiter than Simon Cowell's, so I presumed they were false.'

'Veneers,' Alison snapped. 'Cosmetic dentistry. They cost an absolute fortune.'

Daisy wasn't convinced. 'Well he lost his hair years ago. He's as bald as a snooker ball with a scalp twice as shiny.'

'He shaves his head to be trendy,' Alison hissed.

'I see,' Daisy said. She clearly didn't see at all. She rocked back on her heels and contemplated Alison. 'So are you trying to tell me his willy still works?'

Alison looked affronted. 'Yes, Daisy. It goes up and down. Mostly up. But not for me. Instead he's ga-ga about...'

'Who?' Daisy and I chorused.

'I don't know,' Alison wailed. 'A colleague maybe? He's always home so late.'

'You did say he works hard,' I soothed.

'Not hard enough to achieve full half-year bonus,' Alison's eyes flashed and her mouth disappeared into a tight line. 'Without

25

wishing to go into how much money my husband makes, let's just say that there's always been plenty of the stuff. But suddenly I'm being told to limit my spending. Being asked to use the local hairdresser instead of popping up to Mayfair to see Nicky. Having Tiffany's education compromised with Henry refusing to pay for flute lessons.'

'Well she is already studying clarinet, violin and piano,' I patted Alison's hand.

'Whose side are you on?' she demanded.

'Nobody's!' I assured hastily. 'I'm just thinking of Tiffany trying to fit another instrument into her already busy schedule.' I did sometimes wonder what planet Alison was on when it came to her daughter's education.

'And do you know what he said to me this morning?' she gasped and clutched her chest dramatically.

'What?' Daisy and I chorused.

'He told me to stop shopping at Waitrose and to go to,' she gave a little shriek, 'Asda.'

'I go to Asda,' said Daisy indignantly.

'I'm sure it's perfectly all right for people like you, Daisy,' Alison said patronisingly, 'but I really don't want to shop in a store where people are still wearing their pyjamas.'

'Have you been spying on me?' Daisy narrowed her eyes.

Alison tutted. 'I have better things to do with my time than check out your shopping attire, Daisy.'

I giggled and nudged Daisy. 'You've never gone to Asda in your PJs, have you?'

'Only twice,' Daisy sighed. 'The last time I did it the security guard wouldn't let me in the store.'

'And rightly so,' Alison's chin jutted. 'Don't you ever get fed up of lounging around in your nightwear?'

'No,' Daisy shook her head. 'It's comfortable. Why on earth would I want to wear cashmere in the morning when I'm frying eggs and stirring beans?'

'Well if you slice up some fresh melon, strawberries and grapes on a side plate, and give Tom and the children homemade muesli with organic milk, there's absolutely nothing wrong with being swathed in cashmere. I don't wish to be unkind, Daisy, but how on earth do you attract Tom's attention when you always look like you've fallen into a wheelie bin?'

'Ali, I don't wish to be unkind either, but if you don't shut up insulting me in my own house I might punch your lights out.'

Alison glared at Daisy for a moment, but then visibly crumpled. 'Sorry. I'm a bit stressed.'

Daisy, never one to hold a grudge, leant forward and gave our neighbour a hug before sitting down next to her. 'So tell me and Florrie the reasons why you think Henry is having an affair.'

'Well,' Alison shifted in her seat, suddenly uncomfortable. 'We don't...' Daisy and I looked at her expectantly. 'You know.'

Daisy looked mystified. 'What?'

'You know,' Alison repeated, suddenly awkward. Clearly her prissy upbringing was well and truly coming to the fore right now. 'We don't have...*sex*.' She mouthed the last word again. 'Well, hardly ever anyway.'

'Ahh,' said Daisy, the dawn suddenly coming up. 'Because you no longer fancy Henry.'

'Sorry?' Now it was Alison's turn to look confounded.

'Well, he is fifty, isn't he?' Daisy reasoned. 'And you're only thirty-seven. It's quite an age gap. You're probably still revving up in the loins department whereas Henry probably needs Viagra.'

'I've already told you his dangly bit goes up and down. Why would he need Viagra?'

'Oh. Is it you who needs Viagra?'

'For heaven's sake, Daisy. Neither of us need Viagra. And why do you keep going on about Henry's age?' Alison was getting agitated again. 'He's a very sexy man.'

'Is he?' Daisy looked across at me for confirmation.

To be honest, Henry didn't make me swoon. Not remotely. But I couldn't say that to Alison. I nodded at Daisy. 'Mmm. Henry is very...sort of...Kojak,' I nodded.

'Kojak?' Daisy's eyebrows shot upwards. 'You mean the bald guy with the big nose?'

'The very one,' I tried to give Daisy a discreet pleading look for tact. 'Absolute pin-up in his heyday.'

'Exactly,' said Alison smugly. 'Henry is

28

extremely sexy to lots of women. But somebody out there isn't just finding him sexy, they are getting the full works.'

'The works?' Daisy looked blank.

'Yes!' Alison said impatiently. 'Some woman is availing her services to him.'

'Services!' Daisy scoffed. 'Why can't you just talk like me and Florrie and say that some two-faced tart is bonking him.'

'Daisy,' said Alison in a pained voice. 'We've known each other for a few years now. When have you ever heard me use the word...' she paused before mouthing, '*bonk*?'

'Oh stop being so uptight, Ali,' Daisy pooh-poohed our neighbour's rigid desire to behave like a lady at all times. 'It's high time you loosened up and said things how they are – Henry's todger still works and he's waving it around at some female and rogering her senseless.'

Alison gave a little gasp at such frankness, but Daisy ploughed on regardless.

'If you really think this is the case, then you must confront Henry. Preferably when armed with a rolling pin. But not when you have PMT,' Daisy added hastily. 'You don't want to make a mess over the carpet.'

'Daisy, you really aren't helping,' Alison cried in exasperation.

'So to get back on topic,' I prompted. 'Do you have evidence of this suspected affair?'

Alison took a deep breath. 'I think so. Yes.' She closed her eyes for a moment, as if trying to blot out an awful memory. When she opened them again they were far away, clearly recalling something unpleasant. 'I went through Henry's last few credit card statements looking for clues.' She paused, struggling for composure. 'Last Christmas he spent thousands of pounds at a Hatton Garden jeweller. He bought two bracelets. I received one of them.'

'Perhaps he's saving the other bracelet for your birthday,' I suggested.

Alison shook her head. 'No. You see, I rang the jeweller in question. Both bracelets were identical.'

Daisy frowned. 'Why would Henry buy two identical bracelets?'

'I'm coming to that,' Alison's lip wobbled slightly. 'My bracelet had an inscription on the inside. It said, "To dear Alison with love from Henry." I asked the jeweller if the other bracelet had been inscribed with a message. The jeweller confirmed this to be the case. I asked him what the engraving was.' Alison's voice cracked slightly. 'The jeweller went off to check the paperwork.'

Suddenly Daisy and I were holding our breath.

'And?' Daisy prompted. She looked both fascinated and horrified. There had never been a situation like this on the Jeremy Kyle show.

When Alison next spoke her voice was little more than a whimper. 'The inscription on the second bracelet had said, "To the most beautiful woman in the world with all my love.'"

The breath whooshed out of Daisy and I in one big chuggy gasp.

'Oh,' we chorused.

'I don't know what to do,' Alison wailed.

We contemplated for a moment. What to do indeed.

'Do you still love Henry?' Daisy asked.

'Of course!' she said looking shocked. 'I have a beautiful house, my daughter is in the best school for miles, and I'm accepted into the homes of people like Harriet Montgomery.'

'That's not love,' I said gently. 'That's a lifestyle.'

'Same thing,' Alison snapped. 'I love my lifestyle. And I'm not about to have it jeopardised by some little hussy with a nose piercing and a skirt hem up round her ear lobes.'

'Do you know who she is then?' I asked.

'I've a good idea,' Alison's eyes narrowed. 'One of the secretaries was all over him at the Christmas 'do'. A typical cliché of a woman. Peroxide blonde hair. Cheap red lipstick. I could almost see a flashing neon sign over her head saying "I want you to be my Sugar Daddy."'

'I see,' Daisy puffed out her cheeks. 'So do you actually want to stay married to Henry?'

'Of course I want to stay married to Henry,' Alison snapped.

'Well in that case,' Daisy said conspiratorially, 'we're going to have to catch Henry out.' She looked from Alison to me, her eyes shining like they did when she first opened the door to us an hour ago. 'We're going to set a trap.'

Chapter Four

'Oh for goodness sake, Daisy,' said Alison irritably. 'I'm sure you mean well, but this isn't a scene on the Jeremy Kyle show. This is *my* life we're talking about. Setting a trap for Henry is an absolutely ridiculous idea. And anyway,' she paused, curiosity getting the better of her, 'what sort of trap had you got in mind?'

'I could flirt with him at the May Ball,' said Daisy thoughtfully. 'See if he reciprocates.'

'That's all well and good,' I pointed out kindly, 'but flirting is usually harmless. It's not going to achieve anything. I mean, people flirt all the time, don't they?'

'Do they?' Alison and Daisy chorused. Suddenly two pairs of unblinking eyes had me pinned to the sofa.

'Well, y-yes,' I stuttered, 'to a degree.'

'I thought you only had eyes for Marcus,' said Daisy accusingly. 'So tell us. Who do you flirt with?'

I blotted out the memory of a certain male who had definitely flirted with *me* on numerous occasions in the last few months. He'd had a profound effect on both my knees and insides. The former had turned to jelly, and the latter to mush. Instead I furrowed my brow in apparent concentration.

'Well, I quite like to flirt with ... um ...

with … er … the postman.'

'The postman?' Alison gasped in horror.

'You can't be serious?' Daisy scoffed. 'Trevor's coming up for retirement. Are you like our Alison and get turned on by oldies with saggy jaw lines?'

'Henry does *not* have a saggy jawline,' Alison protested.

Daisy ignored her. 'Spill the beans, Florrie. Tell us how you flirt with Trevor.'

'W-well, he likes to banter about the weather. You know, he says what a lovely warm day it is and…and he gives a little grin and a wink.'

'I see,' said Daisy, clearly not seeing at all. 'And this prompts you to respond in a coquettish manner, does it?'

'Er, y-yes. Last time I said it was a beautiful day to be delivering letters. And then I thanked him for his big packet and he…he said the pleasure was all his because…it had been a joy placing it in my perfectly formed letterbox. It was all…very intense.'

'Good God,' said Alison.

Daisy sucked on her teeth. 'I think you need to get out more, Florrie. All this painting you do cooped up in your loft room day after day isn't doing you any good. The sooner we get you to Harriet's May Ball the better. You clearly need to do some dancing and let off a bit of steam. You might as well do it now while you can still shimmy into a sexy evening dress and aren't huge with child.' She turned to Alison. 'And you leave

Henry to me. I shall ply him with champagne, get him on the dance floor, tell him I've always had a crush on Telly Savalas and flatter all his deepest secrets out of him.'

Alison grunted. 'And what about Tom? Won't he mind his wife taking a sudden interest in a male neighbour two doors down?'

'Not at all – because Florrie is going to distract him.' She turned to me, eyes blazing with triumph. '*You* can flirt with Tom,' said Daisy jubilantly. 'And anyway, it's about time I injected some fire into my marriage. It's gone stale. I mean, look at me,' Daisy got up and flung her arms wide so we could see her properly. 'It's nearly midday and I'm still in my yucky pyjamas. I wouldn't even turn the postman's head right now. It's time to shake things up,' she declared, suddenly fired-up. 'I'm going to dolly myself up to the nines for this ball. I shall drink half a dozen cans of energy jollop so I can stay awake until the early hours. I'm going to show my husband I'm not just a slummy mummy, I'm actually a gorgeous yummy mummy who neighbour Henry has the hots for.'

'And what am I meant to be doing while all this flirting is going on?' Alison pointed out. 'Stand around like a spare part?'

'Nope,' Daisy assured. 'Florrie here is going to have a discreet word with Marcus who will flirt like mad with you and get Henry all wound up!'

'I don't want Marcus flirting with me,' Alison protested. 'I just want to know who Henry is having an affair with.'

'Leave it to me,' Daisy tapped the side of her nose. 'Detective Daisy will get to the bottom of it. Oh, and a few ground rules, girls. No snogging each other's husbands while all this flirting is taking place.'

Alison looked aghast. 'The thought hadn't even occurred to me.'

'I know,' Daisy smiled, 'because our husbands are too young for your sophisticated taste.'

Alison sighed and stood up. 'I really *must* go. Well thank you, Daisy and Florrie, for at least cheering me up a bit and helping me dry my tears. I'm so sorry for raining on your baby parade, Florrie.' I stood up too, accepting Alison's hug. 'It's wonderful news,' she said. 'Truly. Tell Marcus I said "congratulations" too.'

'Thanks,' I said, giving her a quick squeeze back. 'Will do.'

'I must hurry. Harriet will wonder where on earth I've got to.'

I turned to Daisy. 'Thanks for the coffee and the company.' We embraced each other. 'I need to crack on with my painting. The restaurant wants it as soon as possible.'

'Actually,' said Alison, as she proffered her cheek to Daisy for pecking, 'Harriet was talking about commissioning an artist. She wants to surprise Martin with a painting of her for their forthcoming anniversary. I'll mention your name.'

'Wow, that's awfully good of you, Ali. Thanks.'

I followed Alison and Daisy out to the hallway. As Daisy opened the front door for us, our postie just happened to be there astride his red bicycle.

'Morning, girls,' he beamed and handed Daisy an envelope with a wink. 'Nice day for it. I was just about to touch your knocker,' his eyes snagged on Daisy's baked bean and egg stained pyjama top, 'but you instantly came and saved me the effort of dismounting.'

'I see what you mean,' Alison murmured in my ear. 'I've never noticed the innuendo before. I might report him to the Post Office.'

'Please don't,' I paled.

'Hello, Trevor,' Daisy gave our postman a cheeky grin. 'I've been hearing all about you and your enormous package. Who's a naughty boy then! I do hope you're going to Harriet Montgomery's May Ball. There's going to be a bevy of beautiful ladies there, including the three lovely visions standing before your very eyes. You can forget all about the sorting office and sort us out instead.'

Trevor stared at Daisy, suddenly uncertain. 'Ah ha ha ha,' he laughed nervously. 'Yes. I'll be there. With the missus,' he added hastily, before turning his bicycle around and smartly peddling off.

'Oooh, I'm enjoying this flirting lark,' Daisy smiled at us.

Alison shook her head in exasperation while my own thoughts momentarily fragmented and travelled a little way back through time. In my mind I could see his eyes. Dark liquid pools, full of unspoken promises. Without a doubt there had been flirting. But not coarse or brazen, like Daisy had just demonstrated with Trevor. Instead it had been subtle, and wonderful, and had pretty much set my soul on fire.

I didn't dare tell the girls, but privately I thought flirting was a very dangerous game.

Chapter Five

I first met Luca while having a girlie lunch with Alison and Daisy. We were at Serafino's Cucina in nearby Sevenoaks. It was one of those trendy looking restaurants with a rustic New York-style interior where they served bread from a wood oven, and the waiters and waitresses wore long midnight-blue aprons over white shirts and black jeans. That was six months ago. Alison had been keen to try the new bistro.

'I've been to their flagship restaurant in London,' she'd gushed, 'and it was just *the* most amazing food. Henry takes a lot of his clients there, and is very good friends with the owner, Pepe Serafino. Pepe has four sons. One by one Pepe has opened restaurants across the South-East with each son taking charge. Now it's the youngest son's turn. His name is Luca. Pepe said that Luca had been working for his father-in-law but there was a massive falling out after the tragic death of Luca's young wife, Maria. Maria and Luca had had a silly argument and she'd stormed out of the house. As Maria had stomped along the pavement, she'd been hit by a drunk driver. It was absolutely a case of being in the wrong place at the wrong time. Luca blamed himself for his wife's death. His father-in-law blamed him too and wanted nothing more to do with Luca. So despite being broken hearted and bereft, Luca was sacked from his deceased wife's family business and booted out of the matrimonial home. Their house had been a wedding gift from his in-laws, but was instantly reclaimed after Maria's death. Luca didn't contest it. He was burdened by guilt and grief. The last thing he wanted was to hang around being a constant reminder and source of loathing to his in-laws. So Pepe persuaded Luca to come home and take over his own family's latest restaurant. And very well it's doing too.'

Daisy, Alison and I had gone into the bistro and made ourselves comfortable at a table by the window. I'd instantly been distracted by the view. Across the quaint street and behind a low white picket fence, was a large pond. Numerous ducks bobbed about rippling the silvery surface. The peaceful scene was framed by two enormous weeping willows, their boughs draped around the water's edge. I'd immediately wanted to paint it.

'Sorry, she's miles away,' I heard Daisy say to somebody. 'Earth to Florrie, do you hear me?'

I dragged my eyes away from the gorgeous view and, looking up, found myself looking at a completely different bit of gorgeousness. Standing to one side of our table was a devastatingly handsome man. His effect on me was immediate. One moment I was a composed diner in a restaurant, the next I was behaving like a blithering idiot.

'Il menu, Signorina?' he murmured.

With a shaking hand I reached across to take the menu, unfortunately clipping a number of glasses in the process. They fell with a clatter and rolled across the table. Luckily all the glasses were empty so nothing spilt and thankfully none broke either. However, the noise was enough to momentarily hush other diners. They instantly craned their necks to regard the source of disruption to their dining harmony.

'Please, Signorina. It's not a problem,' murmured the man. 'Let me.'

I grabbed the tall laminated menu from him and attempted to hide behind it as the man righted the clutch of wine glasses and squat tumblers. An unattractive blush stained my cheeks as I stared at the writing within whilst failing to actually read one word.

'Are you all right, Florrie?' Daisy whispered.

'Yes,' I mumbled. My voice had shrivelled to nothing, not helped by the fact that someone was smoking. I frowned. Surely there was a no smoking policy in restaurants?

'Florrie, you're smoking,' said Alison.

'Don't be silly,' I croaked.

'Signorina,' said the man urgently, 'allow me, please.' Suddenly the menu was being whisked out of my hands. Smoke trails wisped across the table. 'You had one corner dipped in the tea light,' the man explained, nodding at the ornamental candle centrepiece. 'Have a fresh menu.'

Oh God. How embarrassing. 'Thank you,' I mumbled and leant forward to accept the replacement menu. This time our hands brushed together and instantly the small hairs on the back of my neck prickled. Flustered, I dropped the menu, knocking over a pair of hefty salt and pepper pots in the process. They smacked down against the table top with all the noise of a strike at ten pin bowling.

'Sorry,' I squeaked.

'Please, Signorina,' the man soothed, 'no worries.'

In my peripheral vision I was aware of Alison looking surprised and Daisy frowning. I let out a strangled whimper. The man scooped up the menu and once again offered it to me, but I no longer seemed to have the power to raise a hand and take it from him. Instead Alison did the job for me. She almost snatched it from the man.

'Thank you, Luca,' she said crisply before nearly shoving the wretched thing up my nose.

'And Florrie is a Signora,' said Daisy firmly, 'not a Signorina.'

'Florrie,' the man repeated.

Luca said my name as if savouring it, as one would a fine wine rolling deliciously over appreciative taste buds. My stomach wasn't so much as filled with butterflies as lottery balls whooshing about in their glass dome before picking a winner. This man was having a profound effect on me.

'Is that short for Florence?' he asked.

'Yes,' I whispered.

'A beautiful name. Like the city. Florence is my parents' birth place. Have you been there?'

'Once,' I said hoarsely. 'It inspired me to paint.' Talking was difficult. My vocal chords simply weren't behaving properly.

'You are an artist?'

I nodded, momentarily incapable of any further speech.

'And an absolutely brilliant artist she is too,' Daisy chimed in. 'You won't have heard of her...yet. Our Florrie is on the threshold of having her first show.'

I made a strangled noise. Dear Lord, what was my daft neighbour up to?

'She has a *very* well-known London art gallery pursuing her,' Daisy continued. 'The private art portfolio and gallery manager is preparing a contract as we speak.'

'I would love to buy one of your paintings,' Luca smiled at me. He gestured to the restaurant walls. 'Everywhere is bare. I need to bring the outside *in*. You understand? To give a better ambience and mood.'

'All her paintings are reserved for the art gallery,' Daisy said. 'And I doubt you would be able to afford them,' she added. 'The gallery is starting them at three thousand pounds.'

'Daisy,' I muttered, my face now magenta with embarrassment, 'I know you mean well, but–'

'Florrie does proper art, you know,' Daisy nodded sagely. 'None of this abstract nonsense. You won't find three square canvasses in Florrie's studio block-coloured in red, green and blue. She paints landscapes.'

'That's true,' Alison nodded. 'Whopping great big ones.'

'I like...whopping great big ones,' I added quietly.

'Do you now?' Luca raised an eyebrow. 'Please, Florrie, for now order your lunch and afterwards – if your companions don't mind and you don't have to rush off – you can stay behind. We will talk business.'

And that was how Luca Serafino entered my life.

Chapter Six

After Alison and Daisy had, very reluctantly, gone home without me, Luca had led me to a door at the back of the restaurant. It was marked "Private". Pushing it open, I'd found myself in a narrow hallway with a staircase leading upwards.

'Please,' he'd extended a hand, inviting me to walk ahead of him.

Feeling incredibly self-conscious, I'd made my way up the staircase. Every part of me had been on red alert. I'd felt as though his eyes had been boring twin holes in my back, sizzling right through the skin, muscle and soft tissue, beyond my very bones and into the depths of my soul.

At the top of the stairs a landing had issued straight into an open plan kitchen with dining area and lounge. With its high ceilings and large sash windows, it was wonderfully light and airy. I'd immediately thought it a perfect place to paint. To one side, a couple of doors had been evident, presumably leading to a bathroom and bedroom.

'Please, Florrie. Sit down.' He'd gestured to one of the large, squashy sofas at the far end of the room. 'What would you like to drink. Tea? Coffee? Or wine?'

A glass of robust red to steady the inexplicable nerves had been quite appealing. However, I'd declined on the grounds of needing to drive home later.

'I'll just have water, thanks.'

At least I could keep my vocal cords lubricated if my voice decided to peter out.

Luca had immediately busied himself fetching crystal tumblers. He'd poured chilled sparkling mineral water for us both and finished it off with ice and a slice. The cubes had tinkled against the glasses as he'd brought them over. Placing the tumblers on the coffee table, he'd sat down opposite me and, for a moment, regarded me thoughtfully.

'Well, Florrie, I'm absolutely delighted to properly meet you,' he'd smiled disarmingly.

'Thank you.'

My voice had almost sounded normal. *Hooray.* I'd been very aware of my heart thudding away. It had banged against my ribcage with a loud thwack-thwack-thwack. I'd picked up my glass of water for something to do and my hand had trembled alarmingly as the glass wobbled towards my mouth. *Get a grip, Florrie.* I'd slurped noisily, dribbling some water down my chin, and banged the glass back down on the coffee table. *Geez. Since when had crystal tumblers got so heavy?*

'So!' Thus lubricated, my vocal cords had produced the word like a pistol shot causing Luca to jump slightly.

'So, you paint. And, if your friends are to be believed, your work is exceptional.'

I'd flushed with embarrassment.

Whatever Daisy and Alison thought of my paintings was one thing. What a prospective client thought was quite another.'

'Listen, Luca—'

'I'm all ears,' he'd smiled encouragingly.

'Don't believe everything Daisy said. I don't have anything being exhibited—'

'Yet.'

'Y-yet,' I'd agreed. *Careful, Florrie. Don't talk yourself out of this fantastic little business opportunity.* 'But Daisy was a little out on the pricing.'

'Oh? Not three thousand pounds then?'

'N-no, it's less than that. Much less. More like two—' I'd been about to say two hundred pounds when Luca had cut me off.

'Two thousand is fine, Florrie. Shall I pay you now?'

I'd recoiled, horrified. 'Good heavens, no.'

My vocal chords had started to die again. Quickly I'd reached for the tumbler. At that point my nerves had been well and truly getting the better of me. I'd felt like a major fraud. Grabbing the tumbler, I'd used both hands to lift it to my lips. Luca had regarded me quizzically. An artist with the shakes. For a second I'd caught the doubt on his face about my brushwork.

'Pay me when the painting is finished. If you don't like it,' I'd gabbled, 'then you don't have to pay me.'

'I'm sure I will love it.'

'But you haven't seen any of my work,' I'd

protested and fidgeted uneasily.

I'd had no portfolio to offer Luca. Everything I'd ever painted had been for pleasure and either given away to family or gifted to close friends. The very occasional painting I'd sold had been for little more than the cost of the canvas and oils. I didn't even have a painting hanging in my own home for fear it might seem big-headed. I could just imagine one of Alison's Darwin Prep cronies coming round to mine for coffee and looking down her aristocratic nose at a leafy scene hanging over the fireplace. Annabelle Farquhar-Jones was the worst of them. A divorcée with pots of settlement money, I could almost hear her voice now. "Fancy putting one's own artwork on one's wall. Seems fritefly up oneself."

'Wait!' A lightbulb had gone off in my brain. 'I have photographs of my work on my mobile phone.' A tiny egotistical part of me had digitally recorded what I'd painted so I could be privately proud without seeming like a show-off. I'd rummaged in my handbag for my mobile phone. Touching the icon for photo streaming, I'd flicked back through the catalogue of photographs. 'Ah, here we are.' I'd been on the verge of passing the mobile to Luca when instead he'd moved from his seat and sat down next to me. Instantly the room had seemed to shrink. I'd shifted on the sofa, trying and failing to put an extra couple of inches between us. His thigh had brushed against mine and my thumping had heart had gone into overdrive.

'That's...electrifying,' he'd murmured.

'Mmmm,' I'd nodded in agreement, not quite trusting myself to speak.

Leaning slightly over me, he'd slid a finger across the mobile's screen and viewed the next image. Part of his hand had momentarily touched mine and I'd nearly rocketed off the sofa. Breathing had become a major effort. I'd suddenly seemed to have far too much air in my lungs. Exhaling quietly had been a struggle.

'I like this one,' he'd pointed to a summery scene of fresh blue skies and yellow sunflowers.

'Good,' I'd panted as perspiration started to bead my upper lip.

'And this is lovely too,' he'd indicated an autumn scene with a tree-lined path littered with red and gold leaf fall. I'd had a great time using a palette knife for that one.

'Excellent,' I'd gasped. It was no good. There had been an urgent need to exhale and draw breath properly.

I'd leant forward on the pretext of reaching for my drink, and attempted puffing out gallons of accumulated carbon dioxide before sipping water. I'd been in such a state I'd accidentally inhaled my drink. As I'd sucked in a mixture of air and sparkling water, bubbles had shot up my nose and I'd begun to choke. My eyes had bulged as I'd frantically willed my lungs to accept *aqua con gas*. For an awful moment

I'd thought I might die. I'd had a mental picture of Daisy reading about my death in the newspaper.

Woman Drowns Sitting on a Sofa.

"That's just so typical of Florrie," Daisy would say. "She can't even die without making a spectacle of herself."

"I know," Alison would agree. "Thank goodness she didn't do it at Harriet Montgomery's May Ball. I'd never have lived it down."

Suddenly the glass had been whisked out of my hand and I'd been thumped hard on the back.

'Are you okay, Florrie?' Luca had asked in alarm.

I'd shaken my head and spluttered as water had shot out of my mouth.

Dear God in heaven, this is beyond embarrassing. Just get me out of here – now. Forget the painting. In fact, what on earth was I even thinking of? Daisy's preposterous charade of making me out to be a sought after artist is beyond ridiculous. The moment I've finished either drowning or choking to death, I'm going to have several noisy words with my neighbour.

I'd briefly wondered what Jeremy Kyle might have had to say about it all.

Chapter Seven

Needless to say Luca had gone on to commission me. I'd produced a massive landscape of the Chianti Valley which had graced the immediate wall to the walk-in area of his restaurant. Underneath, in neat calligraphy, Luca had framed a tiny sign which proclaimed: *Florentine Gold by Florrie Milligan. For commissions enquire within.* There had been a smattering of enquiries. There had also been a lot of gasping when Luca had told them my fee. To date he remained my sole client, albeit a very lucrative one. Luca kept me busy. A second and third painting had swiftly followed and now I was working on my fourth, another landscape called *Florence Rooftops.* Unsurprisingly it was a view of some rooftops in Florence painted with umber edges. I was just deepening the pigment when my husband appeared in the doorway. I jumped, as if guilty of something.

'You startled me.'

'Sorry.' Marcus lingered, his face inscrutable.

I looked at him uncertainly. 'Have I forgotten the time or are you home early?'

'I'm early.'

'Oh dear. I haven't prepared any dinner.' I nodded at the canvas by way of explanation.

'That's okay.' Marcus shrugged noncommittally and leant against the doorframe. 'How's my pregnant wife?'

'Fine,' I nodded my head up and down. 'Yes, absolutely fine. In truth I've been so busy, I'd forgotten all about the pregnancy test.' That was a lie. With each stroke of my brush I'd thought of nothing else.

'Really?' Marcus looked at me, as if considering something, and then echoed exactly what I'd been thinking. 'I've thought of nothing else.' He moved across the room and peered at the work in progress. '*Another* painting for Luca Serafino?'

'Yes. You know he likes my work.'

'Mmm. He's the only one who does though, eh?' He paused to examine my effort. 'The guy must be absolutely loaded to pay two grand a pop for all these blobs.'

'They're not blobs,' I said indignantly.

'What's this then?' Marcus pointed to a large blob towering over the surrounding roofs.

'It's the *Cattedrale di Santa Maria del Fiore*,' I said with a flourish.

'Excellent accent,' said Marcus mockingly. 'Is Luca teaching you Italian as well?'

I flushed. 'No. Of course not. He told me about the Cathedral. He loves Florence.'

I felt myself go hot as I recalled Luca gazing at the last finished painting, a look of delight spreading across his face. He'd turned to me, his face animated and his eyes full of ...what? I blocked out the memory.

Something. Just something.

'Beautiful,' Luca had murmured, nodding his approval. 'Utterly beautiful. You know I'm totally in love with Florence.'

Anybody listening would have wondered which Florence he was talking about. Marcus's voice yanked my concentration back to the present.

'You certainly seem to spend ages painting a lot of blobs.'

If Alison could hear my husband right now she'd tell him not to speak to me so condescendingly. However, where art was concerned I knew Marcus was just plain ignorant.

'How long a painting takes depends on the individual artist,' I replied, adding a few more *blobs*. 'It hinges on technical skills, and what the artist visualises the painting to be. Equally, if you fuss with a painting for too long, you run the risk of overworking it. If in doubt, it's better to create a series on the subject.'

'Which is what you're doing?'

'Yes.'

'At this rate, this Luca chappie will surely run out of walls to display your work upon. Still,' Marcus added lightly, 'if he's got a pile of money to spend on blobs, you might as well make the most of it. After all, nobody else is exactly banging the door down for your work.'

I bit my tongue. Marcus had just crossed the line from talking out of ignorance to talking condescendingly. I counted to five before replying.

'Actually,' I murmured, working the blush on a tiny section of brickwork, 'Alison is going to mention me to Harriet Montgomery.' I paused, allowing the name to register with Marcus. He visibly straightened. Ah, that had his attention! 'Yes, apparently Harriet,' I rattled off her name as if she was one of my closest chums, 'is looking to commission an artist. She wants to surprise her husband with a painting of herself for their forthcoming anniversary.' I glanced up. Marcus's jaw had been overcome by gravity.

'How do you know this?'

'I had coffee with Daisy and Alison this morning, remember?' Marcus looked at me blankly. 'Harriet's name came up. It transpires Harriet is good friends with Alison.' I saw a look of relief cross Marcus's face. 'You didn't really think she was *my* new best friend did you?' I chuckled.

'Well I'm pretty damn sure Ali isn't Harriet Montgomery's best friend either,' Marcus laughed, breaking the strange mood between us.

'Not for want of trying,' I added. I smiled, signalling I was happy to move on from the odd atmosphere. 'Anyway, apparently Harriet Montgomery has been a busy bee. She and Martin Murray-Wells are hosting the May Ball. It's a big fundraising affair. Some of the yummy mummies from Darwin Prep are part of the committee. Alison's practically orgasmic to be rubbing shoulders with an ex-movie star. Actually,' I paused and considered, 'I'm not sure if she has a girl-crush on Harriet, or whether she has a woman-crush on Harriet's husband.'

'Surely the former,' Marcus spluttered. 'After all, Martin Murray-Wells must be nearly eighty.'

'Seventy-seven apparently. Alison said he's very debonair. Anyway, she's insisting we support the event.'

Marcus immediately pulled a face. 'Oh no. No, no, no. That's not my cup of tea at all.'

I looked at him in surprise. 'Maybe not, but isn't there a part of you that's curious to have a nosy around the mansion of an ex-movie star and her business tycoon husband?'

'Not particularly. Anyway, I'm sure the whole place will be cordoned off from the public. Everybody will be shepherded into a tent in the garden.'

Marcus, I'd hardly call some big flash marquee in their extensive grounds *a tent*.'

'Marquee or otherwise, I suspect the whole event will be boring as hell. I can't stand luvvy types.'

'I'm sure Martin Murray-Wells isn't *luvvy* at all.'

'I'll bet his wife is. She's meant to have been a massive diva in her heyday.'

'She's a school mum now,' I reminded Marcus, 'albeit an impossibly glamourous one. Anyway, you'll have Tom and Henry to talk to.'

'Oh God,' Marcus raked a hand through his hair. 'Tired-old-Tom and Hooray-Henry? Florrie, whilst you might be best pals with Daisy and Alison, unfortunately I don't have the same rapport with your friends' husbands.'

'It's only for a few hours.' I paused to consider if a rooftop awning needed more warmth. My hand reached for gold ochre. 'Apart from anything else, I could use your help.'

'For what?'

'Alison is convinced Henry is having an affair.'

Marcus gave me an incredulous look. 'Don't be daft. The man works from dawn to dusk. When has he got time for a mistress?'

'Well clearly it's not all work. Alison is positive extra-marital games are going on.' I arched an eyebrow at Marcus. 'Henry has apparently bought another woman an expensive bracelet engraved with a gushing endearment.'

Marcus looked astounded. 'How the hell does Alison know something like that?'

'It was a combination of female intuition, a rummage through his credit card bills, and a conversation with the manager of a jewellery shop.'

My husband blew out his cheeks. 'I'm shocked. And I'm also surprised at Alison going through Henry's stuff, and absolutely flabbergasted at Henry having the balls to do such a thing. But then again, if he truly *is* bonking some ravishing little piece on the side, I can't say I blame him. I wouldn't want a wife like Alison.'

I frowned. 'That's a terrible thing to say!'

'Be honest. Ali is impossibly bossy. Henry has got to be the most hen-pecked spouse in the county of Kent.' My husband had a point. 'And anyway, if anybody was going to have an affair, I'd have thought it would have been Alison herself.'

'Don't be absurd,' I scoffed.

'I'm not,' Marcus folded his arms. A defensive gesture. 'I see the way she looks at us in the mornings, Florrie. She's envious.'

I immediately felt uncomfortable. 'I'm sure she knows that's just you deliberately teasing her.'

'Even so, haven't you seen the way she stares, and the look of longing on her face?'

My brow furrowed. 'Are you suggesting she fancies you?'

'I'm suggesting she wants attention. Let's face it, Henry is never around. He's up at the crack of sparrows, and spends eighteen hours out of the house. At weekends he's either getting reacquainted with his daughter or playing a round of golf. When does he ever take Alison out? Or buy her flowers? Or romance her? Never! Mark my words, Florrie. Alison is ripe for a fling.'

I shook my head and tutted at my husband's fanciful notions. 'Alison would never risk being caught playing away. She's the respectable mother of a star pupil at a highly regarded school. Apart from anything else she's far too busy sitting on umpteen committees and organising the next mega charity event. Like the May Ball,' I added. 'Anyway, I'd like you to buy Henry a drink when we're there. Get a bit cosy with him. See if you can impart any information about this secret lover.'

'Huh. Chance would be a fine thing. The last time I tried making conversation with Henry he bored the pants off me. He prattled on about his brilliant golf handicap, and did I know Tiffany was on her fourth foreign language?'

'Well just try, eh? And anyway, Daisy is going to do most of the legwork with Henry.'

'What do you mean?'

'She's going to set a trap.'

'What sort of trap?'

'You know. Like a honey trap. She's going to ply Henry with wine, flirt with him big time and wheedle out all his sexy secrets.'

'Will she be doing this in her pyjamas covered in baked beans and egg yolk? Tell me, Florrie, do you ever see Daisy wearing any proper clothes?'

'Of course she wears proper clothes,' I said defensively. The fact that Daisy didn't do so much of the time wasn't something I was going to admit to. 'Actually, I'll have you know she scrubs up very nicely.'

'Well she'll certainly need to if she's

planning on being some sort of enticement for Henry.' Marcus rolled his eyes at the very idea. 'And what about poor old Tom? He's going to be quite happy, is he, watching his wife thrust her saggy breasts into Henry's flushed face as they waltz round and round the dance floor?'

'Er, yes, because he's not really going to notice that bit.'

Marcus's eyebrows shot upwards. 'Why?'

'Um, because...because Daisy wants *me* to flirt with Tom. Just to keep him occupied for five minutes,' I gabbled. 'It won't mean anything. Nothing at all,' I reassured.

'Don't be ridiculous. Tom will think you've taken leave of your senses. And anyway, what am I meant to do while you're making eyes at Tom, and Daisy's leading Henry about with his tie in her teeth? Shall I perhaps waggle my eyebrows at a passing waitress as she offers me champagne from a silver tray? Maybe you'd like me to offer her some rumpy-pumpy behind one of Harriet's perfect rosebushes seductively lit by streaks of silver moonlight.'

'Ah, w-well. Now you're talking. If you could actually see your way to doing a spot of eyebrow waggling at Alison in order to make Henry jealous, that would be absolutely brilliant.'

'You do realise, Florrie, you three women clearly have way too much free time on your hands.' Marcus shook his head. 'I've never listened to such hare-brained nonsense in all my life.' He moved away from me and made towards the studio door, suddenly irritable. 'I'm going downstairs. As there's no dinner ready, I'll get us a take out.'

'Lovely,' I called after him.

Later, as we ate dinner, Marcus returned to the subject of the May Ball. 'If nothing else,' he said, popping an onion bhaji into his mouth, 'I suppose I can always chat to Tom and Henry about their children. You know, get some fathering tips from them.'

'Yes,' I said lightly, breaking up a piece of poppadum.

'After all,' Marcus regarded me, 'now that I'm an expectant father, parenting is something us men will all have in common.' His eyes snagged on mine. 'Isn't that so?'

I met his gaze. 'Of course,' I murmured.

My eyes were the first to slither away.

Chapter Eight

The following morning I waved Marcus off to work. It was the usual doorstep display of shenanigans with Alison looking on and tutting loudly. She gave Tiffany a prod in the back.

'Get in the car, darling. Mummy will be with you in two ticks.'

As Tiffany clambered into the car, Alison materialised by our sides. 'I've told you both before. No groping.'

'Marcus is *not* groping me,' I protested.

'Yes he is,' Alison hissed furiously. She turned on Marcus. 'You're like some sort of enormous octopus. Hands everywhere. It's outrageous.'

'Want to join in?' Marcus winked before giving our neighbour a cheeky pinch on the bottom.

Alison squeaked and jumped. 'How *dare* you, Marcus. That is not remotely funny.' She rounded on me furiously. 'I think it's about time you kept your husband under control, Florrie.'

I shrugged helplessly and mentally sighed. The day I managed to keep Marcus under control was not something I could ever foresee. Alison tugged her jacket down over her jeaned bottom. A protective action. Ignoring Marcus, she addressed me.

'I'll see you for coffee, Florrie, when I'm back from the school run. I have news.'

Marcus turned to me wide-eyed. 'Oooh, news!' he said mockingly. 'Don't you really mean *gossip*, Ali?' My husband nudged me in the ribs. 'I'll bet Florrie can't wait to hear all about Annabelle Farquhar-Jones deliberately buying the same jumper as you in Harrods and upstaging you by immediately wearing it at the school gate before you'd even got your own sweater out of that famous carrier bag.'

Alison gasped. 'How did you know Annabelle did that?'

Marcus threw back his head and laughed. 'You're so transparent, Ali. Seriously, I'm not sure my wife is interested in idle tittle-tattle. She has far more pressing things on her mind. Don't you, darling?'

I swallowed, suddenly uncomfortable, but cranked up a smile for Alison's benefit. 'A coffee would be lovely. Just a quick one though, I still have a painting to finish.'

'That's what I want to talk to you about. I've had a word with Harriet Montgomery about the painting commission. She wants to meet you. I'll give you all the details when I'm back from dropping Tiffany off at Darwin Prep. See you in a bit, Florrie.' She bestowed me with a tight smile, nodded curtly at Marcus by way of farewell, then stalked off to her waiting daughter.

'Don't I get a kiss good-bye?' Marcus called after her. Alison flicked her hair by way of response. Marcus turned back to me, lowering his voice. 'And you want me to flirt with her at the May Ball?' He shook his head. 'I don't think I'd even get to first base with our Ali, even if I wanted to. Which I don't,' he hastily added.

'Oh I don't know.' I looked my husband in the eye. 'Try employing some of that deadly charm I've heard so much about.'

Marcus frowned. 'Sorry?'

I bit my lip, thinking of the letter hidden away amongst my belongings. *Not now, Florrie. It's neither the time nor the place.*

'Just...you know...flatter her. You're good at it. Everybody says so.'

For a moment my husband looked unnerved. 'We'll see.' He cleared his throat indicating a change of subject. 'So! The legendary Harriet Montgomery wants to meet my wife.'

'Yes,' I smiled brightly. 'How amazing is that, eh? It would be brilliant to have a second client, and definitely one that's so high-profile.' A part of me wanted to rub Marcus's nose in it after his comment last night about nobody else banging the door down for my work. 'I'm really looking forward to meeting her. Who knows, we might have a few things in common.'

Marcus snorted. 'I doubt it, Florrie. Women like her move in completely different social circles to the likes of you.'

Stung, for a second I couldn't think of anything to say. 'I'm perfectly able to hold my own with the likes of Harriet Montgomery,' I eventually said.

Marcus regarded me for a moment. There was that uneasy tension between us again.

'If she offers you a commission, I think you should decline.'

I boggled at my husband. 'Don't be ridiculous! Why on earth would I do that?'

'Think about it, Florrie. If you did a bum job, she's the type who'd put you out of work forever.'

'Thanks, Marcus,' I said, inwardly seething, 'but if I decline a commission, whether from an ex-movie star, a restaurateur, or Trevor the flippin' postman, it will be *my* decision and *my* decision alone.' For a moment the air crackled between us.

Marcus was the first to speak. 'Of course, my darling. After all, you're not a woman who knows how to say no.'

My eyes flashed. 'What's that remark supposed to mean?'

Marcus shook his head. 'Nothing. Nothing at all.' He leant forward and pecked me on the cheek. I noted the lack of passionate snogs now there wasn't a captive audience. 'I'm going to work. See you later.'

I folded my arms across my chest and watched my husband take his leave. My private thoughts were interrupted by Daisy opening her front door to wave Tom and their brood off.

'Oooh, you're scowling,' Daisy observed. 'What's up?'

I immediately gave my neighbour a mega-watt smile. 'Nothing's up.'

'Don't talk rot. You never could tell a porky to save your life, Florrie.' She looked away for a moment to blow noisy kisses to the children and Tom, before turning her attention back to me. 'Tell me what's upset you over coffee. It's your turn this morning.'

'Actually, coffee will be at Alison's. She apparently has some exciting news for me.'

'Bugger,' Daisy heaved a sigh. 'That means I'll have to get dressed.' She was still in yesterday's pyjamas which were additionally sporting brown marks. She caught me looking. 'Chocolate spread,' she explained. 'I dropped my toast down me. So what's this exciting news Her Ladyship has?'

'It's to talk about a commission for Harriet Montgomery. Apparently she wants to meet me.'

'Get you,' Daisy gave a low whistle. 'Next you'll be having a phone call from the Duchess of Cambridge wanting a portrait of George and Charlotte!'

I grinned. 'Hardly. Anyway, look sharp, Alison's returning.'

We watched as our neighbour parked her immaculate four by four on the drive. Daisy tutted under her breath.

'Fancy driving that petrol-guzzling thing to Tiffany's school. She could walk it in two minutes.'

I shrugged. 'I don't think any of the mothers at Darwin Prep ever walk.'

Daisy rolled her eyes. 'No, the breeze

would ruffle their hundred quid salon blow-dries.'

Alison pushed her driver door open and slid out. 'Morning, Daisy. Would you like to join me and Florrie for coffee?' She paused to look Daisy up and down. 'When you're dressed, naturally. Annabelle Farquhar-Jones will be joining us too.'

Daisy audibly groaned. I was inclined to agree with Daisy. Annabelle wasn't somebody I'd ever managed to warm to, despite my best efforts. She had a reputation as something of a man-eater and seemed to have a new guy on her arm every other week.

'There's no need for that attitude, Daisy,' said Alison firmly. 'Annabelle is a perfectly decent sort.'

Daisy rolled her eyes. 'You only tolerate her because her cousin's husband's best friend knows George Clooney.'

Alison smiled thinly. 'Don't knock it, Daisy. I'm putting in a lot of spadework in that direction. Wouldn't you just be thrilled if George Clooney turned up at the May Ball?'

Daisy's jaw dropped. 'Are you winding me up?' Alison instantly looked affronted. 'Okay, you're not winding me up. Right, give me two ticks, Ali. I'll just get these PJs off and I'll be right with you!'

Alison opened her mouth to say something but her attention was diverted. Turning into our little dead-end road was a sleek Range Rover. I recognised it instantly as Annabelle Farquhar-Jones's vehicle. Sitting in the passenger seat was an unexpected visitor, but with an equally familiar face, albeit not one I'd met before. It was Harriet Montgomery.

Chapter Nine

'Oh Gawd,' Daisy yelped. 'I haven't had time to change.'

Alison gave Daisy a look that dared her not to go and freshen up. She was just about to give Daisy a stern talking to when Annabelle and Harriet stepped out of the car and onto the drive. Alison, ever the gracious hostess, immediately dazzled the two women with her whiter-than-white smile. Distracted, I couldn't help staring. As well as discreet bits of nip and tuck, Ali had clearly been at the dental bleach too. She was certainly pulling out all the stops to win Henry back from his anonymous bit of crumpet.

'Quick, Florrie, shield me,' hissed Daisy.

I turned to face my neighbour. 'Why?'

'Don't ask. Just do it,' Daisy hissed. A second later she'd whipped off her pyjama top just as Trevor, the postman, peddled into The Cul-de-Sac. Spotting a group of women, one of whom was an ex-movie star, the other completely topless, his mouth dropped open and he almost crashed his bicycle into Annabelle Farquhar-Jones's car.

'Aye say,' Annabelle squawked, 'do watch where you're going.'

'He's obviously not used to seeing somebody famous in your little road,' Harriet smirked.

In that moment I knew Harriet would never be a mate.

'Brilliant diversion,' hissed Daisy swiftly pulling her pyjama top back over her head and smoothing it down. 'You can move out of the way now.'

I stared at her in puzzlement. 'Your top is inside-out.'

'Yeah, I know,' Daisy grinned. 'But it looks clean now, so Alison can't moan at me!'

'She'll notice.'

'No she won't. C'mon, let's go and meet a real live film star! I expect Alison will say Harriet's presence has just put our house prices up fifty grand.'

I giggled as we followed the other women into Alison's house. Unlike Daisy's, the entrance hall was uncluttered and devoid of anything other than a pristine doormat on a polished wood floor.

'Do come through,' Alison trilled, clearly in her element. We followed her into the equally immaculate lounge where even the sofa cushions were standing to attention on their points. 'Sit down, ladies, and I'll make the introductions. Annabelle, you've met Daisy and Florrie before.' We bared our teeth at each other. 'Daisy...Florrie...I'm thrilled to introduce you to...Harriet Montgomery.' Alison said her guest's name in the sort of hushed tone one might adopt if God himself had dropped by.

'Pleased to meet you,' I said politely, and gave a neutral smile.

'Can I have your autograph?' Daisy immediately asked.

Harriet's eyes snagged on Daisy's inside-out pyjama top. She inclined her head as if considering. 'I'm ever so sorry,' she drawled, 'but my autographs are far too valuable to give out willy-nilly. However, I will be auctioning one off at the May Ball, if you want to put in a bid.'

'Oh that's all right,' Daisy said sweetly. 'It was for my mother, not me. Mum said she'd watched all your old films, whereas I'd never heard of you until Ali mentioned your background.'

I froze, Alison visibly jerked, Annabelle's eyes widened, and Harriet's nostrils flared. There was a moment's deafening silence where nobody seemed to breathe. I didn't dare look at Daisy, so concentrated hard on Alison's botoxed forehead. She was the first to recover.

'Coffee or tea, ladies?'

'Darjeeling for me, sweetie,' said Annabelle settling into one squashy sofa and making herself comfortable. Harriet sat down next to Annabelle, putting as much distance as possible between Daisy and I who moved to the second sofa.

'Jasmine,' Harriet snapped. It was clear her feathers had been ruffled.

Daisy leant forward, adopting a cosy tone. 'Her name's Alison,' she said helpfully.

'I know that,' Harriet gave Daisy a withering look. 'I was referring to the tea.'

'Ah,' Daisy sat back. 'Sorry,' she put up her hands by way of apology. 'In my house we just drink whatever muck the supermarket has on special offer.'

'I do too,' Annabelle smiled superciliously, 'but only where wine is concerned.'

Harriet gave a tinkling laugh, humour suddenly restored. 'We only drink champagne in our house. Martin insists on stocking the cellar with high quality champers. He has a superb collection. One of the bottles was released in 1961 – the year Princess Diana was born. It was also the official champagne at the royal wedding of Charles and Diana. A limited number of bottles were released to celebrate the occasion, but only a few people in the know managed to get their hands on such an important part of royal history. Martin was one of them,' she smirked.

'How absolutely amazing,' Annabelle gasped. 'I wish I had a husband like yours, Harriet.'

'Hands off,' Harriet gave a throaty chuckle. 'Talking of which, how is the husband-hunting going, Annabelle?'

'I have my eye on one,' Annabelle said slyly. 'But don't worry, not yours. I must say though, Martin is total class.'

'I'll second that,' Alison nodded her head vehemently keen not to miss out on ingratiating herself to Harriet.

Daisy crow-barred her way back into the conversation. 'Actually, I think champagne is very overrated.' She gave a derisory sniff. 'I'd rather have a nice bottle of Asti any day. Don't you agree, Florrie?' I smiled by way of response. 'Not that you can have any for the next nine months,' she waggled a finger playfully at me. 'Florrie here is expecting a baby!' She beamed at Annabelle and Harriet.

Both women looked shocked. For a moment, Annabelle looked almost...furious. Harriet was the first to recover. 'Really? I thought you couldn't have children?'

There was a sudden awkward silence. I gave Alison a searching look. Had she been gossiping about me? Alison didn't meet my gaze. Daisy was oblivious to my dark look at Alison, and happily babbled on. 'It's taken Florrie a while, hasn't it, duck? She and her sexy hubby have been to hell and back trying for a baby.' She nudged me in the ribs. 'Tell everyone how you used to lie on the bed for half an hour with your legs up against the wall.' Daisy gave a cackle of laughter.

'Congrats,' said Annabelle. Her tone was cool.

'Thank you,' I murmured.

'What do your respective parents think about the wonderful news?' asked Alison.

'Er, well, we...um...we haven't told them yet.'

Daisy looked puzzled. 'Why ever not?'

'Oh, you know,' I took a deep breath while my mind raced ahead to think up a plausible answer, 'because... because...we're waiting until I've reached the twelve week stage and...you know... out of the miscarriage danger zone.' I could feel my armpits breaking out in a gushing mess at the lies I was telling. 'We don't want our mothers reaching for their knitting needles just yet.' I smiled weakly as everybody nodded in agreement.

'I really must put that kettle on.' Alison took advantage of the natural break in conversation. 'Daisy and Florrie, neither of you have told me what you want to drink. Coffee?'

'Yes, please,' I said, grateful to be off the baby subject.

'Actually,' said Daisy, 'can I have a hot chocolate instead? I feel like I need something really sweet. I think I've got PMT again.' There was a sudden silence. Annabelle and Harriet stared at Daisy as if she'd just announced she had a particularly nasty case of venereal disease. Daisy looked from one aristocratic face to another. 'It's an absolute bugger. Do either of you get it?'

'No,' Annabelle said faintly. 'I can't say I do.'

'Me neither,' Harriet said. 'And if I did, I don't think I'd be inclined to talk about it.'

'Really?' Daisy looked genuinely astonished. 'Florrie and I talk about it all the time. Don't we, Florrie?'

'Er, well, just occasionally,' I murmured. I cast around the room for something to comment upon and shift the conversation to a topic Alison would approve of. Her coffee table was loaded with all the latest magazines. I noticed Harriet Montgomery's face was on the cover of one of the celebrity weeklies with the by-line: "How I love being a stay-at-home mum and raising money for charity". Excellent, I'd try and turn the conversation back to the May Ball.

'Yeah, Florrie and I talk about all sorts,' Daisy confided. 'Our mood swings...our menstrual flow.' Out of my peripheral vision I caught Alison looking like she was going to self-combust. 'Sometimes I want to murder my Tom. I've actually fantasised about it.' Daisy shifted her weight from her left buttock, to her right, crossing one leg in the process. 'Do you know that if you have three hungry pigs, it will only take them twenty minutes to completely consume one average-sized human, bones and all. The only things they can't digest are teeth.' She looked across at Harriet. 'Mind you, if you were planning to murder *your* husband I'm sure the teeth bit wouldn't be a problem to worry about. I expect your Martin has dentures, eh?'

I sprang up from my seat with such force that Harriet and Annabelle visibly jumped.

'Let me help you with the drinks,' I said to Alison. Anything to get out of the lounge. The air was slowly turning to poison but darling Daisy was blissfully ignorant of it. I left her prattling about the perfect husband homicide and followed Alison's rigid back out to the kitchen.

Alison began rattling porcelain teacups

onto saucers. Her face registered fury.

'I want you to find me three starving pigs and give them Daisy,' she hissed. 'I've never been so embarrassed in all my life. That's *Harriet Montgomery* in my lounge. Not flaming Dot Cotton.'

'Never mind that,' I rounded on Alison. 'Why did you tell Annabelle and Harriet I couldn't have children? That's personal stuff, Ali. I don't appreciate being talked about to the likes of them.'

'As if I'd tell anybody something like that,' Alison huffed.

'Well why did Harriet say what she did?'

'I haven't a clue,' Alison shrugged. She stomped over to her huge American fridge and yanked the door open. Removing a carton of milk, she slammed it down on the worktop. 'But in a village like ours, it strikes me everybody seems to know everybody else's business anyway. I've already had that old biddy at the corner shop, Mrs Thompson, giving me a crafty look and asking if I liked my bracelet from Henry, and how she was sure she'd seen another totally identical bracelet on one of her customers. Naturally when I'd pressed Mrs Thompson to reveal who she'd seen wearing such a bracelet, she'd had sudden amnesia. But never mind that for the moment. What the devil does Daisy think she's playing at? She's talking inane topics to women she hardly knows and who are *waaay* out of her class.'

I decided to give Alison the benefit of the

doubt, and sighed. 'Daisy is just trying to be chummy,' I soothed. I reached for the kettle and peered inside. It was full. I snapped the lid down and flicked the switch.

'*Chummy*?' Alison spat. 'She's a total liability. I'm going to have to rely on you, Florrie, to keep a close eye on Daisy at the May Ball. If she talks like this when she's sober, can you imagine what she might come out with if she hits the vino? She's a loose cannon.' Alison shuddered theatrically as she removed some irregular-shaped cookies from a Fortnum & Mason bag and set them on a pretty plate. 'Here. Take these and offer them around. And if anybody asks, you tell them I made them and say what a brilliant cook I am. Hurry up. Before Daisy starts talking about her second favourite subject.'

As I scampered back to the lounge, plate of biscuits held aloft, I could see from the horrified expressions on Annabelle's and Harriet's faces that I was too late and Daisy was in full flow.

'Premenstrual tension upsets my whole body. I get terribly constipated. It was twice as bad when I was pregnant. My GP gave me this sugary liquid to get my bowels moving. It worked really well though. I do like to have a good pooh.'

'As is evident by the verbal diarrhoea,' Harriet murmured to Annabelle.

I thrust the plate of biscuits under Daisy's nose. 'Here. Alison made them herself. Have several,' I urged. If Daisy's choppers were busy, hopefully she'd be quiet for a while.

Alison appeared in the doorway, hands firmly grasping a beautiful tray set with exquisite china. 'Here we are,' she said in a sing-song voice. She moved towards the coffee table and, with the back of one hand, carefully nudged some magazines out of the way to make room for the tray. 'That's a *lovely* piece on you, Harriet.' Alison nodded at the celeb mag as she set the tray down. 'Your charity work is *so* admirable. I don't know *how* you find time to oversee so many worthy causes when you are kept super busy looking after your beautiful home, being the perfect wife to Martin, and a fan*tastic* mother to Piper.'

Daisy rolled her eyes. 'Oh pur-*leeze*,' she said, spraying biscuit crumbs everywhere. She leant forward to address Harriet. 'I don't believe for one moment you personally put on a pair of rubber gloves and scrub all your own loo bowls in that mansion of yours.'

Harriet bestowed Daisy with an icy smile. 'Of course not. I have help. But running a home like mine, looking after a highly successful man like Martin and tending to Piper – a celebrity child, remember, and incredibly needy – that all requires careful organisation and forward planning, and that I *do* organise totally by myself.'

'And brilliantly too,' Annabelle gushed.

Daisy swiped the back of her hand across her mouth to dislodge some crumbs. She gave Harriet an innocent look. 'It must be a total nightmare having a gardener, a housekeeper and a nanny. I don't know how you cope.' She inspected her chocolatey fingers before wiping them down her inside-out pyjama top. She frowned at the dark smudge marks left across her chest. 'Hell. I won't be able to wear this tomorrow now.'

'How are the arrangements for the May Ball coming along?' I asked.

'Absolutely brilliantly,' Harriet beamed. 'And it's all thanks to my marvellous Events organiser here,' she nodded at Alison who instantly turned pink with pleasure.

'So you've even got somebody doing *that* for you,' Daisy pointed out. She reached for her hot chocolate and slurped noisily. 'Whatever do you do with your free time?'

'Believe me, I rarely have a moment to myself,' Harriet glared at Daisy. 'Time is scarce. Which brings me to why I came here this morning.' Harriet turned her attention to me. 'Alison told me you're an artist.'

The biscuit in my mouth momentarily threatened to choke me. I hastily swallowed, suddenly nervous. 'Y-yes.'

'Do you paint portraits?'

'Mostly landscapes actually. But yes, I've produced one or two small portraits for family members.'

'Good. Well I've seen your work in Serafino's. If your portraits are as good as your landscapes, I'd like to commission you.'

'She's not cheap,' Daisy piped up. 'Florrie charges four grand a painting.'

Harriet raised an eyebrow and looked at me enquiringly. 'Luca told me he paid you two thou.'

'That's for the landscapes,' Daisy interrupted. 'Her portraits are double.'

Alison was giving Daisy murderous looks.

'Whatever,' Harriet shrugged. 'Money isn't an issue.'

Daisy shot me a sidelong glance. I caught her expression. It was one of triumph. Whilst I wanted to kiss her for effortlessly pricing and securing work for me, another part of me hesitated. Four thousand pounds was a huge sum of money. I gulped as Marcus's words floated back from earlier on. *If Harriet offers you a commission, I think you should decline. Think about it, Florrie. If you did a bum job, she's the type who'd put you out of work forever.* 'I'm flattered to be asked, Harriet.' My hands began to anxiously pleat the hemline of the top I was wearing. 'Realistically, I'm someone who paints for a hobby. Wouldn't you like to find somebody more eminent?'

'No,' Harriet replied. 'I haven't the time or the inclination. Apart from anything else, I would prefer to have a female artist.'

'Why's that?' I asked. Somehow I knew the answer to the question before Harriet even replied.

'Because when you paint me, I'll be in the buff.'

Chapter Ten

'Oh God, Daisy,' I snorted into my coffee cup. The two of us were in my lounge, drinking companionably. In the background the television was on. Daisy wanted to keep tabs on Jeremy Kyle's latest dysfunctional guests. 'Fancy telling Annabelle Farquhar-Jones and Harriet Montgomery about your bowel motions yesterday. Did you see Alison's face?'

'Yes,' Daisy nodded. 'Anybody would think Annabelle and Harriet have never so much as farted.'

'They probably haven't,' I replied.

We were now minus Alison who'd been summoned, last minute, to the Montgomery-Murray-Wells' household.

'Rather her than me,' Daisy had said after Alison had picked up a text message, instantly becoming both flustered and elated before gabbling apologies to Daisy and myself as she rushed out of my house. 'Gawd knows why she wants to suck up to Harriet anyway. I mean, what's in it for her? The woman's a nightmare.'

I leant back, relaxing into the depths of my comfortable sofa and sighed. For the first time this week I was feeling a little less on edge. Marcus had left at the crack of dawn for a meeting in London, so there had been no doorstep nonsense for Alison's benefit. Also, Luca Serafino's landscape was finished and ready to be delivered. The painting was still drying, as such, but Luca was chomping at the bit to have it as soon as possible. It would be a relief to be distracted with a new project. I was meeting Harriet this afternoon to discuss where and how she would like to be painted. I paused mid-sip and frowned.

'That's strange.'

'What?' asked Daisy, one eye on Jeremy Kyle's guest who was squaring up to a bouncer.

'Alison took off like a bat out of hell to see Harriet.'

'Yeah. And?'

'Harriet's not at home.'

'How do you know that?'

'Because she told me yesterday, when we were discussing the painting commission, not to arrive at the house until after lunch. You surely can't have missed her boasting about her interview this morning with Holly and Philip on breakfast telly?'

'I think I'd zoned Harriet's voice out by that point. The woman is a crashing bore. She was jabbering on and on about the day she and her husband met the Royal family and how Prince Charles winked at her when Camilla's back was turned. I mean, *really*? The woman is a total narcissist.' Daisy reached for my remote control to change channels. 'Well let's have a look and see how Ms Harriet Hog-the-Limelight comes across on the small screen.' Daisy pressed a button and Harriet's face instantly dominated the television. 'Perfect timing.'

'You have to admit she is a stunning looking woman.'

'Any woman can look stunning, Florrie, if they have the luxury of ten hours sleep at night and somebody waiting on them hand, foot and finger.'

'But movie stars aren't really like the rest of us mere mortals, are they?' I took another sip of my coffee. 'Somehow they're always so...,' I paused, trying to think of the right word, '...glossy.'

'Listen, I can look glossy if I want to,' Daisy waggled a finger at me. She was still wearing her inside out pyjama top smeared in yesterday's Fortnum & Mason melted chocolate. Her hair looked like it hadn't seen a brush in days and her face was shiny and devoid of make-up. She also had a huge spot brewing on the end of her nose. 'Oh, I missed that bit. What did she say?' She turned the volume up.

Harriet was treating Philip to her tinkling laugh. Clearly they'd just shared something terribly amusing. Harriet's face suddenly became serious.

'In all truth, Philip, I was seriously thrilled when Angelina Jolie rang me up. She absolutely begged me to think about starring in her latest project. Naturally it's been written by herself and she will be directing too. Brad is in the lead role, and he's just *such* a fun guy.'

'So the Jolie-Pitts are managing to stay amicable, despite their divorce?' Philip asked nosily.

'They are professionals,' Harriet gently chided, 'so that goes without saying.'

'Whilst I don't doubt they are professional where their work is concerned, nonetheless the paparazzi have been hinting at gin bottles and bongs being hurled at each other long after the midnight hour. There have also been rumours about another woman coming between them.'

'I wouldn't know, Philip.' Harriet was starting to look put out. Her expression said it all. *I haven't come on your programme to discuss the Jolie-Pitt marriage meltdown. I want to talk about me. Me, me, me, me, me.*

'So back to you,' Philip beamed cosily and Harriet immediately perked up. 'Can you tell us what the film is about?

'I can't say too much at the moment, but I have seen the script. It is a high-octane action project with lots of romantic suspense. Obviously I'm Brad's love interest. If I do take the role it will be so nice to play opposite someone who is not just charismatic but seriously good looking.'

'Are you saying,' Phil smiled goofily into camera, 'that you fancy Brad Pitt?'

Harriet threw back her head and gave another tinkling laugh. How on earth did Martin Murray-Wells put up with it? It was beyond irritating. 'Between you and me, Philip,' Harriet paused and winked into the camera lens, 'if you're watching, Angie, look away now!' She turned back to Philip

Schofield. 'I think Brad's divine.'

'Oh for heaven's sake,' Daisy put two fingers into her mouth and mimed puking. 'The woman is beyond ghastly. As if Angelina Jolie would make a point of tuning in to watch Harriet Montgomery on breakfast telly.' She pressed the remote's off button. 'Anyway, enough of her. Tell me more about your baby news. How are you feeling? If you don't mind me saying, Florrie, you don't seem terribly excited.'

Caught off guard, for a moment I could only gape at Daisy. 'That's a daft thing to say,' I said, recovering my composure. 'Firstly, I feel fine. Secondly, I'm thrilled to bits. Ecstatic. Totally over the moon.'

'And Marcus?'

'Yes – obviously!'

'So when are you seeing your GP?'

'Isn't it a bit early?'

'I don't think it's ever too soon. I was hot-footing down to the surgery the moment the tester showed "Positive". It doesn't hurt to get checked over, Florrie. Do you have any idea how many weeks' pregnant you are?'

'No,' I lied. 'It's very early days.'

'And Marcus hasn't gone off the boil yet?'

'Sorry?'

'You know, nudge nudge, wink wink. He's still up for a bit of slap and tickle.'

I flushed. 'Sure.' Another lie.

'That's good. Tom went off sex almost instantly. Men fall into two groups when it comes to their partner getting big with child. There are those who love it, and feel all macho and protective as their woman's body changes shape, and then there are those who make any excuse they can to avoid bonking their partner for the next nine months. I think it's the whole Madonna-whore thing. Pregnant women become saint-like to some men and they just can't lay a finger on their woman as a result. Apart from anything else, Tom just didn't find my elephant ankles terribly sexy.' Daisy sighed.

'Oh,' I said flatly. 'I honestly haven't even thought about whether we'll have a sex life during my pregnancy. I'm still coming to terms with actually being pregnant.'

'Have you and Marcus had a bonk since you found out?'

'Daisy!' I exclaimed. 'What sort of a question is that for goodness sake?'

'A nosy one,' Daisy conceded. 'Well, have you?'

'As it happens,' I rolled my eyes, 'no, we haven't.'

'Ah,' Daisy nodded knowingly. 'So it might well be that Marcus is like my Tom. You'll have to be patient with him, Florrie. It's not personal.'

'It's only been forty-eight hours since we found out. We don't have sex morning, noon and night, you know.'

'Really?' Daisy raised her eyebrows in surprise. 'What's with all the doorstep tomfooleries then? Marcus always acts like he's a walking hormone gland and that you have a constantly arousing effect on him.'

I gave a mirthless hoot. Daisy regarded me curiously. I immediately attempted to inject some oomph into the laugh, as if Daisy's comment had tickled me in some way. Unfortunately I ended up tinkling, and for a second or two sounded annoyingly like Harriet.

'I think a lot of Marcus's doorstep nonsense is simply to annoy Alison,' I said. 'He knows how prissy Ali is, and just likes winding her up.'

'Oh,' said Daisy looking disappointed. 'So how often do you two really do it?'

'Do what?' I asked, feigning ignorance.

'Have sex!' Daisy cried. 'Please tell me it's only once a fortnight. Reassure me that the pace of my love life is normal for a married woman with three kids.'

'Of course it's normal!' I grinned. 'There are millions of women out there,' I waved a hand at the world beyond my lounge window, 'who are worn out looking after their families and simply want to sleep.'

'Ah,' Daisy gave me a crafty look, 'but you're not actually looking after a little one right now. You have yet to deal with the sleepless nights and months of feeling like a zombie. You are still,' she put her head on one side to consider, 'a sleek creature with your boobs above your naval and a stomach that hasn't dropped like frayed knicker elastic. So come on, Florrie. You can tell me. On average, how often do you and Marcus have a bonk?'

'I'm starting to think you're obsessed with sex.'

'Says the woman who flirts with the postman.'

I rolled my eyes. 'Well, if you really must know—'

'I really, really must.'

'It was ... let me see ... last Sunday.' Yet another lie.

Daisy's face fell. 'That's only four days ago. For a moment I thought you were going to tell me you were part of the Every Other Week Brigade.' Her dismay was evident.

I smiled. 'Let's talk about something else. But first, I'll make some more coffee.'

As I walked out to my kitchen, Daisy's question about the frequency of my sex life needled my conscience. The truth was I simply couldn't remember the last time Marcus and I had been intimate.

Chapter Eleven

As soon as Daisy had left, I rang the surgery for an appointment to see my GP. Usually it was a two-week wait to see a doctor, but this morning the Gods were on my side.

'There's been a cancellation,' said the receptionist. 'Dr Baily can see you tomorrow morning.'

'Thanks,' I said and rang off.

Scribbling the appointment in my diary, I then set about carefully loading Luca's painting into the boot of my car. However, when I arrived at Serafino's Cucina, he wasn't there. I didn't know whether to be relieved or disappointed. As I alternated between the two emotions, a member of staff took the painting on my behalf.

'Tell Luca he can settle up with me next week,' I said. 'There's no rush.'

I then headed off to Harriet Montgomery's home. Set high on a hill overlooking Lower Amblegate, it struck me the Montgomery-Murray-Wells' pile was a bit like a castle overlooking its kingdom, with Harriet queen of all she surveyed. As I drove along the winding and seemingly never-ending tree-lined drive I began to feel a little overwhelmed by my surroundings, especially when the mansion was finally revealed in all its sprawling splendour. A couple of gardeners were toiling away on flowerbeds full of colourful promise. For a moment I dithered where to park the car. *Oh for goodness sake, Florrie. Just make up your mind. Anywhere will do. There's loads of room.* Settling for a spot by a clipped hedge with not a twig out of place, I locked the car and walked towards the house. A number of steps led up to a huge double-fronted door. To one side was a rope-pull to operate an old-fashioned bell. I was about to haul on it when the door opened, taking me by surprise.

'Hello, Florrie,' said Harriet.

She looked immaculate. Harriet was still wearing the smart outfit she'd worn on television earlier. I suddenly felt horribly underdressed in my casual top and jeans which were already feeling tight around the waist.

'Hi,' I smiled. 'You must be psychic. I hadn't even rung the bell.'

She waved a dismissive hand. 'Oh that's just a bit of character nonsense in keeping with the place. I saw you approaching. There are cameras in various places around the top of the hill and at intermittent spots along the drive.'

'Ah,' I nodded. Harriet had just cleverly reminded me this wasn't an ordinary human being I was visiting.

'Well do come in,' Harriet said. Her tone was extremely brusque leaving me in no doubt this meeting was most definitely business, and not a social call. 'I'm expecting company in an hour, so I need to get the finer details of this commission sorted fairly swiftly.'

'Sure,' I said, opting for a bit of briskness myself. Nothing wrong in letting her think I was a busy artist with a diary bursting with appointments. I followed her into the hallway which was about the size of my entire house. Without a doubt, it had the wow factor. I took in the high ceilings, flagstone floor and a sweeping staircase complete with ornate balustrade. The surrounding walls were punctuated with huge windows, a feature in their own right. They poured forth the sort of light that turns dust motes silver and touches everything with an ethereal quality. 'This is the most perfect area to paint,' I said, unable to keep the enthusiasm from my voice.

'But not very private,' Harriet pointed out. 'Follow me, please.'

I recognised an order when given one. As Harriet moved towards the staircase, I scampered after her. The stairway swept upwards circumnavigating galleried landings on two more floors. Along an inner hallway and set to one side, a smaller staircase led into the eaves and roof space. A century ago, this would have been the servants' quarters. Today it looked as though nobody ever came up here. The lay-out was almost like a corridor in that you passed through one room straight into another. There were no doors, only doorways. The first room was completely empty, the second had been turned into a bathroom, and the third contained nothing but an enormous wrought iron bed. Harriet caught me looking. She paused.

'Gertrude, Martin's sister, sleeps up here when she visits.' Harriet checked the room over with a proprietary air.

I leant against the doorframe. 'Doesn't your sister-in-law find her guest bedroom rather removed from the rest of the house?'

'On the contrary.' Harriet gave a twisted smile. 'I think she feels quite at home in the rafters. After all, Gertrude is a total old bat.'

'Ah.' I wasn't sure what to say to that, so kept quiet. Even so, it was nice to know that even ex-movie stars sometimes had issues with family members just like the rest of us ordinary folk. Harriet turned her back on her sister-in-law's occasional sleeping quarters and led me into the fourth and final room. This, like the first room, was empty.

'You will paint me in here.'

Harriet marched to the far end where the original dormer window had been revamped into a Juliet balcony. She pulled the door open. Immediately bird song and spring fragrances invaded my senses. I inhaled appreciatively and moved across the floor to Harriet's side to peer out. What a view. From here I could see the whole of Lower Amblegate spread below, including The Cul-de-Sac. I could even see Alison's car on her drive! Which reminded me.

'Did you catch up with Alison?' I asked. Harriet looked at me blankly. 'She rushed off to see you this morning,' I explained, 'but you were in London.'

'You must be mistaken, Florrie. My work with Alison is finished. Regarding the May Ball, I've instructed Alison exactly what I want, where I want it, and how. All that remains to be done is for me to talk to the paparazzi, and tie up a few loose ends with a discreet roving film crew.'

I was stunned at Harriet's breathtaking dismissal of my neighbour. It was clear from Harriet's tone that Alison had served her purpose. My heart squeezed for my neighbour's feelings when she realised her coveted close friendship with Harriet had amounted to nothing more than being taken advantage of.

'So,' Harriet flung her arms wide and turned to look at the loft space. 'This is going to be your studio throughout the duration. It's wonderfully private. I can walk around starkers up here with no prying eyes peering in.'

'That's good to know, but I just want to say I'm more than happy to paint you from a photograph in my studio at home,' I pointed out.

'No, no, no, Florrie,' said Harriet waggling a finger at me. 'No photographs. I can't risk any images falling into the wrong hands and then being splashed across the tabloids.'

I didn't know whether to be affronted at the insinuation I'd stoop so low as to flog a photo to the press, or whether to laugh out loud. Harriet was carrying on like she was Madonna.

'You will have to bring your paints and easel over here, Florrie. My privacy absolutely *has* to be respected.'

I blinked. *Just think of the four thousand pounds she's paying you.* 'Of course,' I demurred.

'Good,' said Harriet giving me a stern look. 'I'm glad we understand each other. I'd like you to start this Saturday, bright and early. Shall we say nine o'clock?'

'Sure.'

That suited me fine. I had a legitimate excuse to be out of the house without Marcus around me or having to endure the strained atmosphere that had developed between us.

'What's more,' Harriet continued, 'I want it finished in time for the May Ball.'

I blanched. One week. Harriet noticed my hesitation.

'Problem?' she frowned.

'No, not as such,' I shook my head. 'But if you want me to paint you as a still life – how available are you actually going to be? After all,' I pointed out, 'you're a very busy lady.'

'If I have to leave you mid-pose you will have to work from your muse...memory... or whatever else it is you artists lean upon when called to do so.' I sensed that Harriet wanted to wind the meeting up. 'Any questions?'

'No, I don't think so.'

'Good. Now if you don't mind, I'll see you out. I'm expecting company in a little while and need to get out of these clothes and into something,' a smile played around her lips, 'more comfortable.'

As we made our way back to the entrance hall, I wondered what on earth she had to do other than change her outfit. She already looked immaculate. Harriet opened the door and I stepped out into the cool afternoon air.

'Right,' I turned back to smile at her. 'See you on Sat–'

But I was talking to the door. Clearly ex-movie stars didn't bother saying good-bye to the likes of people like me. I sighed and walked towards the car.

I'd barely driven a hundred yards down Harriet's grand driveway when, from the opposite direction, a vehicle came hurtling towards me. It was driving far too fast for the likes of this driveway. My foot touched the brake. Surely the other driver was going to slow down, wasn't he? Suddenly realising that this wasn't going to happen, I swerved and frantically steered my car to the very edge of the driveway, tucking it under the branches of one of Harriet's overhanging trees. As the sound of twigs scraped noisily against the length of my car scratching all the paintwork to shreds, I muttered a string of oaths. Furious, I glared at the approaching driver determined to mouth a few profanities his way. But my angry expression swiftly turned to one of surprise. I knew that car, just as surely as I knew the driver behind the wheel. He whooshed straight past my vehicle with barely a millimetre to spare, spinning tyres sending up a spray of shingle and dust as he retreated from sight in my rear view mirror. It was apparent the driver had been totally oblivious to both my car and me sitting within it. I watched, stunned, as the vehicle disappeared around a bend. The driver hadn't so much as glanced at my astonished face. His eyes had been full of excitement, his face a picture of joy, no doubt from the anticipation of feasting his eyes on Harriet Montgomery's change into something "more comfortable". And what would that be, I wondered. A negligee? A French maid outfit? Her birthday suit? I blew out my cheeks and wondered what Alison would make of it all if she knew.

The driver had been her husband. Henry.

Chapter Twelve

The following morning I sat in my doctor's surgery and, whilst waiting to be seen, tried to think of a perfectly innocent reason for Alison's husband visiting Harriet yesterday. Unfortunately all legitimate possibilities evaded me other than the obvious. Henry and Harriet were having an affair. My mind tumbled back to Alison tearfully revealing Henry had bought a diamond bracelet for a mystery woman. The inscription had apparently read, "To the most beautiful woman in the world with all my love." Well there was no doubting Harriet Montgomery was beautiful. On a scorecard of ten, she was an eleven.

Last night, over dinner, I'd nearly told Marcus about seeing Henry at Harriet's, but swerved off at the last moment for fear of him accidentally letting it slip to Alison. The last thing I wanted was her being even more hurt. I could just imagine the possible future doorstep shenanigans:

"Oooh, Florrie, you're driving me mad with desire...mwah, mwah, mwah...oh no, now look what's happened...I seem to have grown a third leg. Ah, morning, Ali. I hear Henry's having a touch of the same problem. According to my wife here, Henry's third leg grew so big it was wedged on his car's accelerator. Isn't that right, darling? Florrie said Henry's car was absolutely hurtling along Harriet's driveway. Yes, that's right. Harriet. Even her gardeners witnessed his excessive speeding. Their eyes were agog, especially when Henry got out of his car. The poor chap had to pogo up Harriet's steps."

Nor could I confide in Daisy. Much as I loved my scatty neighbour, she was a frightful gossip and might let something slip to Alison. Again, my imagination acted out a possible scenario:

"Morning, Ali. Remember when I offended you by saying Henry was over the hill? Well I was right! Henry *is* over the hill...at Harriet Montgomery's place. Shall I ring Jeremy Kyle?"

I realised I was in a horrible situation. I knew something about my neighbour's husband that she most certainly didn't. Should I keep quiet? Or casually mention it? Or talk to Henry myself? Or just forget the whole thing and feign ignorance? I'd read about this sort of quandary on the problem pages of magazines. Many a time I'd settled down with a nice cup of tea only to read: "Should I tell my friend her husband is having an affair?" Perhaps I should write a letter.

Dear Deirdre

I live in a very insular village in which also dwells an ex-movie star (who, incidentally, may or may not be on the verge of a massive comeback). I can't say who she is, but if you want a clue I can reveal the said woman has a highly irritating laugh. Between you and me I'd like to give her a good slap. But the real problem, dear Deirdre, is that this high profile woman is having an affair with my lovely neighbour's husband. What should I do? Tell my neighbour what her cheating hubby is up to? Risk jeopardising our friendship? Or confront her hubby? Maybe give HIM a good slap? Or say nothing? I'm finding the whole situation very distressing. It doesn't help that I'm pregnant which isn't without its own problems. What should I do?

It was a dilemma. I tried to predict an agony aunt's response.

Dear Distressed Person
Every day I receive letters from people whose lives have been turned upside down by their partners having affairs. Affairs can definitely affect friendships, so first and foremost please seek out the ex-movie star and give her that good slap. This is a very difficult situation and your friend's husband has put you in an invidious position. So yes, go ahead and give him a good slap too. It's unforgiveable you should be burdened with this when you are pregnant and clearly having your own personal difficulties. Therefore I recommend you just give everybody, including your entire insular village, a really good slap. It will make you feel so

much better. Good luck with the pregnancy.

'Florence Milligan?'

Dr Baily was standing in her consulting room doorway. Startled, I leapt up and hastened into her room. The GP sat down in her chair and indicated I should do the same on the opposite side of her desk. She gave me a pleasant smile.

'How can I help you?'

I opened my mouth to speak but was suddenly and without any warning ambushed by emotion. From nowhere a mish-mash of jumbled feelings rose up like a tsunami, hitting my tear ducts and switching on the waterworks.

'I-I'm so sorry,' I stuttered, genuinely taken aback at this unforeseen outpouring.

'That's okay. Take your time.'

Dr Baily glanced at a clock on the wall. Outside there was a waiting room full of patients. The doctor had been behind schedule before I'd even stepped over the threshold of her consulting room. Perhaps everybody was having a bad day and breaking down the moment they sat down with Dr Baily.

'I'm s-sorry. J-just a bit...emotional.'

'No worries.' Another glance at the clock.

For goodness sake, Florrie. Just tell it how it is, and hurry up.

'I'm pregnant.'

'Congratulations!'

'Th-thanks. It's come as a bit of a shock.

You see, I was told I had endometriosis and having my own children would be unlikely.'

'Double congratulations!'

'And also my husband pretty much fires blanks.'

Dr Baily was starting to look flabbergasted, but did her best to hide bemusement.

'So triple congratulations, Mrs Milligan. I always say if a baby is meant to be it WILL be!'

'Y-yes.' I glanced down at my shoes for a moment. 'Anyway, I have no idea how pregnant I am. Well, maybe a bit of an idea.' I clasped my hands together, fingers interlacing. A nervous gesture. 'But then again I might be totally wrong.' I unlaced my fingers and foraged up my sleeve for a tissue. Dabbing my eyes, I gave Dr Baily a frank look. 'My jeans are really tight. I can't do up the stud button anymore.'

'First of all, don't worry about your tears,' Dr Baily smiled kindly. 'Heightened emotions are perfectly normal. So, you've taken a pregnancy test?'

'Yes.'

'Good.' Dr Baily peered at her computer screen and began tapping out notes on her keyboard. 'Date of last period?'

'I had a really odd one about six weeks ago. It lasted just one day. But to be honest my body has always been a law unto itself where that's concerned. I can't really remember the last time I had a "normal" period as such – possibly four months ago.'

'Okay.' Dr Baily did a bit more tapping. 'We'll do background history in a moment. I'll also book you in for a dating ultrasound which is very helpful for pinpointing the expected date of delivery.' She stood up and indicated I do likewise. 'Over there, please. Hop on the couch and I'll examine you. I can give you a rough idea how many weeks you are.'

'Oh, good,' I said uncertainly. I kicked off my shoes and pulled down my jeans. Lying down on the hard couch, I gave an involuntary shiver while Dr Baily got to work.

'Well, Mrs Milligan, I'm delighted to confirm your pregnancy.' She beamed at me. 'I would say you're about eight weeks.'

I gulped. 'Are you sure?'

'Like I said, the ultrasound will give a more accurate result.'

'Right. So...so the ultrasound *might* say I'm as much as twelve weeks? Or sixteen?' My brain struggled to remember exactly when Marcus and I had last been intimate.

Dr Baily smiled and shook her head. 'I can tell you're a first time mum-to-be.' She spoke in a humouring tone of voice. 'You are definitely not twelve weeks or even sixteen weeks gone. As such, it's very early days.'

'But my jeans are throttling my midriff,' I protested.

'That's mainly fluid retention. Get dressed and we'll go through your medical background.'

As I hauled up my jeans, I chewed my bottom lip. I'd suspected it all along, but knowing for sure was a massive reality check. Marcus was not the father of my unborn baby.

Chapter Thirteen

Throughout the drive home from Dr Baily's surgery, I felt horribly nauseous. Letting myself into the house, I charged upstairs to the bathroom. Sinking to my knees, I leant over the toilet bowl and threw up and up and up. Was this the dreaded morning sickness – albeit afternoon sickness in my case? Or just a bad reaction at having shocking news confirmed? I reached for some toilet paper and wiped my mouth. Standing up shakily, I flushed the chain, then washed my hands and cleaned my teeth.

Oh, Florrie. What have you done? I went into the master bedroom and sat down heavily on the end of the bed. Leaning forward, I rubbed the heels of my hands into my eyes. Things were a mess. So, what to do? There were a few options.

Firstly, lie. I could tell my husband Dr Baily had estimated the pregnancy to be further along, approximately twelve weeks. I could then omit telling him about the dating ultrasound and, with an awful lot of luck and downright blagging, get through the pregnancy without any doctor telling my husband the real due date. I'd then pretend to give birth to a premature baby. As Marcus had been a very bonny baby boy weighing in at ten pounds, and I'd been not far behind him at a robust nine pounds, I'd have to hope my premature baby wasn't the size of a Christmas turkey. My conscience immediately scattered this train of thought. *You mean to say, Florrie, that you're totally comfortable with the idea of Marcus raising a child that isn't his? That you have no qualms about him bonding with a baby fathered by another man? Shame on you!* I sighed heavily. Some women did just that, but I wasn't one of them.

A second option was to have a secret abortion and pretend I'd had a miscarriage. My brain had barely processed this thought when every particle of my being recoiled. What, get rid of this miracle baby? After five years of trying to get pregnant? After goodness-knows how many failed IVF attempts? No way. Automatically my hands moved over my abdomen, almost cradling the soft swell, instinctively wanting to protect. Abortion was absolutely unthinkable.

Option three was to talk to the real father-to-be. The fact that he was clueless about my predicament and I had no idea how he'd react was pretty monumental stuff. We'd only had one brief encounter for heaven's sake! But then again, didn't he have a right to know? Wasn't it deceitful *not* to tell him? Certainly it was deceitful to let Marcus believe this baby was his. Dear Lord, Jeremy Kyle would have a field day with me. I had a sudden vision of him thrusting a microphone into my face.

"You've taken the lie detector test, Florrie

Milligan. And I can reveal to everybody here in this studio along with our audience watching at home...YOU ARE A LIAR!" And everybody would give a collective gasp and agree as Jeremy turned to camera and declared, "Florrie Milligan is a horrible manipulative woman." Then the camera would pan across a booing audience before settling on me, sitting in a studio chair on stage, hanging my head in shame. Alison would never talk to me again, whereas Daisy would probably text me asking I get Jeremy's autograph. I shuddered.

The final possibility was to simply confess all to Marcus then embark on motherhood as a single parent. I gulped at the thought of sitting Marcus down to stutter out the truth. I didn't want to hurt him, despite the fact that he'd hurt me so many times in the past. The fact was I'd found solace, briefly, in the arms of another man. It had been totally unpremeditated. I squeezed my eyes shut as a memory was evoked, rushing to the surface of my mind like an air bubble pinging to the surface of a pond. Everything about that illicit encounter had felt so right, despite the circumstances being so very wrong. However, unlike me, Marcus had deliberately started affairs time and time again. Indeed, my husband had his own outstanding explanations waiting to be heard. Some of the evidence was right here, in this very room.

I pushed myself up from the bed and

105

went to the wardrobe. Opening one door, I rummaged within until I'd located the correct shoebox. Tugging at it, I lifted the lid. My hands scrabbled within, making contact with the hidden letter. Crouching down, I extracted the notepaper, smoothing it out against the carpet with one hand. The damning message was written in blue ink. The handwriting was almost defiant in its boldness.

Dear Florrie

You and I have somebody in common. Your husband. Some time ago Marcus and I had an affair. I appreciate this revelation is going to come as a huge shock. Can I invite you to now stop reading and sit down before I continue?

We have mutual friends, and that is how I met Marcus. His charm was deadly, and I fell madly in love with him. He told me he loved me too. In snatched moments together, we made plans. Marcus was going to leave you. He promised to move in with me. He vowed we would live the coveted Happy Ever After. Except, unbeknown to me, Marcus had embarked on another affair. It was quite by chance I found out. Thank God Marcus hadn't moved in with me. After all, I have a child to think about. The last thing I would ever want is another failed relationship impacting upon my daughter.

My love rival (sorry, I appreciate that must sound ironic when I've been your love rival) is, by appalling coincidence, also an acquaintance. She has no idea I know about their fling. I can't tackle her about it because, apart from the fact that we move in the same social circle, I don't want to risk confrontation which, again, could impact upon my daughter in the long run.

So, Florrie, the reason I'm telling you all this, at the risk of sounding like a woman scorned, is I think you should be aware what sort of man you are married to. Marcus is a serial philanderer. Truly, it is not my wish to hurt you. However, I can't deny that I want to hurt Marcus. Badly. He swept me off my feet, but the moment something better came along I was discarded like an empty sweet wrapper. So, Florrie, I suggest you start double-checking your husband's movements. When Marcus next tells you he's away on overnight business in London, question it. He's actually not far away. You would be shocked if you knew just how close he is.

With your best interests at heart,
A friend

I rocked back on my heels and puffed out my cheeks. I had absolutely no idea who the author of the letter was. The only clue was that she had a daughter. Nor was I any the wiser about who Marcus was currently having an affair with other than that this second woman apparently lived close by. One thing I *did* know was that my husband was indeed a serial philanderer. And I knew the reason why. Ever since he'd been told his sperm count was virtually non-existent, Marcus had almost immediately gone on the prowl. I suspected that bedding one woman after another made him feel manly.

At first I'd tried to ignore it. I'd told myself things would settle down. Marcus would come to terms with our situation, and the love we had for each other would see us through. Which is all well and good until, after another year of intermittently sobbing into my pillow in a frequently empty marital bed, I'd started to question exactly how deeply in love I was with my husband and whether, in fact, I'd started to thoroughly dislike him. Continuing to live with a man behaving in this way had finally eroded all love. I'd eventually realised that, and come to terms with it. I definitely no longer loved my husband. I'd wept at the full realisation of this, shed tears for all my marriage could have been and now never would be, for I'd already mentally made the decision that I would be leaving. It was simply a case of picking the right moment. Things had to be done properly. Solicitors needed to be appointed. The house would have to go on the market. I also needed to brace up to approaching the subject of divorce with Marcus. He would be furious. This was a man who for years had, as the saying goes, "Had his cake and eaten it". So far, the bracing up on my part had eluded me. And then, deeply unhappy and quite by chance, I'd suddenly and unexpectedly found comfort elsewhere. But, as my mother would have said if she'd known my circumstances, "look before you leap". But I hadn't looked. I'd just leapt blindly. And now I was stumbling around in the dark.

Chapter Fourteen

When Saturday morning dawned I was up bright and early. After loading the car with my artist's paraphernalia, I went back to the house to make a quick sandwich and fill a flask with tea. I wasn't sure how accommodating Harriet might be with refreshment, and thought a packed lunch might be wise. I was just slapping a lid on a plastic container when Marcus came up behind me, catching me unawares.

'How did you get on at the doctor's yesterday?'

I froze. I hadn't told Marcus I'd been to the surgery. 'F-fine.'

'Why didn't you tell me? I'd have taken some time off work and gone with you.'

I gulped. I hadn't reckoned on Marcus wanting to play the supportive husband. After all, half the time he was either not around or locked away in the study "answering emails", but in reality texting his latest mistress.

'I...well I didn't see the point really. Not at this stage. It's very early days, isn't it?'

Marcus moved to my side so he could look at me properly.

'Is it really early days?' he arched an eyebrow. The air in the kitchen was suddenly very still. He gazed at me speculatively. 'By my reckoning you must be, what, about three months' pregnant?'

He looked at my tummy. 'Isn't it about time we rang our respective parents and told them the happy news?'

'How did you know I'd been to the doctor?' When cornered, answer a question with another question.

'I went into the corner shop for a newspaper and Mrs Thompson told me she'd seen you in the surgery waiting room while she was waiting to be seen about her sore big toe.'

'Ah, Mrs Thompson,' I nodded. 'The fount of all village gossip.'

'Indeed. But then again she does rather have her finger on the pulse of the village, doesn't she? It's the only place for miles where you can buy a paper and a pint of milk if you've run out. In the space of a week she must serve the entire population of Lower Amblegate. Anyway, Mrs Thompson asked after you. She said she was concerned. Apparently you were slumped on a waiting room chair looking as though the weight of the world was on your shoulders whilst gazing into space.'

I made a tutting noise. 'I was simply preoccupied.'

'I can imagine,' Marcus said under his breath.

I inhaled sharply. 'What's that remark supposed to mean?'

'You tell *me*, Florrie. Apparently you're the one with the weight of the world on her shoulders.'

'If you really must know, at the time I'd

111

been thinking about Alison.'

'Oh dear, oh dear, oh dear,' said Marcus sarcastically. 'And what's wrong in Alison's perfect world this time? Did Tiffany come home from prep school with an A minus instead of an A star in her latest language assignment? Or is Ali no longer having Christmas in the Caribbean because old Henry can only afford a festive weekend in Benidorm? Or has a major catastrophe occurred whereby Annabelle Farquhar-Jones dared to omit Alison from a coffee morning invitation?'

I pursed my lips. 'Regrettably I don't have time to pursue this line of conversation. Harriet Montgomery is expecting me at nine on the dot.'

I picked up the lunchbox and made to move but Marcus put a hand out to stop me.

'Actually I'm not interested in talking about Alison, Florrie. I'm more interested in what Dr Baily said.'

Ah. We'd gone full circle. Back to the same question.

'She simply went over my background medical history,' I said truthfully whilst neatly leaving out the rest of what had been discussed. 'Now if you'll excuse me, Marcus, I really do have to go.' I busied myself gathering up the tea flask and my handbag, carefully avoiding any further eye contact with my husband. 'See you later.'

'No, you probably won't.'

Startled, I swung round to face him. 'Oh?'

'I thought I'd pop in on my parents later. I gathered you'd probably be painting at the Montgomery-Murray-Wells house until late, so thought I'd catch up with my folks. I might even stay the night if Dad insists I share one of his homemade bottles of wine. You know what that stuff is like. Rocket fuel. Absolutely lethal.'

'Sure,' I nodded. 'Give them my love.'

I turned on my heel and walked smartly out of the house. A mixture of guilt and deceit had me eager to put distance between us.

Needless to say, when I arrived at Harriet's, she kept me waiting for nearly three hours. I'd sat, in the make-shift studio, on a chaise-longue somebody had placed by the Juliet balcony. Bored, and suddenly ravenously hungry, I'd devoured my sandwich within the first hour. The housekeeper, a dead ringer for Les Dawson in drag, had brought me up a coffee and a slice of cake in the second hour. I'd been tremendously grateful for that as the hunger pangs had been returning by that point. My appetite seemed to be revving up. Presumably this was the "eating for two" thing. At this rate I'd be piling on the pounds. The housekeeper had stayed and chatted for five minutes. Long enough for me to ascertain that Harriet Montgomery was enjoying a leisurely bubble bath, her daughter Piper was on a sleepover for the weekend, and Martin Murray-Wells was out of the country on business. I was in the middle of texting Daisy when Harriet finally wafted into the studio on a cloud of perfume.

'Florrie.' She inclined her head by way of acknowledgement.

'Afternoon, Harriet.' I stood up, rather like one would if a headmistress had walked into a classroom. There was no doubting who had the upper hand here. She was wearing a full-length kimono-style dressing gown which made a swishing noise as she walked over to the chaise-longue. She paused, waiting for me to position myself at the easel.

'Shall we begin?'

I gritted my teeth. I'd been ready to begin hours ago. 'Yes, of course.'

She pulled at the kimono's tie-belt. The garment slid off her frame and dropped to the floor in a rustle of silk. I tried not to gasp at the sight of her. Loose hair tumbled over creamy shoulders. She had full, pert breasts. Not one ounce of fat clung to her perfect curves. Her legs were long and, it had to be said, seemingly free from cellulite. Harriet draped herself across the chaise-longue and assumed a day-dreaming pose. No wonder Henry was putty in her hands. Poor Alison didn't stand a chance. I grimaced.

'Are you all right, Florrie?'

'Yes,' I assured. 'Just a bit of...indigestion,' I finished lamely.

'Well don't go breaking wind in here,' said Harriet bossily. 'I'm very sensitive to smells.'

Affronted, I chose not to reply and instead got to work. An hour later, Harriet was bored stiff. She'd turned the heating up twice, and the make-shift studio was stifling hot. Now she was fiddling with her mobile phone, clearly texting somebody. After five minutes, her mobile rang. Whoever it was, her face lit up when she saw the caller ID.

'Dah-ling,' she purred.

I pretended not to be listening and carried on sweeping strokes of paint across the canvas. Harriet had kept still long enough for me to outline her silhouette and put in basic features.

'I feel like I haven't seen you for ages. Yes, me too. Of course I miss you. You're my sooper-dooper growly-wowly coochy-coo teddy bear,' she said playfully. 'Or should I say *beddy*-bear,' she threw back her head and treated her coochy-coo caller to her irritating tinkling laugh.

Annoyed, I gripped my paintbrush and fought the urge to march over to the chaise-longue and give her a good slap. Preferably on her perfectly formed buttocks. Harriet had paused to listen to her caller but when she next spoke she was very animated. Excited even.

'Yes, yes, that could work quite well. I see. Okay, hunny-bunny. Yes, I'll meet you there. Give me half an hour.' She ended the call and looked up at me. 'That was my husband. He wants to take me to lunch.' Harriet clearly wasn't au-fait with my conversation with the housekeeper and Martin Murray-Wells being out of the country. 'Apparently something's come up.' Visions of Henry's third leg filled my mind. 'For now you'll have to carry on without me.'

'Sure.' I paused mid-stroke and regarded her thoughtfully. 'Before you go–'

'Yes?' Harriet was already up and off the chaise-longue, reaching for her kimono.

'I wondered if you'd give me some impartial advice.'

As she shrugged herself into her wrap, Harriet looked momentarily surprised. 'Yes, what is it?'

I cleared my throat. 'I have a very dear friend whose husband is having an affair.'

Harriet regarded me coolly. 'And?'

'I don't know whether to tell my friend what her husband is up to and, more importantly, who he's having the affair with.'

Suddenly I was feeling very fired-up and feisty. To hell with jeopardising a four-thousand-pound commission – Alison's marriage was under threat! I gave the overconfident egotistical woman standing before me a challenging glare.

'Really, Florrie,' Harriet tutted, 'you're asking me?'

'Yes,' I said with steely determination. 'I am indeed asking you.'

Harriet gave another tinkle of laughter. The sound lacked any humour. 'I suggest you ask yourself that very question, Florrie.

After all, a little bird told me you've had your own secret dalliance whilst being a married woman.'

'I beg your pardon?' I gasped.

She smirked and nodded at the canvas. 'Don't let me hold you up.' And then Harriet turned and strode off through the attic rooms, kimono swishing, leaving me mouthing like one of Jeremy Kyle's cornered guests.

Chapter Fifteen

After Harriet had left without a backward glance, I must have stood at the canvas for a full five minutes. Not one stroke of the paintbrush was made. Instead I stared into space, my mind looping over and over. How did she know about my extra-marital liaison? Had she somehow seen me? If so, where? It surely wasn't possible for her to know I'd been unfaithful to Marcus.

Disconcerted, I refocused on the painting. Harriet's face needed defining but the features were loosely there. Her eyes, currently pale and ghostly, looked up at me from the canvas, seemingly straight into my soul. I waggled the paintbrush at her image and frowned.

'You know nothing, Ms Montgomery. You were simply playing a clever mind game with me. A bit of reverse psychology. You barely know me, never mind the ins and outs of my private life. All you can be sure of is that I live in Lower Amblegate in a small cul-de-sac next door to Alison and Henry. I, on the other hand, know quite a bit about you! I've discovered you're having an affair, who you're having an affair with, and that you're with him right now, you treacherous cow!'

Satisfied that Harriet had simply given me some bitchy riposte, I vowed to get on with her painting as swiftly as possible, take the fee and – when the May Ball was over – never see or talk to Harriet Montgomery again. Unfortunately my hunger pangs chose that precise moment to come back with such a vengeance I was forced to leave the easel and go home for sustenance. I needed food. And immediately.

I'd barely walked through the front door when my mobile shrilled into life. Hurrying into the hallway, I dumped my handbag on the floor. Rummaging within, I tried to locate the elusive gadget. Muttering oaths, I tipped the handbag upside down, scattering contents everywhere, and grabbed the chirruping mobile just before it switched to voicemail.

'Hello?'

My mother-in-law's gin-soaked voice crackled across cyberspace. 'Florrie, darling!' I could picture Margaret sitting in her wing chair, afternoon tipple in one hand, phone in the other. 'I was just saying to Phil, we haven't seen you and Marcus for ages.'

'Hello, Margaret.' I smiled into the handset. I absolutely adored my in-laws. They were both charming and lovely. I knew, deep down, part of my procrastination about divorcing Marcus had been because I didn't want my relationship to change with Philip and Margaret. Although now I was up the duff with another man's baby, it might be *them* giving give *me* the sack instead. 'It's lovely to hear from you. How are you both?'

119

'Oh, we flourish, we flourish,' Margaret laughed. 'Since we retired, there's been little else to do but eat, drink, and be merry.'

My parents-in-law had been filled with grand retirement plans – travelling the world, taking up ballroom dancing, improving their golf handicaps. The reality had turned out to be watching Lonely Planet and Strictly Come Dancing and selling their golf clubs on eBay. They'd settled down to an easier life of watching the world from their armchairs, or Phil pottering in the garden while Margaret knocked up mouth-watering dinners and puddings. Together they were embracing ever increasing waistlines.

'And you, Florrie? How are *you*, darling?'

'Oh, I'm fine. Er, flourishing too.' It was definitely time to exchange these jeans for something more comfortable and with an elasticated waist.

'Excellent! Listen, darling. I was chatting to Phil and he says it's simply been too long. You and Marcus *must* come to dinner. What about joining us for Sunday lunch tomorrow?'

I grimaced. Even though I'd guessed my husband wasn't really visiting his parents and staying the night at their house, it was still a small blow to the solar plexus to have it confirmed.

'That would be lovely, but unfortunately Marcus is out tonight and won't be home until tomorrow. I'm not sure what time.'

'Not a problem, darling. Tell you what, I'll give him a ring on his mobile and put the idea to him. I'll get back to you in five minutes.'

'Okay, Margaret, do that and I'll speak to you shortly.'

I hung up and, bending down, began gathering up the strewn contents of my handbag. My mind wandered to Marcus. I tried to picture his face paling when his mother revealed she'd spoken to me, and that I'd now know he wasn't spending time with my in-laws. Distracted, I didn't bother looking at the caller display when my mobile rang again.

'That was quick!' I laughed. 'What did he say?'

There was a pause, and then a male voice quietly spoke my name.

'Florrie.'

All of a sudden my knees began to shake. I sank down to the hall floor, legs splayed out. This man had always had the most devastating effect on me. My hand gripped the mobile tightly.

'H-hello,' I croaked. 'How are you?'

His voice, when he next spoke, was serious and more urgent.

'I really think we need to talk.'

Chapter Sixteen

On Sunday morning I awoke in an empty marital bed. I hadn't slept well. Yesterday's conversation with my caller had rocked me. I lay in bed, staring up at the ceiling as my mind replayed the conversation.

'Talk about what?' I'd asked. My voice had sounded calm, totally at odds to the turmoil raging within.

'Tongues are wagging, Florrie.'

I'd hesitated. 'What idle gossip have you heard?'

'Mrs Thompson doesn't consider herself to be a blabbermouth. Instead she prefers to be the bearer of "news".'

I'd grimaced. 'I see. And what "news" have you heard?'

'That you're expecting a baby.'

I'd gasped. How swiftly did word of mouth spread around a village like mine? And how long before the likes of Mrs Thompson ended up telling both Marcus's parents and mine this "news" which was basically a bombshell? Even worse, how long before Mrs Thompson got wind of the *true* state of affairs. I could imagine my own mother's reaction.

"I only went into the corner shop for a pint of milk, and that awful Annabelle Farquhar-Jones was chatting to Mrs Thompson and – in front of a huge queue of customers – they asked how I felt about not only becoming a nanna, but being a grandma to a baby that isn't even my son-in-law's child. What have you been *up* to, Florrie? I hope this doesn't upset Daddy's angina. I'll never be able to hold my head up at the WI again."

To say my mother was a narrow-minded snob was an understatement. And what of my mother-in-law? Margaret would be devastated.

"Florrie, darling. Is it true? I saw that frightful Harriet Montgomery coming out of the corner shop. She took great delight in telling me you have a bun in the oven and that Marcus isn't the baker. Don't worry I gave her a good slap."

'Florrie?'

At the sound of his voice, I'd come back to the present.

'I think you're right.'

'Sorry?'

'We do need to talk.'

At the other end of the line there had been a pause, an indication that unspoken information was being processed.

'Can I see you tomorrow?'

I'd gulped. 'Yes.' The last few days had passed with me cowardly impersonating an ostrich with its head buried in the sand. It was time to be brave and face up to the consequences, which included telling the man in question. After all, I hadn't got into this predicament all by myself. 'I'll pop over about half seven.'

Margaret had eventually called me back about the Sunday lunch invitation.

123

'I've not been able to get hold of Marcus,' she'd lamented. 'My phone calls keep going to voicemail.'

'Don't worry,' I'd soothed. 'His battery has probably died.' The reality was he'd probably switched off his phone to avoid having his secret rendezvous rudely interrupted. 'Shall we do a rain check?'

'Yes, okay, and tell Marcus not to leave it too long. Cheerio, darling!'

And now, on this early Sunday morning, I wiggled my toes under the duvet luxuriating in its gentle warmth and savouring the moments of calm before the day got underway. I wondered how things might be come Sunday evening. Meanwhile, there was an unfinished painting awaiting my attention. I hauled myself out of bed.

With the duvet no longer plumped around me, the cool air in the bedroom rushed around my bare flesh like a winter breath. Shivering, I reached for my dressing gown. It made a rustling sound as I slipped it on. Something was in the pocket. I touched it. Ah, yes. The anonymous letter. I'd stuffed it into the pocket after reading it again last night.

Downstairs, I was halfway through my breakfast when, from outside, came the sound of a familiar car engine. Marcus was home. A minute later the front door clicked shut and my husband wandered through to the kitchen. He looked animated and was clearly in excellent spirits. Indeed, he exuded happiness. No, that was the wrong word. It was elation. He looked like a man who'd climbed Mount Everest and found a secret door to Heaven.

'Hi,' I gave a friendly smile and arranged my features into one of neutrality before spooning up some cereal.

'Hey,' he replied, dropping his keys on the worktop.

I munched in an oblivious fashion for a moment or two and then casually opened conversation. 'Did you have a good time with your folks?'

Marcus visibly appeared to tone down his euphoria. 'Oh, you know.' He shrugged. 'Duty visits are always a bit boring.'

'How was your dad's wine? It must have been good, you're still glowing!'

Marcus looked shifty for a moment. 'Ah, yes. The wine. Robust as ever. Actually, I have a bit of a hangover.' He went towards the kettle. 'I think a strong coffee is definitely overdue.' He reached upwards and opened a kitchen cupboard, pulling out a mug before foraging in the larder for coffee. 'Mum and dad send their love.' He lifted the lid from the kettle to check the water level before flicking the switch. 'They missed you.'

'Really?'

There must have been something in my tone that caused Marcus to turn and look at me in surprise.

'Yes,' he nodded. 'Really.' He considered me for a moment, and then frowned. 'Are you in one of your funny moods, Florrie?'

I widened my eyes innocently. 'No. Are you?'

Marcus's brow puckered. 'Am I what?'

'In a "funny" mood?'

My husband tutted. 'Okay, you *are* in a funny mood.'

'I don't think so. Am I laughing?'

'And now you're being ridiculous.'

Annoyed, he turned back to the kettle, busying himself with pouring boiling water and adding milk. I stared at his back. Shoulders set. He looked like he might be steeling himself. For what? To think up more lies? I glanced down at my bowl of cereal. The grains had absorbed all the milk. Everything looked bloated and disgusting. I pushed the bowl away.

'Marcus?' I asked softly, addressing my husband's back. 'Why don't we just stop this nonsense?' There was a measured silence as my husband added sugar to his coffee and began to stir. The only sound was that of the teaspoon clinking against china. My voice was unintentionally sharper when I next spoke. 'Do you hear me?'

He swung round and his eyes immediately snagged on mine. 'Oh, yes, Florrie. I hear you loud and clear. And what, my dear wife, is the "nonsense" you wish us both to stop?'

'You know perfectly well,' I said quietly, swallowing hard. There suddenly seemed to be a golf ball lodged in my larynx. 'I'm talking about this...this *sham* of a marriage.'

There. I'd said it. The words hung in the air, like a detonated nuclear bomb, whooshing upwards and mushrooming outwards but with the fall-out yet to be experienced.

'Excuse me?' Marcus spat. He looked livid.

My stomach began to knot with anxiety. Too late to stop now. 'I can't stand it any longer.' My voice sounded odd. Like it belonged to someone else. A part of me felt like the very essence of my being had divided into two. One part had stepped back to watch the kitchen sink drama unfolding at Number 2 The Cul-de-Sac, while the human bit of me pushed back the dining chair and stood up. 'Let's just stop all this...pretending.'

Marcus was suddenly very still. 'Pretending? If there is any pretence, surely you are the guilty one!'

'Me?' My eyebrows shot upwards. 'I don't think so!'

My voice was rising. I was beginning to feel like I'd climbed up a steep hill. My breath was starting to come in ragged gasps, but the reality wasn't anything like as solid as a hill. Instead, the truth was that in the last few minutes our lives together had morphed into a fragile house of cards. Marcus and I were teetering on the brink of everything collapsing...our marriage...our home together...our respective futures. For a moment neither of us knew who would be the first to tap one of the cards and send the whole pack tumbling down so that it was an unsalvageable mess. In the end it was me.

'You haven't been with your parents at all.' My words were shrill and accusing. 'Margaret was on the phone earlier, so please don't waste your breath lying. The lies have just gone on and on, haven't they? Like pretending for years to be in love with me.'

'I *am* in love with you.'

His words, delivered smoothly and convincingly, for a moment wrong-footed me. *Was* he in love with me? I'd assumed, because I'd fallen out of love with him that Marcus had fallen out of love with me too.

'Florrie, I'm aware things aren't right between us, but that doesn't mean I've ever stopped loving you.'

'Rubbish,' I barked. 'My definition of a man in love with his wife is one who is loyal and by her side. You've been bedding other women from the moment you knew the truth about your sperm count.'

'Florrie–'

'And now,' I interrupted, foraging in the pocket of my dressing gown, 'I have solid proof of your dalliances.' I pulled out the letter. 'Look. See for yourself. One of your mistresses deigned to put pen to paper and spill the infidelity beans.' I shook the notepaper at my husband and watched his face pale. 'You say you're in love with me, Marcus, but apparently you were going to leave me and move in with...with...whoever

128

this person is.'

My voice caught. For a moment tears threatened. Not, you understand, over feelings for Marcus, for I knew without a shred of doubt I hadn't loved my husband for a long time. Instead the tears were sorrow at allowing our situation to have gone on – for never having been gutsy enough to broach the subject when the love *had* still been there, when the marriage *could* have possibly been rescued.

'May I?' He leant forward, one hand outstretched to take the letter. As he did so, I caught a whiff of stale perfume. It was somewhat masculine with its musky overtones. A memory stirred. I knew this scent. My heart began to beat erratically as realisation dawned. I'd smelt it before. On Alison. Suddenly some of the words within the letter floated to the surface of my mind.

He's actually not far away. You would be shocked if you knew just how close he is.

Dear Lord. Was Alison having an affair with my husband? But...but...no, surely not. She wouldn't do that to me. Would she?

'Florrie? Can I read it, please?'

Overcome with uncertainty and rage, I tried to throw the letter at Marcus.

'Be my guest,' I snarled. But whilst the written words weighed heavily, the notepaper was as light as a feather. It left my hand with a flipping noise, barely flying out six inches before fluttering down to the floor. Bending down, Marcus retrieved it. Even though I couldn't properly see his face, I knew in an instant he'd recognised the handwriting. His forehead shifted in such a way that indicated eyes widening in horror. He straightened up, reading the note at the same time. I planted my feet wide, hands on hips. An expression of defiance and challenge.

'So,' I sneered. 'Do please enlighten me. Who is this so-called "friend" who wishes me well?'

Slowly, Marcus raised his eyes from the letter to look at me. His body language had changed. Suddenly he seemed contrite. His expression was one of regret.

'It's true I had a fling with another woman. But there haven't been quite as many as you think. And whatever is written within this note, I promise I was never going to leave you for her. There's no comparison.'

'Spare me the pretty words.' My lip curled like an angry Rottweiler. 'You still haven't told me who she is.' My heart was painfully thudding away. 'Is it Alison?'

'You really want to know?'

My mouth went dry. What sort of ridiculous question was that? Didn't an unfaithful man ever realise that a wronged wife was hungry for information about a mistress? I wanted to know everything about this person, right down to her shoe size. My eyes blazed with fury.

'Yes, I really want to know who she is.'

But nothing could quite prepare me for my husband's answer.

'Very well. The author of this letter is Annabelle Farquhar-Jones.'

Chapter Seventeen

'Anna—?'

Her name died on my lips. A part of me was hugely relieved Marcus hadn't bedded my neighbour Alison, whilst another part was ashamed I'd even fleetingly entertained the idea of my friend betraying me. But even so. Annabelle Farquhar-Jones of all people! I stared at my husband, literally gobsmacked. My mind flipped back to the recent coffee morning at Alison's house with both Annabelle and Harriet in attendance. Upon learning of my baby news, Annabelle had looked furious. It had been Harriet who had made a comment about me not being able to have children. So clearly Marcus had told Annabelle about my infertility problems and it had been Annabelle who had repeated the same to Harriet. Alison hadn't been gossiping about me after all. I felt another pang of guilt for challenging Alison when I'd followed her out to her kitchen. This was what infidelity did. It made you paranoid – suspicious about everyone and questioning everything.

'I'm sorry,' Marcus said in a small voice. 'And please don't believe a word about me dumping Annabelle for somebody else. That's just spite on her part.'

'Where were you last night?' I croaked.

'Truthfully? I checked into a cheap B&B for...' he was choosing his words carefully,

'...space. To reflect.' His face was a picture of shame. 'And before you ask, yes, I was on my own.'

I stared at my husband, still unable to find the words for the sheer volume of thought processes spinning at high speed through my brain. Whatever had he seen in a shallow woman like Annabelle? As Daisy had once said, "Annabelle Farquhar-Jones is so up herself she can probably see what she had for breakfast." But then again, the woman was attractive and oh-so-very-available. A divorcée, with a daughter at Darwin Prep, Alison had whispered that Annabelle had the reputation of being a man-eater. It was a well-known fact she was husband hunting. But when had she set her sights on Marcus?

'How did you both meet?' I blurted.

Marcus shrugged. 'Does it matter?'

'I want to know!'

Marcus blew out his cheeks. 'She had a planning application for a roof extension. I was the surveyor sent to her house.'

'I see.' I didn't really see at all. 'So after you'd checked out her upstairs, you whipped out your tape measure and offered to sort out her basement?'

'Florrie, please—'

'So when did it start?'

'Well, planning applications take a little while so—'

'I'M TALKING ABOUT THE AFFAIR, MARCUS.'

My husband visibly jumped as my vocal

cords suddenly boomed back into life. I was pretty sure not only the other two houses in The Cul-de-Sac had heard my roar, but possibly Mrs Thompson at the corner shop. Give it an hour and the village would be whirring with whispers. "Thanks to Annabelle Farquhar-Jones getting her tits out, the Milligans' marriage has gone tits-up."

I glared at Marcus. 'I'll ask you again. When did it start?'

'Well, it was sort of, you know, kind of,' he put his arms out in a helpless gesture, 'like, ah, pretty much, erm...' he trailed off.

I stared at him incredulously. 'Immediately?'

Marcus dropped his eyes to the floor and gazed at a spot somewhere in front of him. He put out his foot and scuffed his shoe gently backwards and forwards. An evasive gesture.

'You had an appointment to see a client, went to her house, and by the time you'd left you'd had a shag?'

Marcus winced at my vulgar turn of words. 'Yes,' he murmured.

I shook my head in bewilderment. 'Is that what you've always done? Gone to see a client and, if they're female, pretty and available, you have a quickie?'

My husband bowed his head. 'Sometimes,' he mumbled. 'Florrie, I'm not proud of myself.'

'Oh, I see, that's good,' I nodded. 'So because you're not proud of that behaviour, it makes everything okay, eh?'

'No, of course not.'

'Right, glad you realise that.'

'For God's sake, Florrie, these things...they just happened,' Marcus suddenly sounded irritable. 'It wasn't premeditated. I didn't get up in the morning and rub my hands together with glee and say, "Well, well, well, Marcus old chap, you're seeing Annabelle Farquhar-Jones this morning. Let's see if you can get to first base with her, or even second or third." The woman practically launched herself at me.'

'As did all the others?'

Marcus remained defiant. 'Pretty much, yes. I don't mean to big myself up, but I think I'm an all right looking guy. Women want me. They bat their eyelids.'

'Well funnily enough, Marcus,' I ranted, 'you had the option of saying no. After all,' I parroted, 'I think I'm an all right looking woman. Men like *me*! They bat *their* eyelids! But the difference between you and me is...I DON'T JUMP INTO BED WITH THEM ALL.'

Dear Lord. Mrs Thompson was going to have a field day with that grapevine.

Marcus's attitude changed in a nanosecond. 'Don't you?' he hissed.

For a moment my mind was a blank. I looked at Marcus in puzzlement. 'What are you talking about? Don't I what?'

My husband took a step towards me. His eyes narrowed and his mouth disappeared into a thin line.

'Whatever I am, Florrie, and whatever I've been, I've never put you in the invidious situation of knowing that another woman is bearing my child.'

I stared at him in bewilderment. And then the penny dropped. Marcus was talking about my pregnancy.

'You see, I *know*, Florrie. I *know* that the child you're carrying isn't mine.'

I gulped. Suddenly the tables had been turned. I was as bad as my husband. Maybe I hadn't slept with umpteen other partners, like him, but adultery was adultery. I'd betrayed my husband. Even worse, I'd doubly betrayed him by conceiving another man's child.

'You're no saint.'

His face twisted with both fury and pain as he took another step towards me. The action was quite menacing. Alarmed, I found myself matching him step for step but retreating in the opposite direction. He glared at me.

'I know exactly when I last made love to you, Florrie. Quite apart from the fact that I'm pretty much firing blanks, please do explain,' he nodded at my stomach, 'why you're not three months' pregnant. Or are you going to try and bluff this pregnancy as the next Immaculate Conception?'

My mouth was suddenly devoid of moisture. I tried to swallow but ended up coughing. I shook my head from side to side, forcing my vocal cords to work. They refused to oblige. I stared at my husband helplessly as he continued to come towards me. I came to a sudden full stop. My spine was against the kitchen wall. Marcus had backed me into a corner, both literally and figuratively. Marcus tilted his head on one side and this time it was *his* lip that curled.

'You see, Florrie, unlike me, you weren't so discreet.'

I continued to stare at him fearfully.

'There I was, parked in a dark side street opposite a very popular restaurant waiting for a certain little waitress to finish work. And lo! In the living quarters above the restaurant, framed clearly in a lamp-lit window, I was amazed to see my wife.'

Understanding began to seep into my numb brain. My expression changed to one of horror.

Marcus nodded. 'It's coming back to you now, is it? Jolly good,' he spat. 'And instead of painting – as you'd led me to believe – you were being embraced by another man. That embrace turned into a passionate kiss. It went on and on and on. I'm surprised neither of you suffocated each other. I watched, mesmerised, as the two of you came up for air and then began ripping each other's clothes off before slowly sinking out of sight. So you see, my dear Florrie, you're not such a goody-two-shoes after all, are you? And when you told me you were pregnant, for a moment I allowed myself to truly believe I was going to be a daddy.'

His voice caught suddenly, and despite

everything my heart squeezed for his feelings.

'You see, there was a small part of me that desperately hoped it just might be possible,' he gulped, 'and that somehow a miracle really had occurred.' His chest was starting to go up and down. He was struggling with his emotions. Seeing the visible depths of his despair made me feel both helpless and ashamed. My husband heaved a sigh that audibly reflected his pain.

'So no more accusations between the two of us, Florrie, because I know who is *really* the father of the baby you're carrying. My congratulations to you and Luca Serafino.'

Chapter Eighteen

Marcus stared at me as I shrank back against the kitchen wall. I was trapped.

'Don't look so scared, Florrie. I'm not going to hit you.'

I burst into tears. His arms were around me in a trice. I began to shake violently, no doubt from both our mutual confrontation and the shock of so many home truths spilling out. My legs were trembling like an invalid without crutches. If Marcus hadn't been holding me, I'd have probably slid down the wall and sprawled across the floor.

'Please don't cry, Florrie.' His voice was suddenly tender.

My face was squashed into his shirt which was taking the brunt of both tears and snot. He buried his face in my hair and held me tight.

'What do you want to do?' he murmured.

The question was little more than a sigh. For a moment I wasn't even sure I'd heard him correctly. I pulled back. My bloodshot eyes met his own, which were full of pain.

'Do?' I whispered.

'Yes. Do.' He raked one hand through his hair. 'Look, let's sit down.'

He led me over to the kitchen table and pulled out two chairs, shifting them so they faced each other. I sat down heavily. Marcus did likewise, shuffling the chair forward so that he was sitting right in front of me. He took my hands in his.

'Florrie, you're my wife. Despite our marriage being reduced to splinters, I truly believe we might still be able to fix things.'

I gaped at my husband. 'You want to stay married to me?'

Marcus gave me an appraising look. For a moment neither of us spoke.

'Yes,' he eventually said.

'Marcus, I'm not aborting this baby.' The words tumbled out of my mouth in a rush.

'I'm not asking you to.' He looked down at my hands in his and rubbed the ball of his thumb over my wedding band. 'For better or worse, Florrie.' He looked up at me under his eyelashes. 'That's what we said to each other when we stood at the church altar. I stand by those words. I can't give you a baby. You have your own fertility issues, so your pregnancy *is* nothing short of a miracle. So,' he took a deep breath, 'I'm going to suggest...,' he trailed off, squeezing his eyes shut for a moment, as if blocking out anguish. When he next spoke the words came out in a hurry, as if the faster he uttered them the more likely they would stick. 'I'm going to suggest we carry on being married, and that I raise your baby as my child too.'

I gasped. My husband had just presented me with an incredible solution to the quandary I'd been in ever since Tuesday morning when he'd seen the blue lines on the pregnancy test and danced me around the kitchen in delight. How many men would be prepared, knowing the bitter truth, to do that? Not many. For a moment I was so overwhelmed at his offer, I couldn't speak.

'That's...that's very...magnanimous of you.'

Marcus nodded. For a moment he looked like a little boy, full of doubt, unsure about carrying out what he'd suggested but refusing to retract the offer because of marriage vows. How very virtuous. I gazed at his fingers now intertwined with mine. His offer, if that's what you could call it, might well be generous but it was also flawed.

'You mentioned our marriage vows,' I said hesitantly. 'For better or worse.' He nodded morosely. I stumbled on, not sure how to collate the thoughts in my head. 'The thing is...we also made vows to love and to cherish.'

Marcus's expression changed to one of bafflement. 'Yes, I know that. What point are you making?'

'The point I'm making is you've never worried too much about the vow of "love and cherish", so why do you feel you have to honour the bit about "for better or worse"?'

He looked thrown. 'What do you mean? Of course I've loved and cherished you!'

'I don't agree. I know I've now broken that vow too, but...,' I shrugged, not wishing to sound churlish about who had done what first or how many times. This wasn't a case of point scoring. Nonetheless it was an

141

integral part of what was going on here. 'From the moment you discovered the truth about your infertility, you were off chasing anything in a skirt.' I stared at him, willing him to understand. 'That's not loving and cherishing *me*,' I reasoned. 'Don't you understand, Marcus, that when I ended up in the arms of another man, it was out of deep unhappiness.'

He inhaled sharply. 'I was unhappy too, Florrie.'

'Yes, unhappy about your psychological hang-ups of manliness and not being able to father a child!' I cried. 'Not unhappy because I was an awful wife!'

'Are you saying I've been an awful husband?' He looked affronted.

'Yes!' I cried. 'Have you any idea how it felt, Marcus, knowing for weeks at a time you were making love to another woman. My arms were always open for you...to comfort you...to share the hand that life had dealt the two of us. But you instead chose to walk into the arms of others. You completely rejected me. Time and time again. I always knew when someone else was on the scene because your interest in me immediately became non-existent.'

'That's not true,' he said vehemently.

'Oh yes it is,' I countered. 'And you know what, Marcus? I don't believe for one moment you were by yourself in a B&B last night.'

'I *was* in a B&B,' he said emphatically.

'Sure,' I nodded. 'But not alone, eh?' His

eyes slithered away from me. 'You haven't laid a finger on me for three, if not four, months. *That* is how I know you're seeing another woman right now.'

My husband removed his hands from mine and silently stared up at the ceiling. When I next spoke, my voice was low.

'Marcus, continuing this marriage would be disastrous. I think you've only suggested staying with me because, by letting others believe you're the baby's father, you think you'd fulfil some emotional void. But *you* would know the truth. It would only be a matter of time before you'd resent raising a child you knew wasn't biologically yours. You'd *still* be looking to prove yourself elsewhere. Even now, when we're meant to be baring our souls to each other, confessing the truth with a view to starting afresh, you cannot be honest. Who is she, this latest squeeze?'

He waved a hand dismissively. 'It's irrelevant.'

I inhaled sharply. No denial this time. Of *course* there was another woman on the scene. There always would be.

Marcus met my eyes again. 'I hear what you're saying, Florrie. And...and I guess you're right. Starting again is almost guaranteed to fall at the first hurdle. I'm not sure I could dance for joy watching my wife give birth to another man's baby. You're right.'

I raised my eyebrows in surprise at his sudden acknowledgement.

'However,' he continued, 'I also think there's another reason our marriage wouldn't work, and it's got nothing to do with fidelity or fulfilling emotional needs.'

I gazed at him, knowing what he was leading up to before he'd even uttered the words.

'You see, Florrie, there's a fundamental difference between you, me and our respective betrayals. I've never loved any of the women I've had an affair with, but I've always loved you. You talk of honesty. Indeed, you're demanding it. But I put it to you now to confess you're not being fully truthful with me.' He paused to give me a frank look. 'If you can't admit it, then I'll say it for you.'

I waited to hear the words that I'd been terrified of admitting to myself.

'I know the real reason our marriage would fail. It's because you're in love. But not,' he concluded sadly, 'with me. Am I right?'

I bit my lip and turned away.

Chapter Nineteen

Marcus's words rang in my ears. I was in love with another man. Yes, it was true. Up until now, I hadn't even dared admit it to myself. I knew, from the moment I'd laid eyes on Luca Serafino, that he'd set my soul on fire. But I'd reasoned such giddy feelings were more to do with the laws of attraction. Simple chemistry. Some people would have been blunter, citing lust. If I'd confessed to Daisy about the effect Luca had had on me from the moment we'd sat in his restaurant, she'd have simply snorted with laughter and told me I'd got the hots for the guy. Alison would have sniffed and told me not to be so ridiculous, and that true love was making sure you lived in a middle-class area with a man who provided a ski holiday in spring and guaranteed you white sand and blue surf in winter. For me it was very different. Whenever I thought of Luca I wanted to breathe the very air he'd exhaled. I was brought back to the present by my husband, who I'd once thought myself totally in love with.

'So, where do we go from here, Florrie?' Marcus asked sadly.

Where indeed? To the local solicitor's office? To the divorce courts? To the front room for discussion about who'd paid for the television and who'd bought the three-piece suite? I shook my head.

'Can we just leave things for now? Currently I don't think we're in any emotionally fit state to deal with the next step.'

Marcus nodded. 'You're right. My wife is always right.' He gave a rueful smile. 'I'm sorry for...,' he sighed, 'just...everything.'

Tears sprang to my eyes again. 'Me too.' I wiped the back of my hand across my face.

'Look, I'm going to...um...,' Marcus stood up awkwardly from where we'd been sitting together at the kitchen table, '...see my parents and break the news to them.'

I must have appeared momentarily sceptical, because he immediately put up both hands in a gesture of surrender.

'This time I mean it,' he assured. 'I think I ought to have a chat with them about...well...us.'

'Sure,' I nodded. But as my husband moved towards the kitchen door, I called out to him. 'Marcus?' He turned to look back at me. 'Can you...for now...leave out the bit about me being pregnant? I think that's something I'd like to explain to your parents myself. I think too much of them to have you doing my dirty work for me.'

'Okay. But don't worry, Florrie. I'll tell them I've been no saint.'

I knew without a shred of doubt that Marcus would definitely be honourable where his parents were concerned. It would be the truth, the whole truth and nothing but the truth.

'See you later,' he smiled ruefully and

shut the door quietly behind him.

After Marcus had gone, for a moment I didn't know what to do with myself. The urge to go back to bed, pull the duvet over my head, and sleep for a year was very tempting. Instead I washed up the breakfast things, wiped the worktops and hastened upstairs for a quick shower. There was an unfinished painting requiring attention. I had no idea whether Harriet Montgomery would once again keep me waiting while she languished in another long, drawn-out bubble bath, or if she'd be standing on her doorstep, tapping a well-shod shoe, absolutely furious about my tardiness.

Inevitably, when I arrived at the Montgomery-Martin-Wells' household, only the housekeeper appeared to be home.

'Go on up to the top floor, love,' she gestured to the sweeping staircase. 'Between you and me I don't know what goes on in this household.' Her hairy chin quivered with indignation as she clutched one hand to her ample bosom. 'That little Piper has taken herself off to someone's house to listen to music. All by herself! It's wrong. And her ladyship isn't even home at the moment,' she sniffed, 'although His Nibs is around somewhere. If either of them asks where I am, tell them the internet's broken and I can't do the on-line shopping. I'm off to the supermarket.'

'Of course,' I smiled by way of response before making my way up the stairs.

In the attic room I set to work squeezing out oils, relishing the smell of linseed and turpentine filling the musty air. Soon I was in another world, totally absorbed in building the image as I stroked paint onto the canvas. At this rate I'd have to leave the finer details of Harriet's face until last. As I worked, my thoughts automatically drifted. Luca's face flooded my mind. He was, without a doubt, the most beautiful man I'd ever laid eyes on. My desire to paint him was overwhelming, and I wouldn't need a photograph to work from. Every cell of his being was ingrained in my memory. But Luca wasn't just gorgeous on the outside. He was beautiful on the inside too.

Luca had his own sad past to deal with. The premature death of his young bride was a well-known fact. Lesser known was that his wife had been having affairs before they were even married. I'd discovered that when we were chatting. Inevitably I'd found myself confiding in Luca about Marcus's dalliances.

'It seems, Florrie, we have much in common. Spouses who have loved the thrill of the chase, regardless of the wounds inflicted on those around them.'

Luca had found out about Maria's many liaisons just days after shaking the wedding confetti from their hair. They'd been arguing about her refusal to give up her latest lover when Maria had slammed out of the house prior to the tragic accident.

I sighed. Every which way I turned,

someone was having an affair. Was nobody happily married anymore? My thoughts strayed to my parents. Henpecked Daddy firmly under my mother's thumb. Had *he* ever had an affair? I had a mental picture of him trying to be furtive:

"Ah, there you are, darling! And if I may say so, your blue rinse is looking exceptionally pretty today. It matches your eyes perfectly. Um, is it okay if I go out for a little while? To the, er, nursery? No, of course I won't be long, dear. Is an hour permissible? Oh. Half an hour? Thank you, dear. Toodle-oo."

I then tried to envision my father making a mad dash by car to seek out the homely lady in charge of garden furniture, before the pair of them sloped off for a breathless grapple behind the flowering petunias. Not exactly pulse-pounding romance.

My mind drifted to my in-laws. Margaret and Phil were both still a handsome couple happily growing old together. But then again, Margaret spent much of her time cuddling a gin bottle while Phil was more content to stride across local fields with a Labrador at his side.

My thoughts returned to Luca. I was looking forward to seeing him this evening, but equally I was dreading it too. My tummy instantly contracted with anxiety about what his reaction might be after I'd told him he was going to be a daddy. But before I could give Luca another thought, I was disturbed by a noise.

Behind me came the sound of frantic footsteps pounding up the last flight of steps. They were coming towards the old servants' quarters. I paused, paintbrush suspended in mid-air, ears pricked. The footfall was heavy and out of time. I then realised it was two people, and they were clearly in a rush. There was nowhere else for them to go apart from here, within the linked row of rooms under the mansion's rooftop. A male voice suddenly shouted out.

'You bloody little tease,' he roared. 'Come here!' His words were instantly followed by a shriek of female laughter and a playful response.

'Catch me if you can!'

Automatically I turned to see who was heading my way, just as the main door at the far end of the attic burst open. Surprised, I was about to greet the two of them when the words died on my lips. The man in question had caught up with his frisky companion. With a speed that defied his years, he launched himself at his playmate who allowed herself to gleefully surrender to his ardent embrace. I paled as the two of them welded their mouths together; eyes tightly closed, and urgently began stripping off in synchronised movements.

There was no way I could speak up without causing major embarrassment for all three of us. Horrified, I realised there was only one thing for it. I'd have to hide.

With a bit of luck they wouldn't wander into my area, instead making use of the spare bed reserved for the scant visits of Harriet's disliked sister-in-law, Gertrude. The man, his lips still glued to his companion's, tossed his trousers to one side and, hopping briefly on one foot, whipped off a pair of designer boxers exposing the full state of his excitement. I nearly whimpered out loud. Horrified, I moved back into the shadows. Dear Lord. Get me out of here. But there was nowhere to go without giving myself away. Even worse, the lovers were now staggering through the connected door-less rooms and heading straight towards my studio area. Oblivious to my presence, their eyes still tightly shut, their kissing went on and on. I gasped. This was dreadful. Truly awful.

Frantically I cast around for somewhere – anywhere – to hide. If I'd been a pin-man I could have tucked myself behind the easel. Regrettably, the only feasible place to try and conceal myself was under Harriet's chaise-longue. I nervously eye-balled the shallow space between its underside and the floor. It wasn't much of a gap. Would I fit underneath? There was only one way to find out, and not a moment to lose. As the loved-up couple staggered past Gertrude's bed, it was quite obvious they were heading my way.

Abandoning my paintbrush, I dived under the chaise-longue. Wriggling frantically, I twisted myself underneath.

Contorting into a horribly uncomfortable position, my head came to rest at an unnatural angle to my shoulders. It was debatable whose breathing was more ragged, mine or that of the unexpected visitors. They were now edging towards the very piece of furniture I was hiding under. If I'd been able to avert my eyes, I would have done so. Regrettably, there was no room to swivel my head away from the scene unfolding before me. I boggled silently as the man, bits and pieces jiggling, finally broke away from his companion's mouth in order for her to divest the last of her clothing. Usually so prim and proper, she whipped off her spotless M&S undies before pausing, briefly, to unhook her sensible white bra. As her unsupported breasts drooped downwards, she paused briefly to wave the garment around like a football rattle. Then, with a cry like Tarzan's Jane, she pushed her lover to the floor. Seconds later she was on top of him impersonating an out-of-control pneumatic drill.

I could have, indeed should have, tightly shut my eyes. I can only presume it was the terror of being discovered that kept my eyelids pinned back so my eyeballs could do nothing else but watch in fascinated horror the graphic scene taking place before me. Just when I thought things were reaching a noisy climax and the two of them might soon bog off, the woman instead jumped up and, hauling the man to his feet, tugged him towards the chaise-longue. The entire frame creaked alarmingly as she threw herself with gusto onto the faded velvet. Seconds later the man collapsed on top of her. I was petrified the ancient piece of furniture would buckle. As the two of them got down to the joyful task of bonking the living daylights out of each other, I tried not to think about the possibilities of me ending up headlining the national newspapers:

WOMAN SQUASHED TO DEATH IN MOVIE STAR'S MANSION!

For a man of seventy-seven years, I had to give it him. Martin Murray-Wells was in pretty good shape. Judging by the ecstatic grunts and groans coming from above, the two of them were thoroughly enjoying themselves. But it was his amorous companion who'd truly astonished me. Never in a million years had I ever anticipated this particular lady would put herself in such a risky situation. As her signature perfume, masculine with musky overtones, reached my quivering nostrils, I didn't think I'd ever be able to look her in the eye again. For above me, in all her naked glory, was my neighbour Alison.

Chapter Twenty

I lay under the chaise-longue for what seemed like an eternity. By the time things came to a juddering, groaning, noisy climax I'd completely lost sensation in my legs, and my neck muscles were in agony.

Finally my neighbour and Martin Murray-Wells rolled off the chaise-longue, collected up their discarded clothing and, exclaiming excitedly at their brazen antics, left the attic rooms. I was just about to come out from my hiding place when Alison returned by herself. Giggling naughtily, she went and stood in front of the easel for a minute. After that I was too scared to come out for another ten minutes in case either of them returned again. When I finally hauled myself out, I felt incredibly shaky. I sat down heavily on the chaise-longue, desperately trying to regain my wits and sense of well-being. It evaded me. Groaning, I put my head in my hands. I don't know how long I sat like that, but a familiar female voice had me jumping off the chaise-longue like a schoolgirl in trouble with the head teacher.

'What the hell's happened to my painting?' Harriet roared.

I clutched my hands to my thumping heart. 'O-oh, Harriet. You took me by surprise.'

'I take it the reason you're sitting on that chaise looking like your world has collapsed is because of *this*?' she snapped.

White-faced, I crept over and peered at the canvas. Alison had finished off Harriet's facial features on my behalf. The image was now sporting blacked out teeth and a pair of Harry Potter glasses.

'Y-yes,' I stammered. 'It was a bit of a shock. I had to, er, sit down and just...take a moment.'

'That child of mine,' Harriet fumed, 'is turning into a delinquent.' She dumped her handbag on the floor and stomped over to the chaise. 'I've told Martin that I'm finding her behaviour more and more rebellious. I'll be having words with that school of hers on Monday. We don't pay thousands of pounds in fees to have our daughter carrying on like some sort of chav.' Harriet's eyes flashed with anger.

'Don't blame Piper,' I soothed. 'It's probably just a cry for attention.'

I desperately hoped Piper didn't get into trouble due to Alison's prank back-firing.

'If Piper wants attention, she only has to ask. After all, her father is downstairs with Alison.'

I looked at Harriet uncertainly. Surely she didn't know of or condone the shenanigans her husband had so very recently been up to with my neighbour? Harriet met my gaze.

'What's up?'

'Nothing,' I said quickly as a vision of Martin Murray-Well's erect private parts instantly sprang to mind. The mental picture faded to Henry and his third leg. Dear Lord, the Montgomery-Murray-Wells' house was certainly seeing a lot of extra-marital action.

'I was, um, just surprised to hear my neighbour is downstairs.'

Harriet flapped a hand dismissively. 'The May Ball. Apparently there was some minor tweaking that just couldn't keep.'

'Ah,' I nodded. So that was the excuse for Alison being here.

'Well shall we get on with it?' Harriet said, suddenly business-like. 'I want this painting finished tonight.'

'Tonight?' my head jerked. 'I'm afraid I'm seeing somebody this evening and–'

'Cancel them,' Harriet ordered.

'It's a long-standing arrangement. Apart from anything else, you told me I had a week's slot for this commission. I'm afraid I can't drop everything to suit–'

'I'll pay you another thousand pounds.'

'Look, Harriet, it's not about the money. It's–'

'Okay, I'll double your fee. Eight thousand pounds.'

I gasped. *Eight thousand pounds*! Dear Lord. Aware that I was staring divorce in the face and would shortly be going it alone, I determined that my meet-up with Luca would regrettably have to be postponed.

'Okay,' I nodded. 'But first, I need to make a phone call.'

'Go ahead,' said Harriet waving one hand in a don't-mind-me gesture.

156

'Ah. I was hoping for a bit of privacy.'

'I'm not listening,' Harriet assured as she began stripping off her clothes. One way or another that chaise-longue was seeing rather a lot of nudity today. 'Just hurry up,' she ordered.

'Er, right.'

I whipped out my mobile phone and found Luca's number. It rang and went straight to voicemail. I hung up and tried the restaurant. A female voice answered.

'Pronto?'

'Oh! Um, hello.' Out of my peripheral vision I could see Harriet was now entirely in the buff and draping herself over the chaise-longue. 'Is the manager there please?'

'Who?'

I really didn't want to say names in front of Harriet.

'The proprietor, please.'

'Il proprietario?'

'Yes.'

'No.'

Bugger.

'It's quite urgent.'

'Luca upstairs. With viz-ee-tor.'

'I see. Look, is it possible to tell him Florrie is on the phone?'

'Do you have mobile number?'

'Yes.'

'Ring mobile. I will shout up the stairs. I will say Flor-ee is calling.'

'Thank you.'

I hung up again. As I redialled Luca's

mobile number, Harriet's fingers began to tap impatiently against one creamy thigh.

'I thought you said you had *one* call to make? This is phone call number three.'

'Yes.' *Thank you for reminding me you can count.* 'I haven't been able to reach the person in question, but I've been assured I now will.'

Harriet rolled her eyes by way of answer just as my call connected to Luca's mobile. As the sound of ring tones once again went unanswered, I had a flicker of doubt. What if Luca had changed his mind about seeing me this evening and was deliberately avoiding speaking to me? Just when I thought his voicemail would kick in again, my call was answered.

'Hello?'

For a moment I couldn't speak. I knew that voice. What on earth was *she* doing in Luca's upstairs apartment? Moreover, why was she answering Luca's phone?

'Er, hello.'

I could imagine her at the other end of the phone, smirking like a cat with the cream.

'Ah, Florrie. It *is* Florrie, isn't it?'

'Y-yes.'

'And what do you want, Florrie?'

Her tone was supercilious. She sounded like Cinderella's step-mother demanding to know why I wanted to go to the ball. It was obvious from her tone of voice that I was intruding.

'Well, clearly I was hoping to speak to...,'

I let my voice trail off. I really didn't want to name names in front of Harriet. It was obvious who I wanted to talk with. But the woman at the other end of the phone was having none of it. Like a game of cat-and-mouse she was toying with me, thoroughly enjoying herself.

'Hoping to speak to whom, Florrie?' she mocked.

I took a deep breath. 'Luca.'

From her position on the chaise-longue, Harriet shifted. I could see her head swivelling in my direction. Evidently she was hanging on to every word I was so reluctantly saying. Irked, I asserted myself.

'Please could you put me on to Luca?'

Out of my peripheral vision I saw Harriet's mouth forming a perfect O.

There was a brief pause before the woman at the other end of the phone deigned to reply.

'I'm afraid that's not possible.'

'Can I ask why?'

'No, Florrie. That's personal. Just understand that Luca cannot come to the phone right now, and even if he could he wouldn't be interested in talking to you. Do I make myself perfectly clear? Luca is with *me*, Florrie.' She waited, letting her words sink in. 'Do you understand? Now please don't embarrass yourself by calling again.'

The line disconnected. I removed the phone from my ear and stared incredulously at it. Its screen blurred as my eyes suddenly swam with unshed tears. How could I have got things so wrong?

Harriet gave a little cough, cutting across my thoughts.

'I couldn't help overhearing you were ringing Luca Serafino.'

I blinked rapidly, willing the waterworks to subside.

'Yes,' I whispered, tucking the mobile away. 'He was ... indisposed.'

'I see.' Harriet inclined her head. 'So you were meant to be meeting Luca this evening?'

'Y-yes. About a painting,' I lied. 'But there must have been a misunderstanding. He wasn't expecting me after all. I can stay for as long as you like.'

My voice was hoarse. There was a huge lump in my throat. It felt as though my airways were being constricted.

'You look visibly upset, Florrie,' Harriet persisted. 'Was it a woman who answered Luca's phone?'

I wasn't in the mood for Harriet's probing.

'It's really not important,' I mumbled, picking up my paintbrush.

Harriet gave me a knowing look. 'If it's any consolation, she told me she's been after Luca for ages.'

I inhaled sharply and looked across at Harriet. 'I really don't know what you're talking about.'

'Yes, you do,' she persisted. 'You've just been warned off by Annabelle Farquhar-Jones.'

Chapter Twenty-One

Ignoring Harriet, I got down to the task of painting her image. The Harry Potter glasses and blacked out teeth were replaced with chiselled cheekbones and a flawless complexion. My brush fairly flew across the canvas and, for the most part, Harriet kept still and didn't complain. She didn't make conversation, and neither did I. I worked on autopilot, paint blurring and building. As I stood in the make-shift studio under the eaves of the Montgomery-Murray-Wells' mansion, another part of me ...the feeling part...lifted up and whirled backwards to that moment in time where the association with Luca Serafino changed from working relationship to close relationship.

'You've been crying, Florrie.' Luca had looked concerned as he'd greeted me. 'What's wrong?'

'Nothing,' I'd sniffed and instantly pasted on a bright smile. 'Just a bit of a cold.'

Luca had looked at me uncertainly. I'd been standing on the doorstep at the rear of the restaurant. My visit was a follow-up appointment to talk about the next landscape in the Florentine series, and which wall in the restaurant the painting would grace.

'Come upstairs, Florrie. The weather is not so good today and you look chilled.'

Luca had stood aside allowing me into

the narrow hallway. I'd stepped over the threshold into immediate warmth. Outside it had been a particularly cold February evening and chucking down with icy rain.

'Follow me,' Luca had said and led me up the staircase to his flat. 'But first, I insist on making you a hot drink before we get down to the business of discussing the new painting.'

'That would be lovely,' I'd said with a shiver. Even now I like to think that shiver was simply due to coming in from the cold, but at that point I'd been acutely aware of Luca's close proximity as he'd taken me into the lounge. I'd sat on a sofa by the window, desperately trying to relax in the comfort of Luca's lounge which had been lit by soft lamplight. Minutes later, he'd sat down right next to me. Two cups of frothy cappuccino had been set on the occasional table in front of us.

'Sugar?'

He'd smiled and immediately my insides had started to melt. I'd gazed at him, momentarily struck dumb, as my brain had sternly told my mouth to spit out the word "yes" or "no". Momentarily I'd behaved like someone who'd had their grey matter abducted by aliens and the space filled with tiramisu.

'That would be lovely,' I'd finally whispered, taking a fat brown cube from the proffered sugar bowl.

We'd drunk our coffees together companionably. Luca had done most of the

162

talking, which had been just as well because I'd felt ridiculously tongue-tied. Eventually we'd drained our cups. Luca had looked at me enquiringly.

'Ready to talk shop?' he'd asked and smiled encouragingly.

I'd nodded and smiled back. *That's better, Florrie. Settle down. Enjoy the man's company. And his beauty. Just don't drown in it. Stay focused.*

'So, another painting of Florence,' Luca had begun, 'but this time a completely different flavour. I'm looking for a piece that conveys a tantalising opportunity to glimpse into another world, one where there might have been intimate conversations and secret moments.' He'd produced a photograph of the Ponte Vecchio. 'This is the oldest and most famous bridge in Florence. It spans the Arno River. Locals and tourists love to visit and browse the jewellery shops located here. And look,' Luca had pointed. 'See all the padlocks around the railings? They're all shapes, all colours, and all sizes. But they mean one thing.'

I'd cleared my throat to speak.

'You place the padlock on the railings with your true love by your side. And when you close it, it symbolizes locking your love for each other, forever.'

'Very good, Florrie. You have been there?'

Suddenly I'd been unable to speak. Instead I'd simply nodded again.

Luca had smiled. 'Me too.' Then he'd noticed the shift in my expression. 'Hey, you're upset. What is it, Florrie? What's wrong?'

I'd opened my mouth to speak but instead found myself sucking in a long breath that had caught at the back of my throat. On the exhale, I'd sounded like a juddering washing machine gathering itself to do a final spin. Suddenly tears had spurted out of my eyes.

'I'm so sorry,' I'd gasped, mortified at my eyes taking it upon themselves to leak like knackered plumbing. 'I don't know what's come over me.'

Luca had quickly put the photograph down on the table by our empty coffee cups.

'Well clearly something has upset you.' He'd frowned. 'Is it the photograph?'

My eyes had cast downwards in misery. 'Yes,' I'd eventually muttered.

Luca had looked at the photograph and then back at me. Understandably he'd been confused.

'Why does such a romantic image move you to such profound sorrow?'

I'd blinked through my tears. 'Its...it's nothing really,' I'd stuttered.

'But clearly it is.' He'd picked up one of my hands. Tentatively he'd cupped it in both of his. 'You can tell me it's none of my business,' he'd said gently, 'but sometimes unburdening to someone you don't know all that well can be very therapeutic. And,' he'd added with a smile of reassurance, 'I have

164

nothing better to do on this miserably cold, wet, winter's evening.'

And before I'd been able to stop myself, the whole sorry saga of my unhappy marriage had tumbled from my lips.

'The photograph is of a place my h-husband once took me,' I'd gulped. Luca had nodded encouragingly, and I'd stumbled on. 'It...it was a surprise weekend. A gift.'

'Your birthday?' he'd asked.

I'd shaken my head vehemently. 'N-no. Nothing like that. It was a...s-sorry present. For...for,' I'd struggled over the words, almost gagging, aware that I'd been divesting information so secret I'd not even told Alison or Daisy, and most definitely not my family. I'd been too ashamed to tell anyone. Too embarrassed. And too furious. And I didn't want my friends or family to be livid on my behalf and, more importantly, I'd not wanted them to be angry with Marcus. Or to think less of him.

'It was a sorry present for my husband being unfaithful to me.'

'Ah.' An expression I'd not been able to read had flickered across Luca's face. I'd yet to hear about *his* marriage, both brief and disastrous, to Maria.

'My husband – Marcus – at the time he'd been seeing a woman at his office. They were having an affair.'

'That's a cause of great hurt,' Luca had acknowledged. His voice had held a note of genuine sympathy.

165

'I'd suspected for a while that somebody else might be on the scene. You see,' I'd lowered my eyes, suddenly feeling awkward, 'I can't have children and...my husband...well he has fertility issues too, so it's unlikely he'll ever father children ...so between the two of us...,' I'd shrugged and let my voice trail off.

'Many couples can't have children, Florrie,' Luca had said quietly. 'But usually they rally together. Acknowledge it isn't going to happen. They're grateful to at least have each other and celebrate the rest of their lives together, without letting despair or sorrow snuff out that love.'

'Yes,' I'd acknowledged, 'some couples do. But regrettably we haven't been one of those couples. My husband, you see, he feels...he feels like he's not a man...in the true sense. If it weren't for me, he might have had a slim chance of fathering a child. But the two of us together...it's...it's a no. It's just not going to happen.'

'So he sought solace elsewhere? Is that what you're saying?'

'Yes. It wasn't his fault. Not really.'

'It wasn't his fault he slept with another woman?' Luca had raised his eyebrows.

I'd considered. 'Not in the true sense of the word,' I'd insisted. 'It wasn't lust or...or deliberately trying to hurt me. It was...well...frustration. Disappointment. Feeling emasculated.'

'You sound like you're trying to justify your husband's actions so you can excuse him. You are a very forgiving woman.' Luca's expression had become slightly incredulous. 'Most men would expect to have paint stripper poured over their car, or discover their clothes hacked to pieces with the garden shears.'

I'd smiled weakly. 'I'm not that sort of person.'

'I can tell,' he'd murmured. 'You are one of life's gentle souls.'

'Oh I don't know about that,' I'd laughed mirthlessly. 'In my head I've confronted the other woman a thousand times. Slapped her too,' I'd added. I hadn't wanted Luca to be under any illusion about me being mild-mannered. At the time I'd been devastated. And as mad as a hornet.

'How did you find out about his...indiscretion?'

I'd sighed. 'Marcus had gone for a shower. It was early evening and he'd left his mobile phone on the kitchen worktop. I was cooking dinner when his mobile began to ring. I didn't know whether to answer it or not. So I peered at the display to see if it was a family member or mutual friend calling. The display lit up with a man's name. John Smith. Unoriginal, but also unassuming. I thought it must be one of Marcus's business clients, so rather than answer it I let it go to voicemail. But a few minutes later the mobile gave a series of beeps indicating the arrival of a text message. I didn't open the text, but from the lit-up display I could read part of the message.'

Luca had nodded. 'So you were able to work out what he was up to?'

'Exactly. From what I could read there wasn't a shadow of doubt about the romantic intention of the person that had written the text. And "John Smith" was most definitely not a man!

I hadn't revealed to Luca the message's specific content. But whoever "John Smith" was, the person had told my husband they couldn't wait to see him later and shag him senseless. The rest of the message was hidden and had only been accessible if I'd opened it, which would have alerted Marcus. But I'd seen enough. As I'd mechanically stirred the gravy, I'd desperately tried to gather my wits. My husband was meeting with a woman. And later that evening.

'So,' Luca had prompted, 'what did you do next?'

'Marcus eventually came downstairs to dinner. I sat there and made small talk with him as we ate. As always, I asked him about his day. He told me it had been really boring. Then he put his knife and fork together and said he hoped I didn't mind but he'd promised a client he'd drop some info around to their house first thing in the morning, but he'd left the paperwork at the office. He said he needed to go back to London and collect the paperwork. So I pretended to go along with it and agreed he must drive back to his office.'

'And then what did you do?'

'Well, I...,' I'd looked shamefaced, '...I followed him.'

Luca had looked astonished. 'Exactly how did you manage that?'

'The moment Marcus left the house and went to his car, I grabbed my car keys off the hall table and belted after him. Obviously I kept my distance. Driving along, I allowed other cars to fall in behind his and separate us, and so successfully managed to trail him all the way to a semi-detached house in Gravesend.'

'So not an office in London,' Luca had grimaced.

'No,' I'd shaken my head as fresh tears had streaked down my cheeks. 'My legs were shaking as I drove. It's a wonder I didn't drive into the car in front of me.'

'So what happened when you got to Gravesend?'

'Marcus parked his car. I drove past him and found a space further down the road. By the time I'd parked my vehicle, Marcus was standing on the doorstep of this unassuming looking house. I saw him ring the doorbell. I got out of my car and, using a long row of parked cars as a shield, stealthily headed towards him from the opposite side of the road. While he was waiting for the occupant to come to the door, he turned and studied the street. I immediately ducked down behind one of the parked cars. Then, shifting my position, I slowly came up and peered through the

169

car's rear passenger windows just in time to see the front door being opened. My husband was effusively greeted by a woman in a plunging dress.' I'd stopped and, foraging for a tissue up my sleeve, blown my nose. 'At that point there was still a small part of me that desperately hoped the woman was a client...that Marcus had perhaps found the so-called missing paperwork in his car, and the two of them were simply having a cup of tea while talking business.'

'And were they?'

I'd shot Luca a look. 'What do you think?'

'I see. So what did you do next? Most women would have been over there like a shot, claws out and kicking the front door down.'

I'd grimaced. 'I went back to my car and sat in it for a while. From my position I was able to see the downstairs lights go out and the upstairs lights turn on. And then the woman appeared at an upstairs window and drew the curtains. I took that as my cue to leave. I drove home, numb and disbelieving, despite what I'd witnessed. Once home, I made myself a cup of tea and sat at the kitchen table simply staring at the wall until Marcus returned. He was all smiles. He apologised for being late. There were excuses about the Blackwall Tunnel being closed and having to divert all around the houses, instead coming home via the Dartford Bridge, which had also been a nightmare due to a massive accident. He was really very believable. Except, of course, I knew the truth. So I nodded, and smiled, and made sympathetic noises. And then he paused. Frowned. Queried why I was sitting in the kitchen nursing a cold cup of tea. And that was when I asked him, outright, why he'd visited a woman in Gravesend.'

Luca had let out a low whistle. 'That was very brave of you. And how did Marcus take that?'

'He looked absolutely stunned. And horrified. And then he broke down. Said he was so, so sorry. That the affair was nothing more than plain gratuitous sex. He didn't love the woman. It was only me he loved. It was because he felt such a failure, but that it would never, ever happen again. Next thing is I was being bombarded with flowers every night, and being told I was his sun, moon and stars, and then two tickets to Florence were pushed into my hands with Marcus insisting I was going to be romanced forever.' Leaning forward, I'd picked up the photograph from the coffee table. 'We walked over this bridge.' I'd nodded at the image. 'Marcus surprised me by producing a large red heart-shaped padlock. He opened it up, held it out before me, and said I was his beautiful wife and he would never stop loving me. Then he reached forward and snapped the padlock around a railing insisting nothing would ever shake our love again.'

'That's a grand gesture. And did you still love him, Florrie?'

I'd heaved a sigh. 'Back then, yes. Back then I loved him very much. But I can't deny I struggled to trust him. I forgave, but found it difficult to forget. And just when I felt like my heart was starting to heal, just when I was beginning to trust, it happened again.'

'With the same woman?'

'No. Someone else. The signs were there from the off.'

'Such as?'

I'd briefly closed my eyes and tried not to look embarrassed. 'The sudden lack of interest in...well...intimacy. There is a pattern. Marcus is distracted and happy. He loses interest in me. I find out. He begs forgiveness. Repeat all over again.'

Luca had looked flabbergasted. 'You constantly forgave your husband for his repeated affairs?'

I'd nodded. 'But each time it happened, a little piece of my love for him died.' I'd given Luca a grim look. 'Unfortunately, there comes a point when there is no love left.'

'Has that point now been reached?'

I'd nodded my head slowly. 'Most definitely. A little while ago I received a letter. It was from his latest mistress. I will spare her blushes, but she's well known in this village.'

'Ah,' Luca had said. 'That's very honourable of you. So many women would be plotting a humiliating revenge.'

'I told you. I'm not like that,' I'd sighed. 'I've lost count how many affairs Marcus has had. But when that letter arrived, the little bit of affection I had left for Marcus had been hanging by a thread. By the time I'd finished reading its contents, I couldn't even cry. Marcus had used up the last of my love.'

'But you're crying now, Florrie. Your face is still wet with tears. Are you sure you don't love your husband?'

'Oh, quite sure,' I'd said emphatically as two more fat tears trickled down the sides of my nose.

'So why are you crying again?' he'd asked gently.

'I'm crying for the memories your photograph evoked. For being lulled into living a lie with my cheating husband. I should have left him a long time ago.'

'But you didn't.'

'There never seemed to be the right moment. And then one of my parents wasn't well and, at the time, I didn't want them worrying about me.'

'That sounds like an excuse,' Luca had said.

'You're right,' I'd agreed. 'Maybe there is also an element of cowardice. I need to psyche myself up to leave. Be brave.' I'd blown my nose again.

Luca had nodded, his eyes full of sympathy. 'Sometimes it's good to prepare yourself for a major life change. Think it through properly. And be very, very brave.'

And then Luca had put one arm around my shoulders and, with the other, drawn me towards him. I'd begun to sob again. Not for the lost love over Marcus, but for a marriage that had started as a dream, then hit the rocks and shattered. Before I'd known what was happening, Luca had cupped my face in the palms of his hands and, using the balls of his thumbs, wiped away my tears. Then slowly, oh so very slowly, he'd lowered his mouth to mine. And so had begun the start of something special that nobody knew anything about. I'd thought.

Chapter Twenty-Two

Afterwards, as I'd lain in Luca's bed staring up at the ceiling, a whirl of different feelings had whooshed through my brain. They'd gathered momentum, seemingly taking on a life of their own before fragmenting into a kaleidoscope of broken thoughts. One thing was clear. I was a hypocrite. A cheat. An adulteress. I was no better than my Casanova husband. I'd wondered if Marcus had been at home, maybe nursing his own cup of cold tea whilst staring at the kitchen wall wondering exactly how long it took his wife to discuss a painting commission with a restaurateur? Or whether he'd thought, "Yippee! I can nip out and see Annabelle Farquhar-Jones!" Or Christine...or Janey... or Carrie? So many women. So many names. Little had I known that my husband had been outside Serafino's waiting for his latest amour and already seen the romantic drama unfolding from the lit window over the restaurant.

Next to me Luca had stirred. We'd been drifting in and out of sleep for half an hour or so, eyes closed, arms wrapped around each other. I'd looked up at Luca's face. So handsome and kind, even in repose. He'd opened his eyes and, slowly, smiled at me. The smile had reached his eyes, crinkling the skin at the corners.

'Florrie, *cara*. I can't tell you how happy

I am seeing you next to me.'

I'd smiled back but hadn't returned any endearments. I'd regarded what we'd done as a one-off. The guy was hot. He probably had women falling over themselves to get into his bed all the time. Indeed, he might have had another woman in his bed just last night. And maybe another woman was lined up, ready, willing and available to take the place I'd then been occupying. This was what years of being married to a serial adulterer did to you. It left you suspicious of everything and trusting no one.

'Florrie?'

'Yes?'

'Are you okay?'

'Yes, I'm...very okay,' I'd nodded. 'And grateful.'

An expression of puzzlement had crossed Luca's face.

'For listening to me burbling on earlier,' I'd explained, 'and then being so kind.'

'Kind?' He'd raised his eyebrows. 'You think I held you in my arms and took you to my bed out of kindness?'

'I...well...I don't want to presume...I mean...I'm sure you have many lady friends. And...er...that's fine by me,' I'd added hastily, feeling myself go a bit pink in the face. 'After all, you're a single man. An incredibly good-looking one at that,' I'd pointed out, 'so you probably have to fight the women off. But that's fine. After all, you're a free agent and can take as many women to bed as you like.' I'd rattled to a

176

stop feeling slightly foolish. Luca had looked at me in amusement.

'So, I have your permission to romance and woo other women. Is that what you're saying, Florrie?' His mouth had twitched.

'Well, it's nothing to do with me. Your love life, I mean.' My already pink cheeks had begun to redden and burn at inadvertently putting Luca's love life under a microscope.

'Ah, but you're wrong,' he'd corrected me. 'My private life has everything to do with you.'

It had then been my turn to be puzzled. 'Well, that's very nice of you wanting to be so honest, but I'd rather not know, thanks.'

My heart had twisted with pain. The thought of Luca with another woman had hurt so much I'd found it hard to breathe.

'Listen to me, Florrie.' Luca's voice had been gentle. 'I am not some cheating immoral man like your husband. There is no string of other women in my life.' I'd regarded Luca sceptically as he'd taken my hand. 'There is a woman though.' He'd looked deep into my eyes and I'd felt my throat constrict.

Here it comes. The truth about another woman.

I'd braced myself. What did it matter whether it was one woman or several? The outcome was the same. This man was seeing someone else. Luca had cleared his throat.

'The woman in my life...I'm looking right

at her.'

The words had hung in the air for a moment. As they'd begun to sink into my brain, my eyes had widened.

'Me?'

'Yes, you. It sounds corny, Florrie, but I promise you,' he'd taken my hand and, placing his other hand over the top, pressed them against his chest. 'You are here. In my heart. The moment I saw you lunching with your girlfriends in my restaurant, you touched my soul. I cannot explain it. And I don't want to, for there are no adequate words to convey how, when I handed you the menu that day, you made my entire world tilt on its axis. I knew I had to find a way for you to be in my life. Learning you were an artist opened a window of opportunity. Discovering you were married was almost unbearable. However, I suspected your marriage wasn't a bed of roses. This is a small village, *cara*. As you know, tongues wag. When a certain woman booked a table for two in my restaurant and openly paraded the latest man in her life, I didn't need to be Sherlock Holmes to deduce who he was. Especially when that man handed me his credit card to pay the bill. His name was plain to see.

'Marcus?' I'd asked, astonished. 'My husband was so indiscreet as to publicly dine out with this lady?'

That had rocked me. I'd thought Marcus had only got down to straightforward gratuitous sex. I hadn't realised wining and dining played a part in his many infidelities. But even that discovery hadn't hurt. My heart had remained immune.

'Seeing your husband with this woman left me in no doubt about the state of your marriage. It gave me a glimmer of hope. That I might be able to get to know you better with a clear conscience. I'm not the sort of man who pursues married women, unhappy or otherwise. And before you ask whether commissioning you to do paintings was out of pity, I can tell you quite categorically the answer is no. But, yes, I did commission you in order to have a reason to get to know you.' He'd leant forward and kissed the tip of my nose. 'And besides,' he'd added, 'my restaurant is starting to feel a lot more ambient with your paintings adorning the walls.'

I'd smiled, and gently cuffed him in mock outrage.

'I should hope so too.' I'd cleared my throat, suddenly serious. 'So, who was the woman my husband was romancing?'

Luca had paused. He'd given me a level look.

'I think you already know the answer to that question, Florrie.'

The cogs of my brain had whirred and spun as thought processes fell into place. I'd frowned, not quite sure who he was hinting at.

'The woman,' Luca had said, 'is the same, I suspect, as the author who penned that letter to you.'

I'd gasped. Of course. Who else but Annabelle Farquhar-Jones.

'What is it about that female?' I'd asked, frustrated. 'Everywhere I go, whatever I'm doing, she pops up in my life.'

'You are not alone, Florrie. She is very popular with the men – married or otherwise. From what I've heard, she pursues her prey relentlessly. But listen, *cara*. Forget about the likes of women like her. I want to talk about you. And how much you mean to me. I know your life is currently,' he'd paused to find the right word, 'complicated. You have a lot to oversee. Separation. Divorce. Taking a marital home apart and undoing all the ties, especially the emotional ones, is very difficult. But I want you to know I'm here for you. And,' he'd raised my fingers to his lips and kissed them one by one, 'I love you.'

Chapter Twenty-Three

When Luca had told me he loved me, I'd immediately wanted to respond with the same words. I knew I loved him too, with every fibre of my being. But the sane, sensible part of me had protested otherwise. How could I love a man I barely knew? Exploring his body between the sheets was one thing, but I'd yet to get to know the real him – his thoughts, hopes, dreams, and what made him tick. All I'd known for sure was that my brain was screaming words like "rebound" and warning me not to leap from one bad relationship to potentially another.

'Luca,' I'd said tentatively. 'I can't commit myself to you just yet. It's...too early.'

'I know. I don't expect anything from you, Florrie. But I will live in hope. And I also want you to carry on painting for me. The restaurant is genuinely benefitting from your beautiful work. If you are looking at being a single lady you will need an income and more clients.'

I was so very, very grateful for Luca's assistance with launching my painting career. And thanks to his framing a little notice about me under each piece, I had received several enquiries. Hopefully at some point they would turn into commissions. Meanwhile there was a marriage to unravel.

Weeks had passed. By the time I'd confronted my husband about the mystery letter, my relationship with Luca had been firmly limited to one of love but in the context of old-fashioned courtship. There was warmth, supportive friendship, very sweet words and gentle kisses, but absolutely no torrid lovemaking. I wanted to listen to my brain and refrain from that leap into uncertainty...to be one-hundred per-cent sure that going from the marital bed – albeit a very cold marital bed – to Luca's bed, was not a hasty decision I'd later come to regret.

And now, standing in Harriet Montgomery's attic rooms, with the movie star openly watching a stream of emotions playing across my face, my devastation was acute. The loathsome Annabelle Farquhar-Jones had not only bedded my husband but also taken my beloved!

Thank God I'd listened to my brain and not my heart, and insisted on keeping Luca at arm's length and not returned to his bed. Erasing Luca's false words of endearment was going to be challenge enough. Thank heavens I hadn't indulged in making further bittersweet memories of our bodies coming together in what I'd fancifully thought as a soulmate connection. As it was, I had a harsh reminder of our single union. I would be carrying that reminder for the next few months until I went to hospital to give birth to our baby. That reminder would continue for the rest of my life as I raised our child alone.

Harriet interrupted my whirling thoughts. 'How's the painting coming along? I'm bored now.'

'Almost there,' I murmured. 'You can get dressed if you like. I can finish this little bit without you.'

'I wish you'd said something sooner,' Harriet grumbled, instantly shifting her voluptuous bottom from the chaise-longue. 'Come down when you're finished and have a cup of tea.'

'Thank you,' I said, genuinely surprised and grateful.

I couldn't imagine the likes of Harriet Montgomery offering to make tea for many people. She had a housekeeper who surely took care of that. Although right now, I could really gulp down something much stronger than tea. A large gin and tonic came to mind. Unfortunately, at the moment all alcohol was off the agenda. Tea it would have to be. I sighed with both frustration and annoyance and began wiping brushes and packing up while Harriet finished dressing.

'Here,' she said, handing me a key. 'Lock the attic's main door on your way out. I don't want my precocious daughter ruining the artwork again.'

Wordlessly I took the key. If Alison sabotaged the painting again it would have to remain that way because, as from tomorrow, I wouldn't be around to put it right for a second time. As I moved around the makeshift studio I determined to get away from it all. I needed to absent myself from the likes of that wretched Annabelle Farquhar-Jones. There was a deep need to retreat now and privately lick my wounds, whilst attempting to come to terms with the bitter realisation that Luca was no better than Marcus. I didn't want to be around to listen to the village gossip and wagging tongues.

I hadn't seen Mum and Dad for a while, and they knew nothing of my predicament. It was time to update them. I'd drive over tomorrow. First thing. Tell them everything. Before somebody else did. Just as soon as I'd had a good night's sleep. I yawned and slowly stretched out stiff muscles. Right now I felt as though I could sleep for a hundred years.

I was just locking up the attic when my phone signalled the arrival of a text message.

Cara, what happened to you this evening?

Without bothering to reply I turned the key in the main door and made my way downstairs to Harriet's vast kitchen. It was late now, so I was surprised to see Alison still here. She was chatting to Harriet and seated at the enormous kitchen table whilst cradling a mug of something hot. When I walked into the kitchen she looked visibly shaken.

'Florrie!' she exclaimed. 'I didn't realise you were here.'

'She's been working on my painting,' Harriet said, 'and a vandalised painting at that. It would seem my young daughter is nothing more than a delinquent.' Harriet pursed her lips together and Alison had the grace to blush. 'I don't know what gets into Piper. Are you having trouble with Tiffany by any chance?'

'Er, yes, a little,' Alison confessed. 'She really isn't performing well enough with her languages. Such a disappointment. She keeps wanting to play out in our road with Daisy's kids. I've told her it's a no. I don't want her associating with the local school's riff-raff.'

My hackles instantly came up. 'Daisy's children are absolutely delightful,' I protested.

'If you like that sort of thing,' Alison sniffed.

It was at times like this that I found Ali an utter cow. She was quite happy to sit in our mutual neighbour's untidy front room accepting tea and sympathy when she needed it, but when Alison was in the company of fake friends like Harriet she really could be quite a bitch.

'Anyway, Florrie,' Alison continued, 'how long have you been here? I didn't see you come in.'

'Really?' I smiled sweetly. 'That's strange, because I saw you.'

Alison blanched and began to choke on her drink, while Harriet looked perplexed at the sudden undercurrent going on. I turned to Harriet.

'Thanks for the offer of tea, but actually I'm rather tired and think I'd like to go home.'

Harriet shrugged. 'Suit yourself.'

'I'll see you out,' said Alison jumping to her feet. 'You stay put, Harriet,' she fawned, 'and enjoy your tea. You must be exhausted after hours of lying so still for Florrie.'

I put up a hand in farewell to Harriet and headed out of the kitchen and back into the huge reception area that was Harriet's "hallway". As soon as we were out of earshot, Alison clamped a hand on my shoulder and spun me round to face her.

'Just a minute, Florrie.'

I looked at her, my face a picture of innocence. 'Yes?'

'What was that remark in the kitchen intended to mean?'

'What remark?' I asked, eyes wide.

'You said you saw me come in. But I never saw you.'

'I know you didn't, Ali. But don't worry. Your secret is safe with me.'

Alison stared at me, her expression inscrutable. 'Secret? I don't have any secrets.'

'Of course you don't,' I replied, patting her hand. 'I'm going away tomorrow to see my parents. For the moment I've had enough of this village.' My eyes suddenly blazed. 'And I've just about had enough of everyone in it too.'

'W-Whatever are you talking about?'

Alison stuttered. She looked panicked.

'You know perfectly well what I'm talking about,' I glared at her. 'I'll see you at the May Ball. Until then, keep your paws off Harriet's painting and make sure Piper doesn't get into trouble.'

And then, leaving Alison looking like she'd been slapped on both cheeks with a particularly stinky wet fish, I walked out of the front door and into the cool dark night.

Chapter Twenty-Four

I hardly slept a wink that night. Having left the marital bed and made one of the spare bedrooms my own, I'd tossed and turned, vividly dreaming that I was back in Harriet's attic rooms. Once again I was painting, this time as if my life depended upon it. But as I'd splashed colour onto the canvas and built the oil into shape and form, my efforts had been constantly hampered by a stream of amorous couples – none of whom were married to each other.

Harriet had been the first to trail through the ether of light sleep. She'd been totally starkers and towing a lascivious Henry along, his tongue hanging out and making him look like a randy panting dog. She'd looked at me and smirked before snapping, "Keep Alison away from my painting." She'd waggled a finger in warning just as the doors to the Juliette balcony flew open. "I don't want anybody making mischief again or there will be trouble." And then both Harriet and Henry had floated out through the aperture, hovering briefly on a moonbeam before being snuffed out by dark clouds.

Alison had been the next to come in, and Martin Murray-Wells had been by her side. The two of them had insisted they be allowed to scribble on the canvas. I'd repeatedly batted their hands away, yelling at them to clear off. They'd managed to shape-shift into blobs of paint and had disappeared into the image, cackling gleefully. But before I could worry about what havoc they might wreak, a cold wind had blown around my ankles diverting my attention.

Spinning around, I'd gasped to see Luca standing there. He'd had Annabelle Farquhar-Jones draped around him. It had been too much and I'd let out a cry of pain. Annabelle had sneered openly. "You see, Florrie," she'd drawled, "I told you Luca was mine. And here he is to prove it. With me." I'd looked up at Luca, my face awash with tears. "Why did you lie to me?" I'd implored. "Please tell me why?" But his face had been devoid of all expression and he'd not answered me. That part of the dream had sent me hurtling upwards, like a diver struggling to emerge from deep waters, gasping for breath.

I'd sat bolt upright in bed, heart pounding, wide awake and drenched in sweat. My right hand had swiped at a real tear threatening to spill, while my left hand fluttered down and curled over my slightly rounded tummy, stroking the growing seed of our sole union.

A glance at the bedside clock revealed it was six in the morning. Flinging back the bedclothes, I crept into the master bedroom I'd previously shared with Marcus, taking care not to disturb him. However, as my eyes adjusted to the gloom, I could see the bed was empty. The quilted covers were piled up, full of uneven mounds, as if an army of moles had been attempting to tunnel through the feathery duvet's innards. Seemingly I wasn't the only one who'd had a terrible night's sleep. Marcus had clearly opted to channel his wakefulness into something productive and taken himself off to work early.

Moving through the bedroom and into the en-suite, I stepped into the shower and blasted away the tiredness. If only it were so easy to wash away problems and despair. Getting dressed, I moved around the bedroom, gathering belongings and folding them into a small case. Zipping up the bag, I then made both beds, had some breakfast and finally penned a message to Marcus.

Need to get away for a bit. Will be at Mum and Dad's. Mobile phone will be off. If you need to contact me, ring their landline. Will be back home in time for May Ball. Shame to waste tickets.

Florrie

Folding the note, I propped it up against the kettle. It was probably a bit presumptuous to expect Marcus to partner me at the ball, but with or without him I certainly had to be there. I'd promised to support Alison, and told both her and Daisy I'd attend. Apart from anything else, Harriet was expecting my presence when her painting was unveiled to both the local press and Joe Public.

Despite the relatively early hour – it was still only just before eight in the morning – I knew my parents would be up and about. They were the sort of folk who rose with the lark and went to bed before ten. As I shut the front door on Number 2, I heaved a sigh of relief. Sometimes, no matter what our age, we still needed to lean on our parents for a comforting hug, a kiss on the forehead, the reassurance that no matter what mess we'd made of our lives, everything would be all right. My mother was very much of the Hyacinth Bucket mould. Whilst I had no doubt she'd be sympathetic about my marriage ending, I wasn't quite so sure what her reaction would be when I broke the news that not only was she going to be a grandma, but her son-in-law wasn't the father. I certainly wasn't looking forward to what her retort would be when I confessed that the real father of my unborn baby was an Italian stud who'd already romantically moved on, and that not only was her daughter up the duff but also up the proverbial creek without a paddle.

Chapter Twenty-Five

'You *what*?' my mother yelped. 'Oh my God. I don't believe I'm hearing this.'

My mother was in full drama queen mode. She made to clutch her heart whilst still holding her teacup, and only narrowly avoided tipping a camomile infusion down her cashmere-covered bosom. Despite the warm spring weather outside, my mother was taking no chances. She was swathed from head to toe in warm clothing with the heating on for good measure. We were both seated at her neat kitchen table. The best bone china was set before us and a plate of biscuits had been neatly arranged over a doily-decorated plate. My mother tipped her chin upward and drew breath.

'Bill?' she bellowed at the ceiling over our heads. 'Get your bottom off that toilet and get down here. Now!'

My father's muffled voice floated through the plasterboard. 'Barbara, I've only just settled down with the newspaper. Can't it wait?'

'Most definitely not.'

My mother's cheeks were now sporting two rose-pink blobs. I could tell she was upset. From upstairs came the grumbles of my father complaining to himself. The sound of a toilet flushing followed shortly afterwards. I could picture him now, carefully folding up his beloved daily rag and placing it carefully on the cistern for a later visit, before moving over to the basin to wash his hands. Sometimes the bathroom was his only place of sanctuary in order to have a legitimate excuse to escape the many chores Mum made sure kept him busy now they no longer worked. They'd taken early retirement, opting for voluntary redundancy from their respective employers when the recession had been at its worst.

I put my teacup down and looked across the table at my mother. She was doing a very good impression of someone who'd popped a chocolate in their mouth only to discover it was ten years out of date. I sighed.

'I thought you'd be over the moon to hear you're finally going to be a grandmother.'

So far things hadn't gone quite as I'd expected. Certainly my mother had yet to wrap her arms around me and murmur reassuring words of comfort. I reached for a biscuit just as Mum gave me a baleful glare. For one moment I thought she was going to snatch the biscuit away and send me to my bedroom by way of punishment.

My father lumbered into the kitchen. His sturdy bulk momentarily blocked the light from the small kitchen window as he moved around the table towards me.

'Hello, love.' He bobbed a kiss on top of my head before pulling out a chair. 'Well this is most certainly a lovely surprise.' He beamed with pleasure and sat down heavily. I caught him glancing around the table, as if mentally counting the number of people present. My father was neither one of life's fast movers nor thinkers. His brow crinkled slightly. He stared at the empty chair opposite him. 'No Marcus?'

'No, Dad.'

'That's good,' he grinned. 'I'll have my best girl all to myself.' He looked very pleased with that.

'Actually, you've got me all to yourself for the next several days. If that's all right,' I added.

'Of course it's all right. We don't see enough of our girl. Do we, Barb?' He regarded my mother, who wasn't looking quite so ecstatic. Dad's brow furrowed again. 'Is there something going on here that nobody's told me about?'

'That's incredibly astute of you,' said Mum sarcastically.

'Oh dear.' My father pushed his chair back and stood up again. 'In that case I'm going to make a proper brew. Will you join me, Florrie? Unless, of course, you're pretending to enjoy that camomile muck your mother's given you.' He winked.

'Thanks, Dad,' I said gratefully. My father was always the gentler one of my two parents. He'd always been the first to pick me up when, as a child, I'd scraped a knee.

'You might want something stronger when you hear Florrie's news,' my mother said pointedly.

'Is that your way of giving me permission to add a drop of brandy to my cuppa?' Dad

194

grinned wickedly.

'Most certainly not,' my mother's eyes flashed. 'You won't believe what your daughter's gone and done.'

I noted the "your daughter" as opposed to "our daughter". Dad turned his attention to the kettle briefly, pouring scalding water into my mother's prized porcelain teapot.

'Do you hear me, Bill?' Mum's voice was starting to sound like a dripping tap.

I put the heels of my hands to my eyes and pressed hard. Perhaps coming back to my childhood home for a few days' respite hadn't been such a good idea after all. I'd join Dad for that cup of tea and then go back to Lower Amblegate. Yes, good idea. Once home I'd get on the phone to a solicitor. Sit down with Marcus. Start dividing up our belongings. I might even have a bit of time left over to follow up with the estate agent Marcus had mentioned.

Dad banged the heavy teapot down on the table making Mum and I jump.

'Hush, Barb,' he said gruffly. 'I think our Florrie can speak for herself.' His tone of voice said it all. *You can boss me around most of the time, but this is one time I'm not permitting it.* He placed two chipped builder-sized mugs on the table which my mother always kept for visiting workmen, then slapped down a plastic carton of milk, both of which had my mother visibly flinching. Before she could protest about not pouring milk into a china jug for the sake of decorum, Dad turned to me. His eyes were like two bright blue headlamps.

'So,' he said, smiling reassuringly and dropping his tone of voice to one that invited confiding in him, 'tell me, darling, what's happened. Properly. From the beginning.'

'She's pregnant,' Mum blurted.

Dad's face changed in an instant from serious to banana-split-grin.

'Sweetheart,' he cooed. 'This is wonderful news! So why the glum face?'

Mum immediately chimed in. 'Tell him, Florrie. Tell your father what you haven't long since told me. Although I could hardly believe my own ears.'

Dad turned his attention to Mum and frowned.

'Why don't you give the lass a chance to speak for herself, eh? Now please, Barbara. Stop interrupting.'

My mother pursed her lips and folded her arms across her chest.

'Well,' I began, picking my words carefully, 'things aren't very straightforward, Dad.' I cradled the mismatched mug of tea in my hands.

'But you've been waiting for this moment for years, darling.' Dad looked perplexed. 'Your mum and I never thought we'd be grandparents. I, for one, am absolutely delighted with the news. Surely you are too, Florrie?' His eyes searched mine for an answer.

'Yes,' I nodded, 'but the thing is, Dad, the baby...well...it's...you see...,' I took a deep breath, 'Marcus isn't the father.'

Dad stared at me. 'O-kay,' he said slowly, desperately trying to make sense of what I was saying. 'I remember you saying Marcus had some...um...fertility problems too...so...,' his expression cleared. 'Ah!' A lightbulb was going off in his brain. 'I understand. You went to a donor. Is that it?'

Opposite me, Mum snorted. She was obviously dying to get her tuppence-worth in.

'That's one way of putting it,' she said under her breath.

Dad gave an exasperated sigh. 'There's nothing wrong with going to a clinic,' he chided, 'so stop your digs, woman, and let our girl talk.'

'Don't you speak to me like that,' Mum's voice quivered with indignation. 'Our daughter hasn't been to some clinic, Bill. The harsh fact is that Florrie hasn't been true to her husband. Not true at all. Our daughter saw a donor all right. Another man. And this man has loved her and left her faster than you can say "ovulation".' She clicked her fingers together emphasising her point before rounding on me furiously. 'Oh I know all about your generation not giving two hoots about having kids with different men and being single mothers with your free love and your social housing, but that's not how we brought you up, Florrie.'

It was too much. I knew Mum was narrow-minded but right now her words

197

were hugely misplaced. I burst into tears.

'Now then. Calm yourself, love.' Dad reached out with a giant paw-like hand and enfolded mine into his. 'I'm sure whatever's happened, and however it's happened, it will all work out.' He gave my hand a comforting squeeze. 'And one thing I *do* know. If my daughter is expecting another man's baby, then things must have been pretty dire in her marriage to have been driven into the arms of someone else.'

I nodded my head gratefully and gave my father a watery smile. Trust him to be the one to see the bigger picture, whilst all Mum worried about was explaining away her newly single daughter's status and the birth of an illegitimate grandchild to neighbours who, it had to be said, were just as pretentious as the likes of Alison and the Darwin Prep mob.

'I've never told either of you what's been going on with my marriage over the years,' I gulped and stared at my tea. 'I'd hoped we'd work things out together. Get through it. Somehow. But we haven't. Not for wont of trying,' I added. 'Basically the whole subject of fathering a child...or not fathering in this case... has been a huge psychological issue for Marcus. He's had one affair after another to make himself feel macho.'

Mum gasped. 'Marcus? Lovely *Marcus*?'

My mother had always thought the sun shone out of her son-in-law's very pert bottom.

'Yes,' I answered, asserting my voice. I

didn't want her being under any illusion that Marcus was the golden boy she'd always thought him to be.

Dad pursed his lips. 'I always did think your husband was a tad too smooth, Florrie. The bloody sod. Why didn't you tell us, love? I could have had a word with him. Put a rocket up his backside and delivered a punch in his no-good goolies for good measure.'

I shrugged. 'Like I said, I thought we'd work things out. And if we had, I didn't want you knowing how he'd behaved and then thinking less of him. But a little while ago I received a letter from his latest mistress. It left me in no doubt our marriage was never going to change. I want you both to know it's been difficult and, at times, pure hell. And it was when things were particularly bad, and I was at my lowest ebb, that I met somebody who...who,' I gulped and reddened, suddenly finding it awkward to be discussing my extra marital love life with my parents, 'well...you understand. I met someone who consoled me. Unfortunately,' my eyes brimmed, 'let's just say I was a poor judge of character. Again.'

'Now you listen to me, Florrie,' Dad said. His voice was no-nonsense and firm. 'You can stay here for as long as you like. And if you need to come home and live here full-time with our little grandbaby, then so be it. I'll be delighted to have the two of you.'

My eyes watered again at Dad saying "the

two of you". My father turned to Mum. 'We'll *both* be delighted. Won't we, Barbara?' his tone left no room for any objection.

Mum sniffed. 'Of course. I just wish I didn't have to tell Beryl and the rest of my rambling group that Florrie is pregnant with another man's child.'

'Bugger Beryl,' my father suddenly roared. His big paw clenched, immediately turning into a meaty fist that slammed against the kitchen table making both Mum and I jump again. 'It's nobody else's business. And if Beryl says otherwise, I'll be having words with her too. Meanwhile if you'll excuse me, I have a phone call to make.' My father pushed back his chair and stood up.

'Who are you ringing?' my mother asked, her expression one of confusion.

'Marcus,' said Dad, his lips disappearing into a thin line. 'I have a few choice things to say to my son-in-law. I'll be in my study, and neither of you are to interrupt.' He turned to Mum and waggled a sausage-like finger. 'And no ear-wigging either.'

Chapter Twenty-Six

I didn't really care that my parents now thought so little of Marcus. They lived on the other side of Sevenoaks, which was far enough away from my more insular village which was full of gossips and wagging tongues. I spent the next few days doing an awful lot of sleeping, and feeding the sudden ravenous appetite that had abruptly developed. My emotions see-sawed from numbness over the ending of my marriage, to weepiness whenever I thought of Luca with that wretched woman, Annabelle Farquhar-Jones.

I distracted myself wherever possible, helping Dad in the garden, pricking out pots of cuttings, and planting frothy flowering foliage in patio tubs. The weather was glorious. Pottering in the garden under a warm spring sun quickly turned my skin to gold, concealing the grey circles under my troubled eyes. On Friday morning, I even joined Mum and her trekking friends and went for a ramble.

'I'd rather you didn't say anything to Beryl and the rest of the girls about...,' Mum paused and looked pained, '...you know.' She jerked her head at my stomach to indicate what she was talking about. We were sitting in her car at the assigned meeting point, the village hall's car park, awaiting the others.

'Mm,' I agreed. 'Goodness only knows what Beryl would think if she found out your only daughter was divorcing her pleasant looking middle-class husband who spends all his free time bedding women and firing blanks.'

'There's no need to be coarse, Florrie,' Mum snapped.

'Well I'm sorry, but I'm getting a bit fed up with constantly being made to feel like some sort of pariah. This isn't the Victorian era we're living in.

'I don't care what *you* think,' Mum's lips pursed like a dog's bottom. 'I just never thought in a million years my daughter would, after just five years of marriage, be in this horrendous predicament. I mean, how on earth are you going to support yourself? We can't help you with finances. Mine and Daddy's pensions aren't huge, you know. And babies are very expensive.' Mum ground to a halt as a succession of cars suddenly pulled up alongside us. The over-sixties female mafia had arrived en-masse, and Beryl was firmly in lead position of *Don*.

'I've already told you that I'm painting and currently earning very well.'

'Not everybody can afford to waste their hard-earned wages on an unknown artist, Florrie. Don't think for one minute you'll make a regular living out of slapping a bit of paint on a canvas.'

'Thank you for the vote of confidence,' I muttered.

'Stop mumbling, child.' Mum undid her seat belt. 'I'd now like to change the subject.' She put up a hand to Beryl and yodelled a greeting through the driver's glass. My mother's meeting-and-greeting smile was now firmly in place on her carefully made up face. Out of the entire group only my mother was in full make-up. She'd rather die than be caught climbing over stiles without wearing her fuchsia-pink lippy. Mum pulled on the driver's door handle and slid out of the car.

'Morning, ladies,' she trilled. 'Lovely weather for today's walk. I hope you don't mind, but my daughter has come along too.'

I clambered out of the passenger side and raised a hand in greeting. 'Hi, everyone.' I smiled at the group of women. There were about a dozen of us in all.

'Morning,' Beryl briskly responded. I wasn't quite sure where Mum fitted in with the pack's pecking order, but was fairly sure it couldn't be too far from the top.

'Florrie, isn't it?' asked a sweet-looking grey-haired lady who was hovering on the outskirts of the group.

'It is,' I nodded gratefully.

'I'm June.' She sidled over to my side as, without further preamble, the group headed off at a cracking pace.

Our footsteps fell rhythmically into time as we strode, like a miniature army on parade, across the road and through a gap in a hedge and into a field full of sheep. Our walking shoes thumpity-thumped against soft rugged turf as we began ascending a steep North Downs hill set against a backdrop of skylark blue.

'I've heard so much about you,' said June keeping up with me. From my peripheral vision I saw Mum flash me a warning look. June matched me pace for pace as we veered towards a track that ominously looked like it would become a vertical ascent. 'You're an artist, aren't you?'

'That's right,' I nodded, puffing a bit now.

Blimey, these ladies might be retired but they could certainly shift. Clearly their leg muscles were in better shape than mine. Things were getting steeper by the moment. I had an overwhelming urge to drop on all floors and scramble, monkey-like, up the gradient. I briefly dared to look over my shoulder. Far below the bucolic scene of a tiny village complete with church and spire momentarily had me wishing I could set up an easel and paint, but then vertigo got the better of me and I was forced to concentrate on the incline ahead.

'Actually, I've seen some of your work,' said June cosily.

'Really?' I gasped. Sweat had started to bead across my brow.

'Me and my hubby were in that new Italian restaurant on the other side of town,' she nodded happily, 'and there were three incredibly striking landscapes on the walls. Your name was underneath. My husband was so impressed, he wanted to buy one. But the proprietor said none of them were for sale. He was a charming man, but very firm about not making a sale. He said my husband would have to get in touch with the artist directly.'

My heart picked up a bit of speed, which was nothing to do with the ridge of chalk trails we were now negotiating.

'What's that, June?' My mother dropped back to walk by our sides.

'I was just saying to your daughter, her paintings are absolutely stunning. Florrie has three landscapes in Serafino's restaurant.'

'O-oh, yes, yes,' my mother nodded her head vigorously, as if she knew all about it – which of course she didn't. 'Florrie's in huge demand. I'm sure she's going to be quite famous one day,' Mum boasted. I inwardly cringed.

'I'm sure you're right,' June agreed. 'After all, you've just done a portrait for Harriet Montgomery, haven't you?'

'How did you know that?' I asked incredulously.

'One of my daughters told me,' June replied. 'In fact, you might even know her.'

I tensed. 'What's her name?'

'Annabelle,' June beamed. 'Annabelle Farquhar-Jones.'

I took a moment before replying, concentrating hard on the abundance of bright yellow buttercups carpeting the rolling hills to our left and right.

'No,' I said lightly. 'I don't think I've met her.'

'Oh, that's a shame,' said June looking crestfallen. 'I'm sure you and she would have so much in common.'

Well we certainly had two men in common.

'Yes,' I gave a tight smile and tried to be gracious. It wasn't June's fault her daughter had tried to poach my husband and then stolen my lover. Correction. Ex-lover.

'Harriet Montgomery?' Mum butted in with a squawk. Her eyes were as round as the late April sun beating down on us. 'You never told me about this, darling.' The last word was said through gritted teeth.

'It's not meant to be common knowledge,' I replied. 'Harriet is keeping everything under wraps, literally, until the May Ball this Saturday. That's when she'll do a proper unveiling with the press in attendance. There might even be a television crew.'

'Are *you* going to this May Ball?' asked Mum.

'Yes. Not that I particularly want to be there,' I added. 'But Marcus and I are meant to be supporting our neighbour more than anything. You remember Alison? She's put a lot of time and effort into the preparations so that Harriet can just get on and play gracious host on the night.' I didn't add that half the time Ali had probably been screwing Martin Murray-Wells on a chaise-longue in Harriet's mansion. I suddenly felt impotent fury at Alison's coercion, and all her tears over her

206

husband's fling when in fact she was no better than Henry with all her lies and deceit.

Careful, Florrie. Careful. No judging. After all, you're no different to Alison yourself now, remember?

'Well,' said Mum quickly recovering her aplomb, 'I had no idea you were such good friends with a movie star of all people. You know, I think I'd like to go to your village's May Ball. It sounds fun.'

I groaned. My mother didn't do "fun". What my mother *did* like to do was socially climb. And what better way than to say she was on shoulder-rubbing terms with a celebrity?

'Yes,' Mum nodded her head vigorously, mind now made up. 'You can introduce me to Harriet Montgomery and get her autograph for me too.'

I sighed. 'She's not very approachable like that.'

'Don't worry, Barbara,' said June smugly. 'My daughter will get you an autograph. Annabelle is great mates with Harriet.'

Mum looked thoroughly put out. In her eyes, someone right at the bottom of the group's pecking order had almost escalated to Top Dog. But nobody was knocking Beryl off her Number One spot. Within seconds the lady in question had fallen into stride with the three of us.

'I couldn't help overhearing your conversation,' said Beryl. 'I think I can speak for everybody here, Florrie. We'd all like to go to Lower Amblegate's May Ball, meet your friend Harriet Montgomery and see your splendid painting of her.'

'Excellent idea, Beryl,' said Mum, clawing herself back into deputy position. 'I was going to suggest the very same thing. Meanwhile,' Mum turned to me, 'your friend Alison will be chuffed to bits that you've sold so many extra tickets.'

'Marvellous,' I said through clenched teeth. 'That's just absolutely...marvellous.'

Chapter Twenty-Seven

'Bill?' my mother shrieked.

We'd barely finished our ramble and said good-bye to Beryl and her gang when Mum had roared home, practically bundling me through the front door in her haste to share "news" with Dad. She stationed herself at the bottom of the stairs and fog-horned in the direction of the landing above.

'Bill! Are you up there?'

'I've only just got myself settled,' Dad's muffled voice floated towards us. He was clearly enthroned in the smallest room.

'Get yourself down here,' Mum ordered.

'Oh for...' There was the sound of muttered oaths followed by the toilet flushing.

'And don't forget to wash your hands,' said Mum bossily.

'I'm not a child, Barbara,' replied Dad with annoyance.

'That's debatable at times,' Mum muttered under her breath. 'Come on, Florrie. Get those grubby trainers off and let's get the kettle on.'

She hastened off to the kitchen leaving me trailing reluctantly behind. I'd never seen my mother so fired up, and all over a wretched fund-raising ball hosted by an ex-movie star with an ego bigger than the Dartford Tunnel.

My father wandered into the kitchen.

'My goodness, Florrie!' he smiled with pleasure. 'That walk must have done you the power of good. You have some smashing roses in your cheeks.'

The "roses" were nothing to do with a brisk walk through the North Kent countryside or gulping in lungfuls of clean fragrant air, but rather everything to do with Mum's rambling group thinking I was Harriet Montgomery's bestie and wanting a slice of whatever action they perceived to be on offer at the May Ball. I felt decidedly annoyed.

Mum plugged the kettle in then turned to face Dad.

'Get your tux out of mothballs, Bill. We're going to a ball.'

Dad stared at my mother as if she'd lost the plot.

'What ball? And don't be daft, Barbara. I've not worn my tux in ten years. Back then I was three stone lighter.'

He reached past Mum for the biscuit barrel languishing next to the kettle. Like a police barrier, Mum's arm shot out instantly barring access.

'You have twenty-four hours to lose the weight.'

Dad looked thoroughly put out. 'I only wanted a couple of custard creams.'

'You're not listening to me,' said Mum shrilly. 'We're going to a posh black-tie event in Lower Amblegate. You need to fit into that tux.'

'Mum,' I sighed. 'It's just a village "do"

organised by some of the mothers whose kids go to Darwin Prep.'

Dad looked horrified. 'I'm not going to some country bumpkin bash.' He slapped away Mum's arm and grabbed the biscuit barrel, hurriedly foraging inside for the forbidden biscuits before she snatched the tin off him. 'I hate those types of occasions. It will be curled-up sandwiches and warm cheap wine. Apart from anything else,' he added, 'I won't know anybody.'

'Actually, Dad, it will most definitely be a champagne-and-lobster affair.'

'Who's side are you on?' he grumbled, but I could tell he'd perked up knowing his favourite food was on the menu.

'Nobody's,' I assured. 'But you'll know me. I'm going.'

'Okay,' said Dad reluctantly, looking a smidgen happier.

'And Marcus,' I added.

'Well he'd better stay away from me,' Dad growled, his eyes suddenly flashing with anger, 'or I'll be telling him his fortune again.'

'What Florrie hasn't told us,' said Mum importantly, 'is that she was recently commissioned by Harriet Montgomery to do a portrait.'

My mother was almost beside herself with happiness. She could dine out on this story with her rambling and bridge friends for a long time to come.

'Harriet Montgomery?' Dad blinked. 'Didn't she used to act?'

'She still does,' Mum replied, her eyes glowing with an inner light. 'I watched her on breakfast telly the other day. She's going to be in Angelina Jolie's new movie!' Dad looked none the wiser. 'So you'd better sort out that tux, Bill, because we're going to that ball even if your belly pops every single button on your frilly shirt.' Mum turned back to the boiling kettle and busied herself making a pot of tea. 'Apparently,' she said over her shoulder, 'Harriet Montgomery paid our Florrie eight thousand pounds for painting her in the buff.'

'Harriet's painted our Florrie in the nude?'

'Really, Bill, do try and keep up,' Mum snapped. 'Harriet Montgomery was the one who was starkers, not our daughter.'

'Thank goodness for that,' Dad muttered.

Mum swung round, her eyes doing a fair impression of a one-armed bandit machine registering jackpot dollar signs.

'*Eight thousand pounds!*' She thumped the porcelain teapot on the kitchen table by way of emphasis. 'It no longer matters that you're a husbandless pregnant woman, Florrie. Not one tiny jot. In fact, it will probably assist your career as an artist. People expect creative types to be a bit ...,' she paused and wrinkled her brow whilst thinking of an appropriate description, 'you know, odd.'

'Gee, thanks, Mum. I'm so glad I finally have your seal of approval,' I said drily as I poured myself a cup of tea.

'Take no notice of your mother, love,' said Dad. 'She's always did have ridiculous airs and graces. I don't know where she gets them from. Bottom line is, I will be delighted to go to this ball, but only because my brilliant and talented daughter is going to be there getting some long overdue recognition as an artist. Well done, our Florrie.'

'Thanks, Dad,' I smiled gratefully. 'And when I've finished this cuppa, I'm going to get my stuff together and go home.'

It had been a lovely break, but it was time to return to Lower Amblegate and face the marital music.

Chapter Twenty-Eight

I returned home to find a very subdued Marcus in the lounge watching the telly. He was munching his way through a plate of toast. It was clear from his expression that he was feeling neglected at having to fend for himself in the culinary department these last few days. When he saw me coming through the front door, he immediately abandoned his make-shift meal. Reaching for the remote control, he switched the television off and stood up.

'Ah, you're home. Have a good break?' he asked tersely, stepping into the hallway.

'Yes, thanks,' I answered politely.

He came towards me. 'You have a nice tan,' he observed. 'Weather good?'

I put down my holdall and kicked off my shoes.

'I haven't been to Spain, Marcus. I've been six miles away. The weather at my parents' house was exactly the same as here.'

'Ah, yes. How are Barbara and Bill? I gather your father is no longer a fan of mine, despite his daughter being knocked up by another man.' His tone was suddenly bitter. 'Rather double standards if you ask me.'

'Well I haven't asked you, so let's just drop the subject, eh?'

Leaving my bag in the hallway, I walked

into the kitchen. Marcus trailed me. Ignoring him, I spotted a small pile of mail addressed to *Mrs Florence Milligan*. The envelopes were stacked neatly on the worktop. Picking them up, I rifled through them.

'I take it they do *know* you're knocked up by another man?' my husband persisted.

'Marcus, I'd rather you didn't talk like that. Yes, my parents are aware of the situation. No, they don't know who the baby's father is. And I don't particularly want them knowing either.'

'Well I'm hardly likely to be the one to tell them who the daddy is,' Marcus said scornfully. 'After all, I don't suppose I shall be seeing them any time soon or at all for that matter. The days of dropping in on my father-in-law and inviting him out for a pint to have respite from your mother's sharp tongue are well and truly over.'

'That's where you're wrong.'

I paused over a large formal brown envelope with the words "Franklin & May Solicitors" stamped in red ink at the top left-hand corner. Marcus had been busy whilst I'd been away.

'You've forgotten about the May Ball. You'll be seeing my parents there, at the event, tomorrow evening.'

'I'm not going,' Marcus quickly replied.

'Suit yourself,' I said with a shrug.

I didn't care whether Marcus attended with me or not. I paused over another envelope. This one was franked by a local estate agent. I ripped it open.

Dear Mr and Mrs Milligan,

Thank you for allowing us to value your property. We would be delighted to market Number 2 The Cul-de-Sac. As discussed, our fees are one per-cent for sole agency and...

I put the letter down and glanced up at Marcus.

'Can I remind you this house is jointly owned? I'd be much obliged if you'd consult me in future before getting estate agents in for valuations behind my back.'

'Too bad,' he said, suddenly bolshie. 'You weren't here. I was.'

But I didn't answer. My hand had paused over another envelope, this one hand-written and addressed solely to me. Out of my peripheral vision I could see Marcus watching me closely.

'Aren't you going to open that one too, Florrie?'

There was a sneer in his voice. I tore my eyes away from the handwriting and looked at Marcus. His mouth was twisted into a caricature of a smile.

'Not right now,' I said lightly. I placed the letter on top of the other correspondence.

'Oh but you should,' Marcus insisted.

I regarded my husband steadily. 'Why?'

'Because it's from Lover Boy,' he said coldly. 'I had him on the doorstep at the start of the week demanding to know where you were.'

'And did you tell him?'

'Yes, I told him all right. I told him to bloody sod off or I'd punch his lights out, and I also put him straight about being a marriage wrecker.'

'Now you're being ridiculous.'

'Ridiculous, eh? I don't think so, Florrie. You might as well know I've filed for divorce. I'm the Petitioner and I've cited Luca Serafino as Co-Respondent. After all, I'm not the one who's gone out and impregnated another man's wife.'

I lost my temper.

'Not for want of trying,' I screamed. 'Don't you dare try and play dirty with me, Marcus, or I'll be presenting a letter to the Court written by one Annabelle Farquhar-Jones and citing her as one of your conquests before you can say "hypocrite".'

'Leave Annabelle out of this.' Marcus's eyes narrowed. 'She's got nothing to do with you.'

'Defending her, are we?' My eyes blazed. 'Well don't bother. She's not interested in you. She's moved on. And now, if you'll excuse me, I'm going to unpack my bag, and I'd like to be left alone.'

I scooped up my mail and stomped back to the hallway. Grabbing my holdall, I thumped up the stairs to the spare room and slammed the door after me. The house walls momentarily reverberated. Flopping down on the bed, I tore open the A4 envelope from Franklin & May Solicitors. As Marcus had forewarned, it was a stapled court document, a petition for divorce.

My eyes flitted across the typed text...*the marriage has irretrievably broken down...on the basis of adultery*...blah blah...I flipped over the page...*my client is seeking...the marriage to be dissolved...Mrs Florence Milligan to pay the costs.*

My mouth pursed. Bloody cheek. Fuming, I tossed the Petition to one side and instead turned to another envelope. It was cream manila, the paper stiff under my trembling fingers. Marcus had wanted me to open it in front of him. I recognised the handwriting immediately. Luca's. Carefully I peeled back the glued-down seal. Inside was a note and cheque.

Darling Florrie

Why did you not meet with me Sunday evening as arranged? I have been calling your mobile without success. Forgive me, but I was so concerned I came to your house in an attempt to see you and make sure all was well. Your husband would not tell me your whereabouts, or explain your sudden disappearance. Please, cara, you must realise I am worried. If you have had a change of heart about me then I promise I will respect that decision, but at least let me know you are okay. I miss you, cara. Meanwhile, here is your payment for the last painting commission.

Please call me, Florrie. Please.

I love you.

Luca

I stared at the letter. It didn't read like the words of a duplicitous man who was embroiled in a torrid affair with another woman. But then again, Marcus had always carried on uttering sweet words of crap to me whilst out shagging his numerous conquests.

Reaching into my handbag, my fingers curled around my mobile phone. I pulled it from the folds and switched it on. It immediately flashed up with a number of voicemails, texts and missed calls. Some were from Daisy and Alison. One was from Harriet. Over one hundred were from Luca. I was astonished that Annabelle hadn't intercepted them and deleted my number from his mobile. I heaved a sigh and tapped out a message to Luca.

Thank you for the cheque. I am fine. Do not worry.

My finger paused over the on-screen keyboard. There was so much I wanted to say. And so much I couldn't. What I really wanted to do was pour my heart out to him in one great gushing splurge...to say how much I loved him...how much I needed him. I also wanted to call him several rude names for being such a smooth, silver-tongued, lying bastard.

Mentally I shook my head. No. I would not engage in texting words of vitriol. I was better than that. I gave my brief text message a final glance and then, feeling utterly miserable, pressed "send". I chucked the phone down on the bed and slumped back against the pillows until I was staring up at the ceiling. It was white, like a blank canvas. Tomorrow was Saturday. A new day and a new month. The first of May. Tomorrow evening was the May Ball. I wondered what both would bring.

Chapter Twenty-Nine

The following morning I was awoken by the doorbell ringing. It rang in staccato bursts invading the dark and safe womb of sleep. I turned over, shifting my backside off the lumpy bit of mattress that was the spare room's bed. With eyes still tightly shut, I groped for the duvet's edge and pulled it up and over my head, determined to ignore this rude wake-up call. It was probably the postman. Marcus could answer the door. But seconds later the ringing became frenzied. Where the heck was my husband? The racket was inducing a headache. There was the sound of the letterbox clattering followed by a familiar fog-horning voice.

'Florrie? I know you're in there. Open up! If you don't come to the door right now I'll keep my finger on the button so the noise drives you totally nuts.'

Huffing in annoyance, I pushed back the covers just as the doorbell began to sound like a fire drill.

'Argh!' I yelped and clapped my hands to my head. 'Stop it.'

But the person on the other side of the door either couldn't hear me or was hell-bent on giving me tinnitus. Sticking my fingers in my ears, I scampered out to the landing and hastened downstairs to the front door. Releasing the catch, I hauled the perpetrator into the house.

221

'Ouch,' Daisy protested, 'you're hurting me.'

I released my neighbour's wrists and massaged my throbbing temples.

'I was in bed!'

Daisy looked astonished. 'But it's nearly noon. You *never* sleep until this time of day. What's wrong with you? Are you ill? And where have you been? I've been trying to get hold of you, and Marcus wouldn't tell me where you'd gone. He was quite weird actually. Very un-Marcus-like. No flirting. No smooth talking. Just tight-lipped and rude. He told me to go away and mind my own business. And then Alison turned up also asking after you, and he told her to sod off. Can you imagine? Marcus was bloody lucky Ali didn't clobber him with her Mulberry handbag.'

My neighbour rattled to a stop and peered at me, her kind face full of concern.

'Florrie, if you don't mind my saying, underneath that lovely honey tan you look like something my cat dragged in.'

'Thanks.'

I gave my temples a final rub and let my arms drop limply to my sides.

'I'm going to make a cup of tea.' I wandered towards the kitchen. 'Want one?'

'Definitely.' Daisy trotted after me. 'Tom's taken the kids to swimming club, so I don't have to rush back.' She pulled out a chair from under the kitchen table and sat down. 'I spotted Marcus when I was waving Tom and the kids off. He told me you were back, but wouldn't be drawn into any conversation. Florrie, what's going on?' Daisy regarded me beadily. 'Mrs Thompson at the corner shop is gleefully spreading all sorts of tittle-tattle. It would seem that Mrs Thompson is great pals with Harriet Montgomery's housekeeper. Together the pair of them are having a field day telling anyone who cares to listen exactly what's going on at The Cul-de-Sac *and* up at Harriet's mansion.'

'Ah.' I paused to pour boiling water into cups and dunk teabags. There was no ritualistic porcelain teapot in this house. 'So do tell. What news is buzzing on the village grapevine?'

I placed the mugs on the table, and then foraged in the larder for biscuits. The only thing available was an out-of-date packet of Jaffa cakes.

Daisy puffed out her cheeks. 'Well, according to rumour, all sorts of wife-swapping is going on. Mrs Thompson is telling anyone who cares to listen that Alison is having an affair with Martin Murray-Wells, and Harriet is having an affair with Henry. I mean, honestly, what a load of tosh,' Daisy scoffed. She paused to slurp noisily at her tea. 'I know Ali likes older men, but Harriet's hubby practically has one foot in the grave.'

'He's seventy-seven,' I protested, 'not one-hundred-and-seven.'

'Whatever,' Daisy flapped a hand dismissively. 'All I know is I wouldn't bonk either Henry or Martin. Not even for a million quid.' Daisy reached for a Jaffa cake.

'As it happens,' I began, but then hesitated.

Daisy pounced. 'What?' She stuffed the entire Jaffa cake into her mouth. 'C'mon,' she said spitting crumbs across the table top, 'tell me!'

Ah, so what. As my mother liked to say, "The truth will always out." I dunked my own Jaffa cake in my tea and then regarded Daisy levelly.

'Those rumours are true.'

Her eyes bulged and she began to choke on her biscuit.

'You what?' she gasped, struggling for breath.

I got up and patted her on the back until she'd properly recovered.

'It's true.'

'How the hell do you know that?' Daisy's face was a picture of incredulity, but her expression rapidly turned to one of annoyance. 'So why didn't you tell me?'

'I didn't think anybody else even knew,' I protested. 'And regarding Alison, I was desperately hoping it was just a one-off.'

'But how did *you* know?'

'I saw them.'

Wh-a-a-a-t?' Daisy looked like she was in danger of choking again.

'It was in the attic rooms. Harriet had turned part of it into a makeshift studio for me. I was up there painting when Martin and Alison burst in. They were welded together at the mouth, half undressed, and far too absorbed with each other to even spot me gaping at them in horror. I didn't know what to do...whether to embarrass them both by making my presence known, or hide and keep schtum. In the end I did the latter.'

'Just a flippin' moment,' said Daisy slapping the table top with one palm. 'Where was Harriet when all this was going on? Surely she had plenty to say about it!'

'She wasn't there. I was working on the painting without her.'

Daisy looked astounded. 'So...so,' she frowned, 'what about Henry and Harriet? How do you know that's true?'

'Because, on another occasion, I was driving away from Harriet's place and spotted Henry. He was in his car, zooming up Harriet's drive. He didn't even register me passing him in the opposite direction. I'll never forget the expression on his face. He looked like a little boy who'd had all his Christmases come at once.'

'Blimey,' Daisy said, slack-jawed. 'So if Mrs Thompson was right about the four of *them*, is the rest of her gossip true?'

I raised an eyebrow. 'Depends what else you've been hearing.'

'Well, apparently you've been having threesomes with Alison and Martin Murray-Wells. The housekeeper said the three of you enjoyed an afternoon bonking in the attic rooms.'

I rolled my eyes. 'Not true.'

'And apparently you're also having a threesome with Henry and Harriet.'

I snorted. 'Again, not true.'

'*And* you're also having a threesome with Marcus and Annabelle Farquhar-Jones.'

'Seriously?'

'You tell me!'

'Rest assured, Daisy, if I ever felt so inclined to try a "ménage à trois", the last person I'd invite to the party would be Annabelle Farquhar-Jones. I cannot stand the woman.'

'My thoughts exactly,' Daisy agreed. 'I was most indignant on your behalf. I told Mrs Thompson you'd only ever do things like that with me, because I was your bestie.'

'Oh my God, you didn't?' I said in horror and dropped my head into my hands. 'You've just inadvertently started a fresh rumour circulating. Everyone will be whispering behind their hands that the two of us are a pair of bi-sexual swingers.'

'I'm not finished yet, there's other chit-chat.'

'More?'

'Yup. Apparently Marcus isn't the father of your baby, and both Henry and Martin Murray-Wells are insisting on taking paternity tests after the birth.'

'I don't believe I'm hearing this.'

'Oh the best is yet to come,' Daisy grinned. 'Finally, Annabelle Farquhar-Jones told me herself that the story involving her having a threesome with you and Marcus was absolute drivel because the only person she's snuggling up to at night is Luca Serafino!'

I straightened up. 'You spoke to Annabelle?'

'Yes. I gate-crashed a coffee morning at Alison's while you were away. Both Harriet and Annabelle were there. Annabelle gave me a smug smile, like a cat that had been after a budgie then landed a pheasant. She said to be sure to tell you Luca was her man.'

'I see.'

'And I retorted you weren't remotely interested in Luca, or anybody else for that matter, because you were happily married to Marcus. Right?'

'Er–'

'And then she laughed in my face and announced you and Marcus were getting divorced.'

'Ah–'

'So I jumped up and called her a lying two-faced bitch and flung my coffee at her.'

Now it was my turn to have wide eyes. 'You didn't.'

Daisy looked sheepish. 'Unfortunately my aim was off.' She gave a bark of laughter. 'Even in the school playground I couldn't throw a ball to save my life. All these years later it turns out I can't throw coffee in a straight line either. It ended up going all over Harriet.'

I gasped. 'No!'

'Yes. She was absolutely livid. Told me

she couldn't afford to be burnt or scarred for life, especially as she was now starring in Angelina Jolie's new film.'

'Oh dear.'

'Stupid pretentious cow. And then Ali chucked me out. Actually, she was horrible to me. She told me to never darken her doorstep again, and that I was no longer welcome at the May Ball.'

I shook my head. 'What a kerfuffle. Listen to me,' I said, reaching across the table and giving Daisy's hand a quick squeeze as my expression became serious. 'It was very sweet of you to stick up for me. You are one of my dearest friends, and I know you meant well. But regrettably, what Annabelle said is ...well...it's actually true.'

Daisy froze. For a moment she simply gawped. When she finally spoke, her voice was little more than a murmur.

'You can't possibly mean that.'

I sighed and helped myself to another Jaffa cake.

'I'm sorry to confirm that Marcus and I are indeed divorcing. Throughout our entire marriage he's been having affairs. It transpires one of his mistresses was Annabelle. Some time ago she wrote to me anonymously. It was an act of whistle blowing. She wanted revenge on Marcus. Firstly, he'd failed to leave me for her. Secondly, she claimed he'd dumped her for somebody else – although Marcus denied that last bit.'

Daisy looked aghast. 'This is ridiculous.

Please tell me you're winding me up.'

'I wish I were. And the reason Annabelle wanted you to tell me Luca was her man is because—' I broke off. 'This isn't easy for me to say, Daisy...'

My neighbour stared at me, her thought processes visibly whirring as she worked out where the conversation was heading.

'Don't tell me,' Daisy hissed, 'because I think I know the answer. Annabelle was warning you off because...you and Luca have had a walk-out.' Suddenly she clapped a hand over her mouth. Her eyes widened. 'Oh my goodness,' she said in a muffled tone, and then dropped her hand back down. 'Is Luca the father of your baby?'

I nodded. 'Yes.'

Daisy sucked on her teeth, for a moment too shocked to speak. Then she rallied.

'Why didn't you confide in me?' she wailed, clearly stricken. 'You've obviously been having a terrible time.'

She jumped up and stumbled towards me, knocking the table in the process so our teas slopped. Stooping, she flung her arms around my shoulders. Suddenly I was enveloped in the sort of hug my mother should have given me. I hugged her back, hard.

'Darling Daisy,' my eyes brimmed at my neighbour's affection and concern. 'I had to put my own house in order before I could confide in you. I've only just told my parents what's been going on.'

'Oh God!' Daisy released me and flopped

back down on her chair. 'How on earth did Barbara take the news? I bet she's been having the vapours worrying about what everybody will think of her married daughter having another man's baby.'

'Spot on. However, she was a smidgen more accepting when she found out I'd painted Harriet in the noddy and been handsomely rewarded for doing so. For Mum, social climbing is all. In her mind celebrity status is only one rung below royalty. Incidentally, Mum will be at the ball this evening. She's dragging Dad and her rambling cronies along too.'

Daisy leant back in her chair, still struggling to make sense of everything.

'Then there's only one thing for it,' she declared. 'If you and your folks are all attending tonight, so am I. Stuff Alison and her warning me off.' She rubbed her hands together gleefully and gave a mischievous grin. 'I suspect any fireworks going off at this ball tonight will be nothing to do with Harriet's pyrotechnics team. And I, for one, am not missing it for the world.'

Chapter Thirty

When Marcus returned home I was in the lounge "doing a Daisy" and still in my pyjamas. Jeremy Kyle's face filled the television screen. I could see exactly why my neighbour liked dossing about in her nightwear watching car-crash telly all day long. My problems faded to insignificance as I listened to a thirty-five-year-old mother tell Jeremy all about her useless husband drinking the dole money so she couldn't feed their seven kids. Worry was etched on her face and she looked two decades older than her years.

As my husband came through the front door, the atmosphere in the house immediately dropped several degrees. Marcus was exuding hostility. Like an invisible cape, it swirled around him, polluting any previous ambience.

Ignoring me, he went straight upstairs to the master bedroom. Above me came the sounds of wardrobe doors and drawers opening and closing. Minutes later Marcus was back in the hallway, a weekender bag at his feet. He cleared his throat. Reluctantly, I tore my eyes away from Jeremy's distressed guest who was now dealing with a toothless mother-in-law threatening to punch her lights out. Looking up at Marcus, I inwardly flinched. His face was full of loathing.

'I'm going away for a few days,' he announced. His voice was clipped, the tone cold. 'I've phoned my boss to let him know I won't be in the office next week. I'm taking some annual leave. While I'm gone I'd appreciate you signing the estate agent's paperwork so this house can be sold as soon as possible. And, if it's not too much trouble,' sarcasm began to creep into his voice, 'please could you get yourself a solicitor first thing Monday morning and reply to my Petition.'

'Of course,' I said keeping my tone carefully neutral. I nodded at the holdall. 'Going anywhere nice?'

'What's it to you?' His jaw jutted belligerently.

'I'm just making polite conversation, Marcus.'

'Polite?' he asked incredulously. 'There's nothing polite about you.'

I sighed. 'Look, we both know this marriage is over. But until everything is signed, sealed and delivered, can't we just rub along together as we always have done and make the best of a difficult situation?'

His lip curled. 'You're very like your mother sometimes, Florrie. Appearances are everything, eh? I'll bet when you were rolling around on Luca Serafino's sheets, you never begged for it like a decent whore would. I can imagine you now, spreading your legs for that tosser and saying,' my husband immediately adopted a falsetto voice, '"Oh, Luca, baby, if it's all right with you and it's not too much trouble, would you fuck me...*please*".'

The air in the house was rapidly turning to poison. I stared at my husband, partly astonished and partly afraid. There was something about him I didn't recognise.

'Marcus,' I said evenly, 'never in our five years of marriage have I insulted you for your extra marital affairs. I've forgiven you over and over and over again. Don't put this on me just because, for the first time, I've allowed myself to be comforted by another man.'

'*Com*forted?' he sneered. 'Is that what you're telling your family and friends? That another man has "comforted" you? Get your head out of those candy-floss clouds, Florrie.'

He began to walk slowly towards me, his whole demeanor becoming one of menace.

'There are lots of words for what you did with Luca Serafino, but not one of them falls into the category of "comforted".'

He was two steps away from me, his face a mask of vitriol. Alarmed, I jumped to my feet and scurried behind the sofa.

'The correct word for what you did, Florrie, was "shag". Good old-fashioned shagging. Banging. Screwing. Fucking.'

'Stop it,' I protested, and moved swiftly to the left as he manoeuvred around the arm of the settee. Although I'd now put some distance between us, it wasn't nearly enough to feel safe.

'"Stop it",' Marcus mimicked. 'I'll bet you

didn't say that to your lover, did you?'

'This is ridiculous,' I protested and hastily shifted to the other end of the sofa as Marcus took two swift paces in my direction. 'Why the hell are you carrying on like this?' My voice sounded feistier than I felt. 'You know perfectly well it's not justified. You've behaved like a male tart. Before now I've even been to our GP to have an STD treated, all thanks to you sleeping around and not using a condom for safe sex!'

'Don't you have the audacity to talk about safe sex to me,' Marcus roared.

Two red marks stained his cheeks, fanning outwards and turning his entire face a blotchy magenta.

'If my wife had practiced what she's now preaching to me, she wouldn't be up the duff with the local rake's bastard seed in her belly.'

He darted towards me, one hand outstretched to grab my wrist. I snatched my hand away in the nick of time and fled across the room to the dining table. It was a lot more solid than the sofa and, thanks to eight sturdy chairs planted around the wooden oblong, afforded more distance between us.

'Marcus,' I gasped, 'this is crazy.'

I grabbed the back of one of the chairs and clung on to it for support. My legs were starting to feel weak. They trembled slightly, as if some invisible transformation was going on under the skin, liquefying the

234

very bones within.

'Only a few days ago you were suggesting we stay together...that you'd raise this baby as your own!'

For a moment his face crumpled, as if he might break down. Seconds later he recovered his composure.

'Yes, Florrie,' he said, his voice chillingly calm. 'I could have so easily done that,' he nodded slowly, eyes not leaving mine as he began to move stealthily around the table towards me again.

I stumbled to the right this time, willing my legs to work as I tried to match him pace for pace and maintain the distance between us. On the table a vase of flowers rocked unsteadily as our bodies bashed against chairs and knocked against the solid framework. A part of me hoped the vase didn't topple. If water slopped it would cause the polish to bloom and spoil the wood. Another part of me wondered how on earth my brain could detach and come up with such a trivial thought when, right now, my husband was stalking me like some sort of modern-day Jack the Ripper after his quarry.

'So what's caused you to now behave like this?' I squeaked before scooting smartly to the left as Marcus whipped round to my right.

'What's changed, Florrie,' my husband enunciated through clenched teeth, 'is that when I suggested being your baby's daddy, I didn't have the entire village knowing my wife had been bedded by Luca Serafino. I didn't have Mrs Thompson taking my money for a newspaper before casually asking, as she doled out my change, how I felt about being a cuckolded husband?'

'I'm sure a know-it-all like Mrs Thompson is more than up to speed with your own playing away,' I retorted.

'Maybe,' he nodded. 'And before you hear it from Mrs Thompson or Annabelle Farquhar-Jones, I might as well confess about my fling with Harriet Montgomery.'

For a moment I was so shocked I couldn't move and only narrowly avoided Marcus's hand swiping after me. We paused at opposite ends of the table, me panting and out of breath, Marcus simply smiling nastily.

'Don't look so gobsmacked, Florrie. Harriet's a complete man-eater.' He tilted his head to one side as if considering. 'Not a bad fuck as it happens. But she carries on in the bedroom like there's a hidden camera. Lots of hair flicking and pouting and diva-like behaviour. It got a bit bloody boring after a while. Not that it matters. She's moved on. Can you believe she's switched her attention to old Hooray Henry next door?' Marcus gave a peculiar high-pitched laugh. 'Harriet clearly likes old men. Just like Alison. Meanwhile,' his eyes glinted with fresh malice, 'I have a wife to punish.'

In a split second Marcus changed his stalking strategy and grabbed a chair.

Yanking it backwards, he climbed onto the padded seat, knocking his head on the ceiling light in the process. The lampshade swung backwards and forwards like a demented metronome. I let out a blood-curdling scream as realisation dawned that Marcus was going to catch me by simply walking across the table top. As he sprang onto the wooden surface the vase of flowers immediately toppled over. It fell sideways with a hollow clunk, dripping upturned stems as rivulets of water ran in all directions.

Darting forward, I snatched up the vase and brandished it like a sword. A few remaining chrysanthemums plopped onto the floor. I cowered and stared up at him.

'Stay away from me, Marcus,' I warned.

My voice was shaking so much I hardly recognised it.

'I hate you, Florrie,' Marcus growled. 'I detest the very sight of you.'

'Then go away and leave me alone,' I whimpered.

He crossed the table expanse in two strides. Shrieking again, I made to dash away but tripped over a chair leg.

'That's it, Florrie,' Marcus jumped down in front of me, 'you scream. Squeal your little head off.'

With one hand he lunged at me, and with the other he caught a fistful of my hair. Suddenly my head was being wrenched back so hard I thought all my vertebrae would pop and break, one by one. Before I knew what was happening, Marcus had pinned me against the wall.

'Is this what you did for Luca, eh? Did you scream?' His breath on my face was hot and sour. 'DID YOU SCREAM FOR LUCA TO FUCK YOU, FLORRIE?' he bellowed.

Spittle flew from his lips, speckling across my cheeks. I tried and failed to shrink into the brickwork as my husband continued to impersonate a madman. For a surreal moment it felt like we'd become characters playing parts in a horror movie. Except this was no play-acting. This was reality. And it was going on right now in our innocuous looking front room.

'Please, Marcus,' I begged.

'Please? PLEASE?'

Suddenly I was being violently shaken and my head banged hard against the wall.

'Did you plead with Luca, you bloody bitch?'

He shook me again causing my head to repeatedly whip backwards and knock against the wall.

'Did you plead for him to stop?'

Suddenly his hands were all over me, pawing at the front of my pyjama top. Buttons snapped and pinged, bouncing off the arches of my bare feet. My pyjama top gaped open exposing my breasts.

'Did Luca do it like this, Florrie?' he hissed, one hand grabbing soft flesh, fingernails digging painfully into a nipple. My head slammed back for the umpteenth time as Marcus's mouth suddenly came down hard on mine.

I couldn't take any more of this. A part of me couldn't believe this was happening. Marcus was panting like a marathon runner, his breath coming in great chuggy gasps as his teeth bit into my bottom lip. One thing was clear. I was about to be raped by my own husband.

Without pausing to think of the consequences, I raised my hand high over Marcus's head and swiftly brought the vase down with all the strength I could muster, praying to God it met its target. There was a stomach-flipping thwack of china against bone. Marcus grunted in both confusion and pain as, without missing a beat, I raised my arm again...and again...and again. I was still smashing the vase against Marcus's skull when he'd long since slumped to the floor, and I only stopped when the vase finally broke in half and I was one-hundred-per-cent sure Marcus wasn't moving.

I leapt backwards, away from his inert form, dropping the remaining shards from my hand as if they were suddenly molten. My lungs were pumping air in and out at a rate never experienced before and my heart felt like it had transformed into a trapped bird bashing under my ribs. As I stood over the inert form of Marcus Milligan, my hands fluttered up to my face and I began to uncontrollably shake.

Dear God. I'd only gone and killed my husband.

Chapter Thirty-One

Standing over my husband's body, I became aware of terrible screaming. Shock was in full play now and it was several moments before I realised the ear-piercing din was coming out of my mouth.

Turning on my heel, I fled. I had to get out of that lounge. As fast as possible. I skidded out into the hallway, almost tripping over Marcus's packed bag. Yanking at the catch on the front door, and without even bothering to lock up, I roared across the landscaped space that separated Daisy's house and mine. In my peripheral vision I was aware that Alison had pulled up and was getting out of her car on the driveway of Number 3. Tiffany was with her. The two of them regarded me in astonishment. I avoided their stares as, whimpering now, my body shivered and shook like a junkie suffering major withdrawal. As I skittered to a stop on Daisy's doorstep, too late I realised my breasts were still on full display.

'Good God, Florrie,' Alison thundered, mouth pursing. 'Cover yourself up! What a disgraceful example you are to Tiffany.' She grabbed hold of her daughter's hand and frog-marched the child towards their own front door. 'Come on, Tiffany. Get inside now. And stop gawping at Florrie. She's clearly lost the plot.'

I attempted pulling my pyjama top

together with one hand whilst thumping on Daisy's front door with the other.

'Help!' I shouted feebly. 'Help me!'

My voice dried to a croak as the last vestiges of strength left my body. My attempts to rouse Daisy were reduced to simply patting her front door.

'Help,' I moaned into the letterbox flap.

Alison had now ushered Tiffany into her house. She turned back to have some final stern words.

'You need help all right, Florrie.' Her tone was furious. 'Daisy and you make a bloody good pair spending your days dressed in bed clothes and, according to Mrs Thompson, your nights in each other's arms. Talk about leading a double life. I hope the pair of you are thoroughly ashamed of yourselves.'

My legs would no longer hold me up and I dropped to my knees on Daisy's outdoor Welcome mat, palms still flailing uselessly against the wood panels. My throat was drier than sandpaper, and my heart had apparently relocated to my oesophagus and was now fluttering like a tiny butterfly determined to choke me. I couldn't speak properly. Even breathing was difficult. A weird light-headedness was making its presence known. Passing out was imminent.

Suddenly Daisy's front door flew open. I fell into her hallway, nose-diving onto the strip of carpet that acted as a runner.

'Florrie!' Daisy exclaimed. 'Dear God in

heaven, whatever's the matter?'

She bent down to help me up. She was wearing a face pack and two towels – one wound around her head like a turban, the other wrapped about her body. She clutched the latter with one hand to maintain her modesty whilst helping me up with the other.

'Help,' I rasped, collapsing against her.

She shut the front door and led me into her lounge, speaking all the while in a low soothing voice, as if she were addressing somebody of limited intelligence.

'It's okay, darling. This way. That's it. Good girl.' She patted the sofa. 'Down you go. There. Well done.'

She held my hand and crouched down in front of me. Bits of her face pack cracked and fell onto the carpet. I'd evidently interrupted her making the most of Tom and the kids being out of the house. My neighbour must have been enjoying some rare pampering time in readiness for the May Ball later this evening.

'Help,' I mouthed, eyes wide and staring.

'Do you need an ambulance, darling?' She peered at me anxiously. 'Is it the baby? Are you bleeding? Take a deep breath, sweetheart. Try and tell me what's happened.'

I nodded, my eyes huge with the horror of everything that had happened, mentally still seeing Marcus sinking to the floor, replaying in my mind the vase continually cracking against his head until both china and skull fractured. The imagery was playing on an endless loop, like some sort of horror film that wouldn't turn off. Except this was no horror film. It was real life. I took a deep shuddering breath.

'Marcus told me he hates me and he went and bought a newspaper but dumped Annabelle for Harriet and packed his bag and Mrs Thompson has told everybody everything and he ran around the sofa and jumped on the table and the wood is all spoilt and I broke the vase and now Marcus is dead and Alison thinks we're lesbians.'

Daisy regarded me silently for a moment. Then she patted my hand again before standing up and going to her drinks cabinet. She returned with a large brandy.

'Drink,' she ordered.

'The baby,' I gasped.

'Drink,' she said again and pressed the glass to my dry lips.

Obediently I took a sip, gagged, swallowed, and took another sip.

Daisy nodded her approval.

'You're in shock,' she declared. 'Now then, how about you try and tell me again what's happened, Florrie, but this time a little slower. From the beginning, please.'

Chapter Thirty-Two

Sipping the brandy I stuttered, shrieked, wailed and wept as I told Daisy how Marcus and I had started a row which had swiftly escalated into nasty words and, finally, a full-blown violent domestic with his attempted rape only halted by my bashing his brains out with a vase of chrysanthemums.

'I've killed him, Daisy,' I sobbed into the brandy glass. 'I'll go to jail for this. I'm a murderer.'

'Calm down, Florrie,' Daisy said sternly. 'Now you listen to me. You are not a murderer. You haven't got it in you.'

'Oh but I am. And I have,' I howled.

'Did you see bits of brain everywhere?'

I paused, studying the mental imagery still playing in my head.

'No,' I shook my head, 'but he's definitely dead. I bludgeoned him, Daisy. I'll go down for this. You'll see.'

'You've probably just knocked him out.'

'I don't think so.'

'Well why don't we go and look?'

I recoiled, shaking my head vehemently. 'I'm not going back into that house. There's a corpse on the floor of my lounge.'

I shuddered violently. I'd never seen a dead body before, much less a living person morph into a dead one right before my very eyes. I could feel hysteria getting a grip again.

'Florrie, stop,' said Daisy firmly. 'Now sit tight, sip your brandy, and don't move. I'll go and check for myself. Where's your house key?'

'I don't have it,' I sobbed. 'I just legged it and left the front door wide open.'

I could imagine a police officer having a field day over this.

"So, Mrs Milligan. After you cold-bloodedly killed Mr Milligan, you fled the scene of the crime? That is so typical of a guilty person. You'll be behind bars for the rest of your life."

I whimpered into my brandy glass. Margaret and Philip would never speak to me again. I'd snuffed out the life force of their only child. And what of my own parents? I could imagine Dad, lowering his posterior onto the loo, shaking out the local newspaper for a peaceful read and then staring in confusion and horror at the headline.

LOCAL ARTIST REDUCES HUSBAND TO A STILL LIFE

And what of Mum? She'd be mortified. I could see her visiting me in prison, her lips so permanently compressed she could no longer physically apply lipstick.

"Beryl and the girls have banned me from the rambling group. I'll never be able to go out in public again. As it was, I was forced to travel here with a coat over my head."

'Florrie?'

Daisy gently touched my arm. I realised

she'd been speaking to me and I'd not taken in a word.

'Do not move,' she instructed.

She stood up and, as she did so, the doorbell exploded into life. I jumped, slopping brandy everywhere.

'That'll be the cops,' I bleated. 'Daisy, help me. I don't want to go to jail and be somebody's bitch.'

From the other side of the door came a voice of authority.

'Open up!'

'That's no police officer,' Daisy grimaced. 'It's Alison.' There was a series of raps on the door punctuated by doorbell rings. 'Just a flippin' moment,' Daisy yelled.

She gave one final reassuring pat on my hand, checked her towel was firmly in place, and padded off to the front door. Moments later Alison was in the front room, berating the pair of us.

'Thanks to you, Florrie, the television crew that should be setting up at Harriet's place are now hanging around outside your house.'

I paled. 'Oh God. Have they come to film me being arrested?'

Alison frowned. 'Arrested? Why? What have you done?'

I gulped. I wasn't sure who was more terrifying. A police officer bearing handcuffs, or Alison. I'd just have to spit it out and tell her straight.

'I've killed Marcus.'

Alison tipped her head to one side and

regarded me as if I were educationally sub-normal.

'What on earth are you burbling on about?'

I took a deep breath. 'My husband is dead.' I was starting to feel oddly calm. Either the brandy was kicking in or I was now in such deep shock I was no longer feeling emotion. Now it was my turn to address Alison in the sort of patronising and enunciated tones she favoured.

'Marcus has departed this world. Passed away. Passed over. Passed on.'

'Passed out, you mean,' Alison tutted. 'Really, Florrie. I know you artistic types can be a bit theatrical, but don't overdo it.'

I glared at her. 'I can quite categorically state that I've killed him. Ah, that's got your attention, hasn't it! I can see it now, you and your bitchy friends discussing me for weeks on end at your exclusive coffee mornings. "Oh yes, she was a murderer, you know. Who would guess something as innocent as a china vase could put somebody in the morgue faster than you can say *coffin*. He died in the front room. Nobody wants to buy Number 2 because of its sordid history. And it's all Florrie Milligan's fault that house prices in The Cul-de-Sac have crashed."'

Alison stuck her hands on her hips and looked extremely put out.

'Well it's nice to know what you truly think of me and my other friends, Florrie.'

'Don't look so pained,' I growled,

warming to my task. 'Only half-an-hour ago you were berating me for wearing my pyjamas in the afternoon and having a fling with Daisy.'

'Eh?' Daisy was looking as stumped as a co-guest on a Jeremy Kyle show.

'Ah, that's what I came over about,' said Alison suddenly looking shamefaced. 'To apologise. If the pair of you want to be partners, then it's not for me to put you both down. I expect you'll both make a splendid couple. Although I'm not so sure your Tom will be thrilled to bits, Daisy.'

'For Gawd's sake, Ali,' Daisy huffed. 'Florrie and I aren't lesbos, so will you put a bleedin' sock in it and stop listening to village gossip. Quite frankly I've a good mind to borrow what's left of Florrie's vase and go and visit Mrs Thompson at her corner shop and knock *her* flamin' brains out.'

I perked up slightly. 'Then we can go to prison together.'

'Florrie, do stop twittering on about being locked up,' Alison said in annoyance. 'I've not long since seen Marcus. He staggered out of your front door holding an ice-pack in one hand and clutching a small suitcase in the other. He gave me your house keys, and when I asked what on earth was going on, he told me to keep my aristocratic nose out of his business and to fuck off.' Alison looked suitably outraged as she handed me the house keys. 'So I can promise you Marcus is still a member of the human race and walking amongst us.'

I stared at Alison, not quite daring to believe what I'd heard.

'Really?' I asked. '*Really*, really?'

'*Really*, *really*, really,' she assured.

The relief was so immense I burst into tears.

'Sorry,' I blubbered, 'but you just don't know how awful it was in there. I'm going to have to move out.' I wiped a hand across my face. 'I'll have to go and live with my parents until the house is sold.' I glanced at Alison, aware she probably wasn't up to speed on my new marital status. 'We're not together any more. That's one piece of village gossip you might have heard and, if so, it's true.'

She nodded, her face sad.

'Yes, I had heard. And I'm quite sure the two of you are aware of the gossip circulating about me and Henry, and also Harriet and Martin.'

Daisy and I both arranged our features into suitably innocent expressions.

'No,' we both said together.

Alison looked surprised, and then pleased.

'Well if you do hear anything, as far as I'm concerned absolutely none of it is true,' she said firmly, 'and I'd be much obliged if you would emphasise that to all the gossips who say otherwise. Sometimes marriages go through a stale patch and need a little shake-up.'

'So all your worries about Henry having a

fling with someone are groundless?' asked Daisy.

Alison's face turned peony pink. She wasn't a good liar.

'Not entirely.' She studied her fingernails for a moment. 'Henry did pursue somebody else, and he *did* buy a bracelet engraved with a gushing message.'

'Oh, Ali,' said Daisy, her voice full of sympathy.

Alison looked up from her nail inspection.

'It's all fine now,' she assured, 'and let's just say the lady in question has had revenge exacted, whether she's aware of it or not.' Her eyes snagged on mine as she added, 'And I'm not talking about tampered portraits.'

'Your secret is safe with us,' I assured.

'Good,' she nodded. 'I'll be at the May Ball tonight with Henry by my side. It's a fund-raising event and I've worked my socks off ensuring all goes to plan on behalf of Darwin Prep. And I'm sorry I banned you from attending, Daisy. It goes without saying that I want you there to support me. Both of you. And preferably dressed,' she eyeballed Daisy's towelling attire and my pyjamas, 'and ideally in sparkling frocks and full make-up.'

'We'll be there, and we won't disappoint you, eh, Florrie?' grinned Daisy.

'Definitely,' I replied, cranking up a weak smile.

I was still trying to come to terms with

Marcus's resurrection. Right now I felt like somebody who'd been on Death Row for the last hour suddenly receiving a pardon.

'Right, that's settled then,' said Alison briskly. 'In which case all I need you to do now, Florrie, is meet and greet the television crew stationed outside your house, and tell them you're an eccentric artist who spends all day in her pyjamas for creative inspiration and that you'd be delighted to see them at Harriet's a little later for the unveiling of her anniversary portrait to Martin.'

I closed my eyes and inhaled deeply. I definitely wasn't a murderer. My soon-to-be-ex-husband was unquestionably alive. I wasn't going to prison. And if I played my cards right, I was just about to have my career as an artist well and truly launched. I stood up like Bambi testing out his limbs for the first time. My legs were still wobbly from spent adrenalin and drama. Carefully I made my way to Daisy's front door.

'Oh, and Florrie?'

Alison called me back. I paused. Turned around.

'Yes?'

'I'm very sorry to say that Annabelle Farquhar-Jones and Marcus are an item.'

I smiled sadly. 'That's one bit of village tittle-tattle that's definitely wrong. Annabelle is seeing Luca Serafino.'

Alison shook her head. 'She was never seeing Luca, Florrie. It's your husband she's been after all along. She only said she was after Luca to make Marcus jealous when he briefly switched his affections,' she paused, 'elsewhere.'

'What? *What!*' my voice was like a cracked whip in a tart's boudoir. 'B-but Marcus was playing away with Harriet.'

'Oh, you knew about that, did you?'

'I only found out this afternoon. How on earth did *you* know?'

'I walked in on them in the attic rooms,' Alison gave me a knowing look. 'Ironic, isn't it? I'd gone up there to...um...see how the portrait was progressing.'

Alison couldn't quite meet my eye. In that moment it was obvious she'd previously sought to spoil Harriet's precious painting prior to eventually defacing it when I was hiding under the chaise-longue.

'I walked in to find the two of them at it. They were rolling around on that pretentious lounger in the back room. I crept away before either of them spotted me. Your husband was only ever a distraction for Harriet. She's actually a very insecure woman who just needs to be adored.'

'You don't say,' I retorted sarcastically.

'The main thing is that Annabelle isn't with Luca. And never was. And if village chatter is to be further believed, you mean much more to Luca Serafino than somebody who paints Florentine landscapes for his restaurant.'

Alison's words were like marbles rattling through a run. As they quick-fired into my brain, it took a second to process their meaning. My God! Luca *hadn't* had a fling with Annabelle! I had no idea why she'd answered his phone that night when I'd been due to meet him, but the main thing for now was grasping that Luca was a free agent.

Feeling my battered heart soaring quicker than a Victoria sponge in a microwave, I tottered outside to greet the television crew.

Chapter Thirty-Three

'There she is!' said a man with a battery pack clipped to the back of his trouser belt. He hastened towards me with one arm extended and thrust a large fluffy microphone at my face. 'Florrie Milligan?'

'Yes?' I smiled nervously as another man, a huge camera hoisted upon one shoulder and trailing thick black flex, began filming.

'Good afternoon. I understand you're the artist chosen exclusively by film star Harriet Montgomery. It's a pleasure to meet you, Florrie.'

'Thank you.'

'How does it feel knowing your portrait is going to be unveiled this evening at the annual May Ball in front of an audience of thousands watching television at home?'

'Amazing and somewhat overwhelming,' I smiled into camera, adopting an expression more sincere than Hughie Green's. 'I can honestly say being commissioned by Ms Montgomery was an eye-opening experience, and I'm really looking forward to attending the May Ball this evening.' In my peripheral vision I could now see that Alison was standing outside Daisy's house and hastily swiping a lipstick across her mouth. 'In fact,' I smiled at the camera lens, 'here is one of the key organisers.'

I turned and waved to Alison who

instantly feigned surprise before hurriedly dropping the lipstick back into her handbag. She smiled graciously and, giving her best Miss World walk, sashayed over to the anchorman.

'A very good afternoon to you,' she beamed. 'I'm Alison Fairweather, project manager for Lower Amblegate's exclusive annual May Ball which is a fund-raiser for worthy causes, predominantly Darwin Preparatory – intake from age three but, parents, please get baby's name on the waiting list as soon as he or she is born.'

Alison was well and truly in her element and glowing brighter than a set of neon highlighter pens. No doubt she was privately thinking some telly exposure might add another ten grand to house prices in The Cul-de-Sac.

'How did you feel, Alison,' asked the anchorman, his smile not wavering for one second, 'when you discovered your husband was having an affair with Miss Montgomery?'

'W-What?' Alison's glow instantly dimmed.

'According to our source, Lower Amblegate is a hotbed of sex and scandal, so much so that it's attracted the attention of scriptwriters. They're looking at making a spin-off of our favourite soap, but more upmarket. Indeed, I believe it's provisionally being called "The Cul-de-Sac".

Alison appeared to have suddenly lost the power of speech. The anchorman turned to me.

'You, Florrie, are to be played by up-and-coming actress Eleanor Coveney.'

'M-Me?' I stuttered. 'Why would scriptwriters be interested in me?'

'Because you are a high-drama individual. Eleanor isn't remotely fazed by portraying you as the victim of a wife beater.'

I blanched. 'My husband doesn't beat me!'

'That's what all victims of domestic violence say. How do you explain staggering out of your house earlier looking visibly distressed? We captured everything on film. Is it true you sought revenge by trying to murder Mr Milligan?'

I opened my mouth to speak but no words came out. Instead Daisy materialised by my side, still dressed in her towels with the remainder of her face pack clinging by thin powdery threads. She looked like an escaped extra from *The Curse of the Mummy*.

'Now you listen to me,' she said furiously to the anchorman. 'I'm personally telling you and your crew to chuff off right now, or I'll snatch that fluffy microphone and shove it right up your–'

'Ah, you must be Daisy?' The anchorman's smile was as fixed as a horse in a bent race. 'I've heard so much about you. A big fan of both Jeremy Kyle and Primark pyjamas, is it true you and Mrs Milligan have been having a secret romance?'

'Bog off!' Daisy screeched.

'That's a yes then,' said the anchorman smugly.

'I have kids, you know,' Daisy raged, 'and I'm not having some smarmy little twerp upsetting my family.'

'But I do believe you and Mrs Milligan are starting your own family,' said the anchorman ignoring her. 'In fact, I have it on good authority that you, Florrie,' he turned his attention back to me, 'visited a sperm donor who operates privately from a restaurant in nearby Sevenoaks. A Mr Luca...' he paused to listen to his earpiece, 'Serafino. It is rumoured that Mr Serafino charges two thousand pounds a time for impregnation services.'

'This is utterly preposterous,' said Alison, regaining her voice. 'Luca is a delightful restaurateur who was, and still is, a client of Florrie's.'

'Surely you mean Florrie is a client of Mr Serafino's? I must say, girls,' the anchorman swivelled back to Daisy and myself and nodded at our attire, 'I absolutely love the outfits. Later on, will you be attending the May Ball dressed like this?'

'I've had enough of your nonsense,' Daisy huffed, 'and I think it's about time you heard the *real* story of what's been going on around here.'

'Please don't,' Alison murmured, 'I've only just got my marriage back on track.'

Daisy ignored her and rattled on like a high-speed train with no brakes.

'The person truly responsible for Lower Amblegate being a hotbed of sex and scandal is a woman by the name of Mrs Thompson. That's Thompson with a "p",' Daisy enunciated to camera. 'She runs the village corner shop which is actually a front for a high-class brothel providing sexual favours and escort services.'

Alison looked like she was going to faint. She flapped a hand at Daisy and made a strangled noise. I just managed to catch the last two words. House prices.

'Mrs Thompson?' asked the anchorman looking puzzled. 'But she was *our* source for what's been going on in The Cul-de-Sac.'

'Smoke and mirrors,' said Daisy smugly. 'Mrs Thompson is a Madame.'

'But she's got to be about sixty years old,' said the anchorman looking perplexed.

'Don't be fooled by the corrugated perm and apple-pie-smile,' Daisy narrowed her eyes. 'This is a woman who, in her heyday, would take a customer behind the counter, happily show off her pear drops and demonstrate the real meaning of a gobstopper. Behind the façade of newspapers and sweets, upstairs there is a boudoir decorated in black-and-silver flocked wallpaper. Trust me, if you ask for a sherbet dab and a Daily Mail, what you're secretly signalling for is an afternoon romp with the village siren, Annabelle Farquhar-Jones...'

'Oh God,' Alison murmured.

'...whereas a barley twist is the discreet code for Marcus Milligan who, incidentally, is Florrie's soon-to-be-ex-husband because he's serviced so many women he's used up all his wild oats and is firing more blanks than Wayne Rooney attempting goals for Manchester United.'

'Are the script writers aware of all this?' said the anchorman turning round to the crew.

'Be sure to tell them,' said Daisy, 'because it will be pure television gold.'

The anchorman pulled out his earpiece and signalled the cameraman to stop filming.

'Let's get over to the corner shop, chaps, and interview Mrs Thompson. Get a runner to hunt down both Marcus Milligan and Annabelle Farquhar-Jones. I want their stories too.'

'Do give them all my love,' Daisy called after the departing crew, 'particularly Annabelle who will do anything for a toffee crisp.'

'I don't believe it,' said Alison sounding like Victor Meldrew as she clutched hold of my arm for support. 'I just can't believe you spouted all that rubbish, Daisy. Although I do think Mrs Thompson is well overdue her come-uppance. And Annabelle deserves all she gets too.'

'I thought she was your good friend,' said Daisy slyly.

'Not anymore,' Alison shook her head

vehemently. 'My true friends,' her voice suddenly caught with emotion, 'are right here, standing by my side.'

'Aw, Ali,' Daisy smiled, 'that's very decent of you.'

Alison inclined her head graciously. 'True friends don't judge each other. Instead they judge other people. Together.'

'Only you could say something like that,' I grinned, 'and totally get away with it.'

'C'mon girls,' said Alison. 'Let's get ready for this wretched May Ball. I have a feeling that after tonight I won't be on Harriet Montgomery's Christmas card list.'

'Who cares,' said Daisy cheerfully. 'As long as we're on each other's, nothing else matters.'

Chapter Thirty-Four

Back home, I hastily set about dollying up for the ball, but every time the house squeaked or creaked I jumped like a kangaroo on energy drinks such was my worry about Marcus unexpectedly returning.

Stepping into the steaming shower, the emersion heater had noisily clanked, causing me to rocket out of the cubicle trailing water and wet footprints in order to lock the bathroom door. My ears strained and analysed every little sound as I wound my hair into a towel-turban and set about quickly applying make-up to my flushed face. I was too scared to use the hair dryer in case the whoosh of hot air drowned out my husband kicking down the front door and materialising in front of me, spitting venom as he launched his own flowery weapon at me – probably something considerably heftier than mine. One of the patio pots came to mind.

Whimpering slightly, I left my hair to dry naturally. It began to kink and curl into a mass of unruly waves. I slid into an old red evening dress I'd bought not long after Marcus and I were first married. I'd last worn it to a dinner dance hosted by his employer. The silky material gathered under the bust, flaring out nicely over my rounding tummy. Grabbing my sequined evening bag, I popped a lipstick inside its velvety depths then rammed my feet into a sparkly pair of stilettoes.

I made my way downstairs. After checking the back door was locked and bolted, I let myself out of the front door but then paused. I hadn't left any lights on. If Marcus *did* return, the last thing I wanted was him appearing out of the shadows and scaring me half to death. I went back inside and strode around the house flipping lights on in every single room. Locking up, I stepped back and surveyed the house. It was lit up like Buckingham Palace. Good. Feeling more reassured, I gathered up my skirts and walked over to Daisy's house.

Tom greeted me at the front door. His eyes gave me the once over.

'Good evening, Florrie. If I may say so, you look both beautiful *and* desirable. I can see exactly why my wife is having an affair with you.' His lips twitched with amusement. 'But if you could refrain from eloping with Daisy, I'd be much obliged.'

I scowled. 'Is that what the rumour mill is now spewing?'

'Actually, no. I made up the bit about eloping. Trying to be funny,' Tom said with a smile and gave a little shrug.

'Ha ha,' I said mirthlessly.

'In fact, it would seem the grapevine has taken a massive U-turn,' Tom whispered conspiratorially. 'If you can believe this, Mrs Thompson is apparently running a brothel over the corner shop. I'm not sure who started that little gem, but the place is crawling with reporters.'

'How bizarre,' I said innocently.

'Seemingly Martin Murray-Wells was there earlier, repeatedly asking for sherbet dabs and a Daily Mail, much to both Mrs Thompson's puzzlement and Harriet Montgomery's fury. The reporters were having a field day. I've heard that Harriet had to physically drag Martin out of the shop *and* she has told the security team handling tonight's event that if Annabelle Farquhar-Jones shows up, she's barred.'

'I don't think there's any chance of that happening,' I grimaced.

'Me neither,' Tom smiled sympathetically. 'I gather Annabelle has done a disappearing act with your husband.'

'Yup,' I said carelessly, 'and she's welcome to him.'

'Brave words, Florrie.'

'And every single one true,' I assured.

'Attagirl,' said Tom with approval. 'Chin up.'

'Oh it is, Tom,' I nodded. 'Look.' I jutted my jaw out. 'Not a wobble in sight.'

'Lucky you,' said Daisy appearing by Tom's side. 'I'm wobbling all over the place. It's a wonder I managed to squeeze myself into this dress,' she lamented. 'It's awfully snug over my tummy. What do you think?'

She gave us both a twirl. She looked like a particularly porky sausage in the grip of a very tight bandage, but even a few too many chocolate bars whilst overdosing on Jeremy Kyle couldn't spoil her pretty face.

'You look beautiful,' I said truthfully.

'A vision,' said Tom leaning forward to kiss his wife full on the mouth.

'Don't smudge my lipstick,' Daisy protested and immediately batted Tom away. 'However, if you play your cards right, it'll be rumpy-pumpy when I'm home.'

'Is that so?' Tom raised his eyebrows. 'In that case, I shall wait up.'

'It's a shame you're not coming to the ball, Tom,' I said.

'On the contrary, I'm very relieved to be staying at home. I don't mind telling you,' he blew out his cheeks, 'I've been absolutely flabbergasted by recent events, not to mention the awful tittle-tattle and downright lies whizzing around the village.'

'Even though some of it is true?' I pointed out.

Tom immediately looked mortified.

'I do apologise, Florrie. Me and my big mouth. I quite forgot about you and the baby and Luca Ser–'

'Tom,' Daisy interrupted, 'stop now before the hole you are digging gets any deeper.'

'Yes, darling,' said Tom dutifully. 'No offence, Florrie.'

'None taken,' I assured before turning to Daisy. 'Come on. Your carriage awaits.' I jingled my car keys at her. I was the driver tonight on account of being pregnant and abstaining from alcohol.

'See you later.' Daisy bobbed forward to

lightly peck her husband on the cheek.

'I'll be keeping the bed warm,' Tom winked at her. 'Have a lovely time, girls.'

'We will,' said Daisy, just as her eldest wandered into the hall.

'You look beautiful, Mummy!'

'Thank you, sweetie,' Daisy smiled nervously. Her body language had shifted and she was suddenly full of anxiety. 'Be good for Daddy.' She turned and pushed past me. 'Quick, Florrie,' she muttered, 'before the kids realise I'm going out.'

'Where are you going?' the eldest wailed. 'Dadd-eee! Where's Mummy going?'

The other two children suddenly appeared in the hallway, stricken that their mother was going out without them. A monumental din immediately broke out.

'Mumm-eee, don't leave us,' said the middle child.

'Come back, Mumm-eee!' cried the youngest and promptly burst into tears.

'Go!' said Tom pushing us firmly out into the night.

The front door slammed shut behind us. From the other side of the wood panels it began to sound like Kim Jong-un had shown up and was launching a number of nuclear missiles.

'Dear God in heaven,' Daisy sighed. 'You have all this to come,' she nodded at my little bump.

'Bring it on,' I grinned as we hitched up our hems and tottered over to my car.

'Where's Alison?' asked Daisy.

'She's already there,' I replied, pressing the button on the key fob and releasing the car's locking mechanism. 'She and Henry went earlier. I think she's staying just long enough to oversee the raffle and do a bit of plugging for Darwin Prep before she and Henry make their excuses.'

'Sometimes,' said Daisy sounding grateful, 'having a mild-mannered unexciting hubby like my Tom is an absolute blessing.' She settled herself in the front passenger seat and reached for the seatbelt. 'I don't know where everybody gets their energy from in order to carry on with all these extra-marital affairs.' She caught my expression as I reversed the car off the drive. 'Present company excluded,' she hastily added.

'Daisy, truly I'm not offended.'

'Good.'

'But you're right,' I nodded. 'It is exhausting. And mentally draining too. Marcus was always tripping over his lies as he tried and failed to keep track of all his illicit bonks.'

'Do you reckon he and Annabelle will make their relationship work?'

'Honestly?' I paused to shift the gears into first. 'I really don't know. I think they are both as devious as each other so it could be a match made in heaven.'

Turning the wheel, I swung the car out of The Cul-de-Sac. The night was only just beginning, but already I couldn't wait for it to be over.

Chapter Thirty-Five

Burly security guards waved Daisy and I into the Montgomery-Murray-Wells' mansion grounds. We were both momentarily brought up short by the stunning vista before us. Alison had certainly delivered a five star job organising the event. The marquee looked regal enough to welcome royalty – which Harriet probably thought herself to be. Vast chandeliers glittered and winked like upside-down snow domes suspended from a ceiling of billowing silken folds. A string quartet was seated in one corner; three men in matching tuxes were melodically scraping bows across violins whilst a woman in a ball gown straddled a huge cello. The musicians' eyes were closed, their faces serene as they savoured the notes of Dvorak's *Serenade for Strings in E Major*. The music floated up into the air, mixing with the excited chatter of guests greeting one another, men shaking hands and giving hearty back claps whilst the women noisily air kissed and exclaimed at each other's evening dresses. Lavish flower arrangements, which wouldn't have looked misplaced at St Paul's Cathedral, were in abundance everywhere, their fragrance mixing with the heady scents of a hundred different perfumes and aftershaves. A champagne bar was set up opposite the quartet. Crystal glasses twinkled under golden light. At the far end of the marquee uniformed staff were busily overseeing the catering which would be served in another hour or so.

'Not bad,' said Daisy nodding her approval. She immediately appropriated two champagne flutes from a passing waiter.

'Not for me,' I reminded her.

'No,' she grinned, 'but definitely for me.' She drained the first flute in seconds and smacked her lips appreciatively. 'Nice plonk.'

'I think Alison would have a fit if she heard you being derogatory about her carefully chosen bubbly.'

'Oooh, look,' Daisy pointed. 'I can see the telly crew through that bit of open flap. Come on. Let's go and have a nosey and see who they're filming.'

We worked our way through the crowd and slid out into the main grounds, instantly espying Harriet talking to camera. She looked every inch the movie star, from her flawlessly made up face to her figure-hugging evening gown and sexy Louboutins. We moved closer to hear what she was saying.

'Despite this event being hosted on my estate, it is very much the local people's event.'

Harriet said the words "local people" with the same inflection as one might say "dog pooh".

'Just because I'm a famous film star, it doesn't mean I'm not a normal person.'

Daisy elbowed me in the ribs. 'Normal my arse,' she chuntered, before tugging on her second flute of champers.

'I'm a firm believer in mixing with everybody, from the milkman and window cleaner–'

'What a patronising cow,' grumbled Daisy.

'–to Brad Pitt and Angelina Jolie, whose next film I'm starring in. And incidentally there is absolutely no truth in me having an affair with Brad or a row with Angie. Despite their marital situation, it's business as usual for the Jolie-Pitts.'

'Pick up those names dah-ling,' said Daisy, a little too loudly.

'I'd also like to thank my team of gardeners for doing a splendid job on the grounds. The topiaries are particularly stunning.'

Daisy nudged me again. 'Just think. That's about a dozen men who can truthfully say they've all had a go at trimming Harriet Montgomery's bush.'

'Ssh!' said a voice in the shadows.

'Is that you, Ali?' I whispered.

'Yes,' said our neighbour stepping forward. 'I shall be talking to camera in a moment saying a few words on behalf of Darwin Prep and, of course, Harriet and Martin.'

'What happened to that earlier interview fiasco outside our houses?' I asked.

269

'All sorted thanks to Martin's legal team.'

'Oh,' Daisy pouted, 'I was looking forward to watching a new soap on the telly.'

'Ah, that's still going ahead,' Ali grimaced, 'but under a different name and in another location. At least we can save our blushes. I, for one, am very grateful.'

'Oh I don't know,' said Daisy airily as she grabbed two more flutes from a second passing waiter, 'I was quite looking forward to seeing Eleanor Coveney playing the part of Florrie.

'She still is,' Ali whispered. 'But Florrie's husband is now not just a wife beater and womaniser, but also a pimp.'

'Well that's not far from the truth,' Daisy sniffed. 'Sorry, sweetheart,' she patted my arm, 'I don't mean to be rude about Marcus, but I always thought the guy was smoother than a bar of wet soap. All that snogging and pretending to grope you every morning when you were seeing him off to work. What was he trying to prove?' she tutted, tossing more champagne down her neck.

'That he was a macho man,' I sighed. 'And take it easy on the drink, Daisy. That's your third on an empty stomach.'

'Yes, Mum,' Daisy giggled.

'Actually, Florrie,' said Alison turning to me, 'as you're here we might as well have the painting unveiled and get that bit out of the way. Then Harriet can have the piece safely stowed away.'

'Before I scribble on it,' Daisy sniggered.

'Er, been there and done that,' Alison muttered. She signalled to one of the TV crew who caught on and nodded. 'Come on, Florrie.' Alison gave me a little prod. 'Follow me.'

'Wait, I'm coming too,' said Daisy tripping over her too-long hem and slopping bubbly over her ample cleavage. 'Ooh, look at my boobies. They're all wet. Better not let Mrs Thompson see. She might expect you to lick it all off, Florrie.'

'Do pipe down, Daisy,' said Alison in exasperation.

Stepping over thick black cable winding across the grass like a monster snake from a cheap horror movie, Harriet caught sight of me standing to one side. She nodded imperceptibly at a crew member and, without missing a beat, moved seamlessly into talking about the painting commission for her wedding anniversary gift to her darling husband Martin.

'Which brings me to mega-talented local artist Florrie Milligan, recently discovered by yours truly–'

'The lying bitch,' Daisy huffed.

'Ssh,' both Alison and a member of the crew hissed at the same time.

'–and immediately snapped up by me of which *this* is the result.'

With a flourish Harriet whipped off the purple velvet drape that had been concealing her portrait on a nearby easel. There were dutiful gasps from a hand-picked group chosen precisely to do just that. A member of the telly crew led me forward to a ripple of polite applause.

'I give you…Florrie Milligan,' said Harriet graciously.

'Over here, Florrie,' said an anchorman.

I was relieved to see it wasn't the same man who'd been at The Cul-de-Sac earlier.

'This is a particularly splendid piece, Florrie,' said my interviewer. 'How did it feel to be painting such a huge celebrity on your very first commission?'

I smiled and opened my mouth to speak but for some strange reason a completely different voice came out.

'She's done a smashing job,' gushed Daisy, 'but I want to set the record straight – as Florrie's agent – she was first commissioned to paint a series of Florentine landscapes which I personally secured on her behalf for the very charming Mr Luca Serafino, proprietor extraordinaire of Serafino's Cucino in Sevenoaks. Which reminds me, Harriet,' Daisy waggled a finger playfully, 'my twenty-per-cent commission still hasn't been paid, but I am willing for you to forego paying me and instead write your cheque out to St Mildred's Primary School of which my beloved husband, Tom Mitchell, is headmaster and toils tirelessly on behalf of his pupils to achieve the best Ofsted report in the area.'

'Oh God,' Alison paled. 'This is meant to be a fund raising and trumpet blowing event for Darwin Prep.'

The anchorman looked confused and turned to Harriet.

'Does your daughter Piper attend St Mildred's?'

'No,' said Harriet glaring at Daisy but then turning back to camera with a big smile, 'but it is absolutely true that St Mildred's is a first-class primary school and Piper has many playmates from the school. Thank you, gentlemen, and I shall look forward to talking to you again later.'

'I suggest,' hissed Alison in my ear, 'that you get Daisy out of Harriet's way *tout de suite*.'

'Consider it done,' I muttered.

Grabbing Daisy's hand I tugged her back inside the marquee, where we promptly cannoned into my parents.

'Florrie, darling,' said Dad beaming in delight.

'Dad!' I exclaimed with pleasure as he squashed me into his barrel chest.

He looked both ill at ease and out of place in his too-tight tuxedo standing like a lonely island amongst Mum's rambling friends, none of whom seemed to have brought their husbands along.

'You look smashing, sweetheart.' He squeezed me hard before greeting Daisy. 'Hello, love,' he kissed my neighbour on both cheeks. 'You're looking fabulous too.'

'You mean flab-ulous,' Daisy grinned ruefully.

Mum immediately removed herself from Beryl's side and glided over to properly

273

greet the two of us.

'Hello, girls. I hope you're not flirting, Bill,' Mum chastised Dad, her mouth pinching into a pencil line of disapproval as she clocked Daisy's billowing décolletage.

'I only have eyes for you, Pumpkin,' said Dad dutifully.

'You look nice, Mum,' I said leaning forward to kiss her on one heavily rouged cheek. 'You remember my neighbour, Daisy?'

'Of course,' Mum smiled thinly. 'And I must say, dear, it's so nice to see you dressed for a change.'

'Oh, I don't know,' said Daisy airily, helping herself to yet another glass of champagne as a smiley waiter stopped by. 'I think wearing clothes is very over-rated. Later on, when the dancing begins, I might strip off and demand Florrie paint me forthwith. It can be called "Daisy's Delights".' She sipped her champagne thoughtfully. 'In fact, my hubby's got a birthday coming up. Consider it your next booking, Florrie.'

Mum looked thoroughly put out. She'd never entirely approved of Daisy, much preferring the airs and graces of Alison instead. Before Mum could give a waspish retort, Harriet strode in, immediately appropriating the musicians' microphone and telling everybody to take their partners for the traditional first May dance before dinner.

'Ooh 'eck,' said Daisy.

She necked the rest of her bubbly then flung her arms around me, nearly bashing me in the eye with her empty champagne flute.

'C'mon, Florrie. Let's give all the chinwags something to tattle about. Let's have a dance together. But no snogging,' she cackled, now clearly the worse for wear. 'Although I've just spotted Mrs Thompson over there, so maybe one passionate lip-lock just for her benefit, eh? But definitely no tongues,' she said giving a shriek of laughter.

But before I could reply, I was tapped on the shoulder and a familiar voice murmured in my ear. Instantly my heart began doing the conga around my ribs. I knew that voice. At night it haunted my dreams.

'Florrie...*cara*...please may I have the pleasure of this dance?'

Chapter Thirty-Six

I turned and, as I did so, felt emotion rise up and catch in my throat. Luca stood before me, impossibly handsome in his tuxedo. He looked like the love interest in a romantic film and surely far more suited to partnering the likes of Harriet Montgomery than me. My arms didn't care about that though. Without consulting my brain, they sprang up like two jack-in-the-boxes and wound around his neck. I was acutely aware of heads turning in our direction, and the air was thick with whispers behind backs of hands.

'That's it, Florrie,' said Daisy approvingly. 'Give 'em all something to talk about. I'll leave you two lovebirds to it. I've just spotted Mrs Thompson. I'm going to ask her to dance. I'll tell her that I like older women and ask if she's recruiting for her boudoir of bondage and bosoms.'

Cackling to herself, Daisy drunkenly staggered off across the marquee. But I barely registered my neighbour's words or mischievous plans. Instead I was mesmerised by Luca's eyes, thickly lashed, pupils dilated, and full of concern.

'Florrie, what's been going on?'

'Not now, Luca. Not here. It's hardly the place to talk properly.'

'Yes,' he insisted, 'Right here, and right now. Never again am I making arrangements to meet up with you at a later date. You've dropped off the planet once. I won't risk it happening a second time.'

'There was a reason for me absenting myself.'

'So tell me. I'm all ears.'

Around us couples were wrapped up in each other, swaying slowly in time to the smoochy music. To my left, Alison and Henry were nose to nose, completely immersed in each other. To my right Harriet and Martin appeared to be fully reconciled. One could almost see the cartoon hearts filling the air around them. Luca and I were barely moving, simply holding each other, staring into one another's eyes.

'So what happened to you?' Luca persisted.

I took a deep breath. 'On the evening we were due to meet, I was at Harriet's and painting her portrait.'

'Yes, I know. And?'

'And the portrait had been vandalised.' I skipped over the details of Alison's handiwork. 'Harriet insisted I stayed until whatever time it took to finish the painting so it could be safely locked away.'

'So why didn't you telephone and let me know that? Why the silence?'

'I *did* telephone you. I called to rearrange our evening, but your phone was answered by Annabelle Farquhar-Jones. Look, Luca. I'm not up for playing double-crossing games. At the time Annabelle categorically stated that you were her man. She told me to stay away.'

Luca's eyebrows disappeared into his hairline. 'You're joking.'

'Hardly. She warned me off. Harriet overheard me on the phone to Annabelle and saw I was visibly upset. She worked out the gist of my conversation and confirmed Annabelle had set her cap at you some time ago.'

'And that's why you disappeared?' Luca asked incredulously.

'Yes! I don't mind telling you I was absolutely dev–'

I suddenly shut up, fearful of giving away my feelings.

Luca pounced. 'Devastated?'

For a moment I didn't answer. Just looked at him silently. His eyes practically pinned me to the canvas marquee wall, demanding an answer.

'Yes,' I said reluctantly. 'I was devastated.'

His face lit up. 'But this is music to my ears, *cara*. It means you *do* care about me.'

'Of course I care about you,' my eyes flashed, 'I–'

I stopped abruptly, mouth hanging open, refusing to finish the sentence.

'Were you...were you about to say that you love me?' Luca asked.

Hastily I shut my mouth. I'd almost uttered those very words. But it wasn't fair to say them. And I had to tell Luca why.

'Listen...there's...there's something you

don't know about me.'

'Actually, Florrie, for a moment *you* listen. Regarding Annabelle. The night she came to my apartment, it was on the pretext of asking me about a recipe of all things. But she was never interested in me. I gather you now know she had been involved with your husband.'

'Yes,' I nodded. 'The rumour mill has been very busy.'

'When I opened my apartment door to her, I had a towel around my hips. I'd just got out of the shower in anticipation of seeing you later. So I made my excuses to Annabelle and briefly left her so I could pull some clothes on. I could only have been gone two or three minutes. When I returned I had no idea you'd telephoned, and certainly didn't suspect Annabelle of intercepting your call. Later, when I realised you weren't going to show up, I telephoned you only to discover your mobile was switched off.'

'Yes, it was. I have since worked out Annabelle was simply rattling my cage whilst also trying to make my husband jealous. You see, Marcus had briefly switched his romantic pursuit to Harriet.'

'So Annabelle's plan worked. Marcus is back with her, right?'

'Yes,' I grimaced. 'They are a couple.'

Luca caught my expression. 'And you care about this? About them being together?'

I bristled. 'Not at all. I don't give two

hoots about them. Give me an orange pen and a piece of paper and I'll draw a sunset right now for the pair of them to walk off into. They totally deserve each other.' I removed one hand from Luca's broad shoulder and made a criss-cross sign over my heart. 'I promise you it is the biggest relief to be out of a desperately unhappy marriage.'

'Good,' Luca murmured. 'Which neatly brings me to a question I have to ask, Florrie.' He looked at me searchingly. 'Is it true you're expecting my baby?'

My body stiffened. 'Look, I agree we need to talk but...but not now...it's not approp–'

'Yes it *is* appropriate, Florrie. If this is true, I have a right to know. And immediately.'

His tone of voice left me in no doubt he wasn't going to take no for an answer. Suddenly the fight went out of me. My whole body sagged.

'It's true,' I whispered. I wanted to lower my eyes. Look away. Instead I fought the urge to do so and held his gaze. His expression changed from one of questioning to pure shock. I took a deep breath. 'I can see you're horrified. *That* is why I didn't want to tell you here.' When Luca didn't reply, I ploughed on. 'But rest assured, it wasn't deliberate on my part. I honestly thought I couldn't have children. And I expect nothing from you at all.' I was starting to gabble. 'You don't have to support me. Or the baby. It's my mess. My responsibility. You have my word.'

Luca's shocked expression changed to one of outrage.

'You're expecting my child, yet you think I'm the sort of man who would walk away?'

'I just don't want you to feel trapped or–'

'Listen to me, *cara*,' Luca's voice softened. 'I *want* to provide for you and the bambino. But more importantly, I want to *be* with you and our child. Do you understand?'

'W-What?' I stammered.

'I'm overjoyed. Delighted! Unless,' his face clouded and for a moment he faltered, 'u-unless you don't want me in your life?'

My eyes brimmed. 'Nothing could be further from the truth,' I whispered.

'Then why are you crying, *cara*?'

I sniffed and wiped a rogue tear that had managed to whizz down one cheek.

'I'm crying because I'm happy.'

The music came to a sudden stop. Harriet walked over to the band's microphone and requested everybody make their way to the banqueting table where dinner would be served. Couples began to peel away, drifting towards the stack of bone china plates and crisp white linen napkins, but Luca and I remained transfixed on the dance floor. Gently, I touched his cheek.

'You're sure about this, Luca? Everybody will say I'm rebounding. Maybe they will say you are too. The gossips will whisper our relationship is a disaster waiting to happen.'

'So let them gossip. I'm not interested in Lower Amblegate's grapevine. Listen to me, Florrie. You are the woman of my dreams. You're beautiful, funny, kind, caring, and you make my heart sing, okay? I want to spend the rest of my life with you and watch our baby grow up. And why stop at one? We'll have a whole brood! But as long as you are in my life, *cara*, that is all that matters. In fact, to prove just how serious I am, Florrie,' Luca grabbed both my hands and furled them tightly within his own, 'will you make me the happiest man on this planet and say that one day you'll be Mrs Serafino?'

I gasped, and then started to laugh. But the laughter, like a kitten chasing a ball of wool, got all tangled up with my diaphragm. The sound turned to a strangled sob and suddenly tears were once again coursing down my cheeks. But before I could give Luca my answer, a shadow fell upon us. We turned, as one, to regard my father blocking out the twinkling chandeliers. His face was cold. His eyes glittered like twin flints of ice. It was as if winter had arrived early.

'Dad?' I said uncertainly.

My father took in my pink eyes and wet cheeks and then furiously rounded on Luca.

'So you're the man this village has been gossiping about?'

'Er, Dad,' I interrupted, 'I'd like you to meet Luca Serafino. He's—'

'I know exactly who he is,' my father roared. 'He's the man who thought you were good enough to take to his bed, but nothing more than a piece of rubbish to discard afterwards.'

All around us, people were starting to turn and look at what was going on. The band had long since stopped playing. With the absence of background music, Dad's rant was audible across the entire marquee.

'Dad, you don't understand,' I said in a low voice.

'Oh I understand all right,' said Dad menacingly. 'But the thing is, Mr Serafino, I need *you* to understand *me*.'

And with that my father raised a balled-up meaty fist and punched Luca hard in the face.

Chapter Thirty-Seven

As Luca fell backwards, somebody screamed loudly. My mother rushed over, swooping like a malignant bird of prey.

'I've a good mind to give you a bashing myself,' she yelled and raised her handbag threateningly. 'You've reduced our daughter's reputation to shreds and should be thoroughly ashamed of yourself.'

'Mum, please!' I implored. 'And Dad, you have got things totally wrong.'

My father's chest was still heaving from the exertion of flattening Luca. As the enormity of my words penetrated his brain, his face began to register horror. The atmosphere in the marquee was suddenly more highly-charged than the national grid. The hum of chatter rose like a swarm of bees, gathering momentum, until the whole marquee was abuzz about what had happened. However, one voice – trained for the stage as well as the big screen – rose above it all.

'What the bloody hell is going on here?'

Harriet. She strode over to our little group, her face flushed with anger. As Luca slowly stood up, one hand gingerly touching a very bloodshot eye, Harriet clicked her fingers. Instantly the security team leapt to attention.

'Nobody ruins my ball,' Harriet hissed furiously.

'Let me in...let me in,' said a shrill voice.'

Suddenly Daisy was ducking under a security guard's elbow. Her eyes were on stalks as she looked from my father's stricken face to Luca's injured one.

'Oooh, Bill,' she said and clapped one hand to her mouth. 'What have you done to Florrie's beau?'

'Florrie's *what*?' Mum gasped. 'This man is no suitor of my daughter's. He's a complete and utter bounder.'

'And that's putting it mildly,' mumbled Dad. He was rocking backwards and forwards on his heels and looking rather pale. He glanced at the security men. 'I don't regret giving this scoundrel a pasting,' his voice quavered. 'He's used and humiliated my beloved daughter. But I know what I did was wrong.' He held out his hands and put his wrists together. 'Go on, son,' he said to one of the guards. 'Arrest me.'

'Just a minute,' said Luca. He pushed my father's hands down. 'Sir, you have the wrong impression of me, and for that I don't blame you for wanting to deck me. I would feel the same way if your accusations were true. But they're not.'

'I don't understand,' said Dad, puzzled.

Luca ploughed on. 'Thanks to whispers, rumours, gossip and scandal, it seems there has been a lot of misunderstanding.'

'Misunderstanding? You mean you're not the man who loved and left my daughter?'

I put my head in my hands and groaned.

'Dad, I thought Luca was in love with another woman. But it turned out the woman in question was actually in love with Marcus.'

In my peripheral vision I caught sight of June, Mum's rambling friend and Annabelle's mother. She was looking very shifty. Clearly June had known all along about her daughter and my husband having an affair. I mentally sighed. It was pointless saying anything to June. It wasn't her fault her daughter was a husband-thieving man-eater.

'To put the record straight,' I continued, 'Luca is not with anybody.'

'I beg to differ,' said Luca.

'I am so confused,' my father wailed.

'*Cara*, would you please introduce me properly to your parents. Let's start this whole thing again.'

'Good idea. Dad...Mum...this is Luca Serafino. Luca...meet Barbara and Bill, my parents.'

'Delighted to meet you both,' said Luca stepping forward, one eyeball still pouring tears like a mini Niagara Fall. He kissed my perplexed mother on both cheeks before grabbing one of my father's hands and pumping it up and down.

'Luca,' I explained to my parents, 'is the father of my unborn baby.' Both my parents stood stock still and slack-jawed. Even my mother for once seemed at a loss for words. 'And Luca is the man I love.' My parents nodded but remained dazed. 'And,' I smiled as a heavenly warmth began to flood my whole being until I felt like I was single-handedly heating the entire marquee, 'he's just asked me to marry him.' My smile became a full-on beam. Life was too short to be miserable. It was also too short not to take risks and find one's own slice of happiness. 'I'd like you both to meet your future son-in-law.'

From the edge of the gawping crowd, a watching Mrs Thompson audibly gasped.

'Well I didn't know that!'

Chapter Thirty-Eight

Two years later

'I have to say, Florrie,' said Daisy, 'you look absolutely amazing.'

I was seated at Daisy's kitchen table, our habitual morning coffees set before us. In the background Jeremy Kyle's audience were roaring their disapproval at the latest guests publicly playing out their private disasters.

'Thanks,' I smiled.

To my right was Alison, sipping Fortnum & Masons' Earl Grey tea that she'd brought over from her own kitchen larder on the grounds of not being able to stomach common supermarket beverages.

'So how's married life?' asked Alison.

'Still wonderful,' I sighed.

After a very messy divorce from Marcus that had seemed to take an eternity, Luca and I had eventually wed. For the last two months I'd been Mrs Florence Serafino. Luca hadn't rushed me though.

'*Cara*, if you would prefer to – as my mama likes to say – *live in sin* then I'm more than happy to do so. You are the only woman for me. I don't care what the future throws at us just so long as you are by my side. I can't wait to go to sleep with you every night, and for your smiling face to be the first thing I see every morning. I want to grow old with you, Florrie. You're my life partner. I don't care whether you ever permit me to make you Mrs Serafino, although,' his face had grown wistful, 'I'd be very happy if you were no longer Mrs Milligan.'

'Darling Luca,' I'd grinned. 'Rest assured that I am definitely not keeping Marcus's name.'

Knowing that Luca wasn't pressuring for marriage had the desired result. I'd awoken one Saturday morning to baby Milo's cries and, as I'd put our treasured little miracle to the breast, had suddenly been overwhelmed with a huge desire for Luca to make an honest woman of me. Corny? Hell, yes. But wonderful too. And a fortnight later we'd been married in our local registry office surrounded by only our immediate family and closest friends with the wedding breakfast taking place at Luca's restaurant. It had been the second happiest day of my life – the first being the day our precious son had burst into the world.

From the playpen in the corner of Daisy's kitchen, toddler Milo was playing happily with Lily, Daisy's fourth child. It had transpired that when Daisy had shoe-horned herself into her gown for the May Ball, her blossoming figure hadn't been entirely due to over-indulging on chocolate bars whilst watching morning television.

'I'm so glad you didn't move from The Cul-de-Sac after the divorce,' said Daisy. 'Who else would I have had to turn to when

Lily's colic became unbearable or the last sleepless night reduced me to a blubbering mess?'

Alison eyeballed Daisy's grubby PJs covered in Lily's dribble and this morning's baby porridge.

'Speaking of which,' said Ali, 'those pyjamas, Daisy, are an utter disgrace.'

'It's called *being a mum*,' said Daisy placidly.

'*I'm* a mum,' said Alison, looking hurt.

Daisy waved a hand dismissively. 'But not a normal mum. I mean, you never have a hair out of place. I don't know how you and the Darwin Prep mums always manage to look so immaculate. It's not natural. Or normal,' Daisy added, helping herself to a biscuit from the plate in the centre of the table. She dunked it in her coffee.

'It's called "grooming",' said Alison, her tone becoming a little frosty as she added, 'along with having some pride in one's appearance.'

'Oooh, ouch,' said Daisy, pretending to duck flying arrows. 'Don't get your tweed skirt in a twist.'

Tweed was Alison's latest favourite attire, ever since Harriet Montgomery and Martin Murray-Wells had sold up and moved out of their mansion, and an eccentric young designer by the name of Jolly Jones had moved in along with her equally eccentric family. Jolly had been an almost overnight hit in the fashion world with her tweed signature designs. She'd recently extended into soft furnishings too. The fabric was no longer seen as a boring garment just for pensioners or crusty school teachers, but instead had become a style sensation. Certainly all the yummy mummies at Darwin Prep didn't entertain you on their coffee rota if you didn't at the very least have a Jolly Jones tweed tote bag hanging off one shoulder whilst on the school run.

'Anyway,' said Alison ignoring Daisy and turning her attention to me, 'I, too, am glad you didn't leave The Cul-de-Sac. Apart from anything else, Jolly wants me to introduce you to her. She's after a family portrait.'

'Wonderful,' I purred.

My painting had gone from strength to strength over the last two years and was so easy to flex around little Milo.

'So does Luca have any regrets about buying out Marcus's share of the house?' asked Daisy.

'None at all,' I shook my head.

'Most men would want a fresh start,' Alison pointed out.

'True,' said Daisy giving her biscuit another dunk and then looking dismayed as it went into soggy overload and sank to the bottom of her mug.

'We kind of feel there *has* been a fresh start. After all, Luca and I gave the whole house an internal face lift,' I pointed out.

'And fabulous it looks too,' Daisy nodded approvingly. She shifted in her seat. A regrouping gesture. 'What do you think about Mrs Thompson's latest bit of gossip?'

Alison and I turned to stare at Daisy. 'What gossip?' we chorused.

'That Jolly Jones is planning on hosting this year's May Ball.'

Alison fidgeted in her seat. Daisy and I looked at her expectantly.

'Is it true?' I asked with wide eyes.

'News certainly travels fast in this village,' said Alison wryly. Then she smiled at us both. 'Yes, it's true. And *moi* is helping to organise it.'

'Blimey,' Daisy sucked on her teeth. 'I'd have thought, after how it all ended at the last May Ball, you'd have been put off for life from organising another event. After all, nobody even wanted a May Ball last year.'

'Actually that's not strictly true,' said Alison. 'It was more to do with the fact that Harriet and Martin had moved out the previous Spring and Jolly was still getting sorted out with settling in and...' Alison paused, choosing her words carefully, '... was busy turning the whole place into a home that ... um ... reflected her taste.'

Daisy pulled a face. 'Mrs Thompson said she knows Jolly's new housekeeper, and that the inside of the mansion is one big tweed nightmare.'

'I've seen it actually,' said Alison looking smug.

'Really?' I asked. 'Go on, spill the style beans. I can see you're dying to.'

'Essentially it's not too bad,' Alison

smiled. 'I love her huge tweed sofas and they work really well with the matching drapes that she's splashed through with a bright red fabric paint.'

'Sounds bloody awful,' Daisy said. 'Like somebody's been murdered and their blood has been sprayed everywhere.'

'Y-e-s,' said Alison nodding, 'there is that too.'

'Well I for one hope there *is* a May Ball,' I said warmly and squeezed Alison's hand. 'I'm sure you'll do a splendid job assisting. Count me and Daisy in. We'll make sure our husbands look after the kiddies and go together, like the last time.'

'Just don't start Mrs Thompson's tongue wagging about the two of you again,' said Alison with a sigh. 'And you'd better keep Daisy away from the champers,' she warned. 'That episode in the toilets was a bit embarrassing for Harriet, not forgetting how the whole thing ended.'

For a moment we fell silent, sipping our drinks and munching on biscuits as pages of memory flipped backwards to Daisy staggering up the steps of the very swish hired portaloos. Not realising that one of the three toilets was occupied, she'd caught sight of her reflection in the long mirror and, champagne goggles firmly in place, had proceeded to loudly tell her reflection just how hot she looked and anyone could give her a sherbet dab any day of the week, whereupon Martin Murray-Wells had lurched up the steps and tried to steer Daisy into one of the cubicles just as Harriet had emerged from another suitably outraged and breathing fire.

'He was a bit of a goer, that husband of Harriet's,' said Daisy in hushed tones. 'He'd got it out you know,' she stage-whispered, 'and it was *this big*.' She held up her hands by way of indicating size. 'No wonder you were sold on him, Ali.'

'I'm sure I don't know what you mean,' said Alison inspecting her fingernails.

'Someone's got amnesia,' said Daisy winking at me.

'Well I don't think any of the villagers have forgotten how the ball ended,' Alison raised her eyebrows at Daisy who had the grace to look embarrassed.

'I've told you a million times I'm sorry for making the marquee collapse.'

'Mm,' said Alison. 'And please remember that next time, no matter how much champagne you guzzle, there must be no more drunken attempts to dance erotically around the marquee's main support pole. Harriet Montgomery had a massive panic attack. She thought Angelina Jolie had succumbed to believing rumours about her and Brad Pitt having a fling and sent someone to assassinate her.'

'I think some things we need to forget,' I pointed out diplomatically.

'That reminds me,' said Alison, 'did you know that Marcus is single again? It transpires Annabelle Farquhar-Jones has upped and left him.'

'Has she?' Daisy looked astonished.

'Who told you that?' I asked curiously.

'Ah,' said Alison, suddenly looking shifty. 'I'm not sure I remember.'

'How convenient,' said Daisy mockingly.

At that moment there was a knock on Daisy's front door.

'I wonder who that can be,' Daisy frowned.

'Probably Trevor, the postman,' I said. 'I'll go.' I scraped my chair back. 'You put the kettle on, Daisy. I'm ready for a refill.'

'Okay,' said Daisy grinning. 'But make sure you behave yourself. No flirting and asking about his big envelopes filling your letterbox, remember?'

'Don't worry,' I giggled. 'I'm totally impervious to Trevor's parcels and packets.'

I made my way into Daisy's hallway. But upon yanking the door open, it wasn't Trevor the postman on the doorstep but instead a young woman. She was eccentrically dressed in a torn t-shirt teamed with oversized tweed trousers. Her tiny waist was cinched with a fuchsia-pink belt bearing the initials JJ.

'Hello,' she said and gave a toothy grin. 'I was looking for Alison. Is this her house?'

I stared at her. I'd never met her before but there was something about the shape of her face, the slant of her eyes and the tilt of her perfect nose that smacked of familiarity.

'Wrong house,' I said, smiling back, 'but you're in luck. Alison is here. We're both having coffee with our mutual neighbour.

Would you like to come in and join us?'

'Thanks,' the woman stepped over the threshold. 'I'm Jolly Jones by the way.' She extended a hand and I immediately shook it.

'Pleased to meet you,' I said pleasantly.

Alison suddenly materialised in the hallway looking disconcerted.

'Jolly,' she said. I could tell Alison was flustered. 'How lovely to see you, but what are you doing here?'

'Sorry to gate crash your coffee morning,' said Jolly throwing up her hands in a gesture of apology, 'but I've been sitting at home having the most godawful time deliberating about which marquee company should be used for dove-tailing the May Ball with one of my fashion shows.' She looked at me by way of explanation. 'I'm a designer and thought it might be rather good fun to get some of the Darwin Prep mums to model.' She looked at me hopefully. 'Are you a DP mum?'

'Er, Florrie is neither a model nor one of us,' said Ali, instantly isolating me from the cliquey group of yummy-mummies at the posh private school.

I rolled my eyes at Alison and turned to Jolly. 'However, I *am* a mum so if you're looking for models with post-baby waists and a challenged bust line then I am happy to volunteer.'

Before Jolly could reply, Daisy appeared in the hallway. 'Hello,' she cooed, holding out a hand which Jolly instantly shook. 'I'm

Daisy. Why are we all having a mothers' meeting in my hallway? Come in and have a coffee with us.'

'But,' Alison protested, distress apparent, 'you're not dressed, Daisy, and I'm sure Jolly doesn't want to be held up.'

Alison gave Daisy a beseeching look, her eyes flicking over Daisy's grubby bedtime attire. Our neighbour's look said it all. "Please, Daisy, this is very embarrassing for me. You're neither dressed nor groomed."

'Oh, honestly, don't mind me,' Jolly laughed. 'I'm only dressed myself because I had to come out and find you, Alison. You see, I stupidly forgot to program your mobile phone number into mine,' she explained, 'so had to hunt you down.'

'Come on through,' said Daisy.

Jolly followed Daisy into the lounge leaving me and a very twitchy Alison to bring up the rear.

'Oooh, Jeremy Kyle!' Jolly exclaimed. 'I love his shows.'

Daisy grinned in delight and linked arms with Jolly.

'I think you're about to be my third bestest friend,' she said as she led Jolly to the table. 'How do you like your coffee?'

'Black, please,' Jolly smiled and pulled out a chair to sit down.

'I must say,' said Daisy as she busied herself getting fresh cups and opening cupboard doors in the hunt for more biscuits, 'there's something about you that seems awfully familiar.'

'Really?' said Jolly looking puzzled.

'I was thinking the same thing,' I said, sliding into a seat beside Jolly.

The television was playing Jeremy Kyle's signature tune which was starting to reach a crescendo. In the studios something dramatic was about to happen.

'It might be,' said Jolly innocently, 'that I seem familiar to you both because you possibly know my older sister? She lives in Lower Amblegate too. Heavens, just think, you could even be really good friends with her,' she clapped her hands together happily, 'how brilliant would that be! Then we can all have coffee mornings together!'

Alison was looking more and more agitated with every passing second.

'Who's your sister?' Daisy and I asked together.

'Annabelle Farquhar-Jones. Does the name ring any bells?'

Daisy almost dropped the kettle and I nearly fell off my chair. In the background Jeremy Kyle was now addressing his audience.

'Today we have someone in the studio who wants to slap a woman who keeps invading her life and causing trouble.'

Jolly glanced at Daisy and then me, oblivious to both our horrified faces and stunned silence.

'You know what?' she beamed happily, 'I've got a feeling we're all going to get on just famously.'

THE END

ALSO BY DEBBIE VIGGIANO

Stockings and Cellulite

As the clock strikes midnight on New Year's Eve, Cassandra Cherry's life takes a turn for the worse when she stumbles upon husband Stevie lying naked, except for his socks, on a coat-strewn bed with a 45-year-old divorcee called Cynthia. Suddenly single, Cass throws herself into the business of getting over Stevie with gusto. Her main problems now are making her nine-year-old twins happy, juggling a new social life with a return to work and avoiding being arrested by an infuriating policeman who always seems to turn up at the most inopportune moments. Then, just when Cass is least prepared, and much to Stevie's chagrin, she crashes head over heels in love with the last person she'd ever expected.

AVAILABLE NOW AS E-BOOK AND PAPERBACK

Flings and Arrows

Steph Garvey has been married to husband Si for twenty-four years. Steph thought they were soulmates. Until recently. Surely one's soulmate shouldn't put Chelsea FC before her? Or boycott caressing her to fondle the remote control? Fed up, Steph uses her Tesco staff discount to buy a laptop. Her friends all talk about Facebook. It's time to get networking.

Si is worried about middle-age spread and money. Being a self-employed plumber isn't easy in recession. He's also aware things aren't right with Steph. But Si has forgotten the art of romance. Although these days Steph prefers cuddling her laptop to him. Then Si's luck changes work wise. A mate invites Si to partner up on a pub refurbishment contract.

Son Tom has finished Sixth Form. Tom knows where he's going regarding a career. He's not quite so sure where he's going regarding women and lurches from one frantic love affair to the next.

Widowed neighbour June adores the Garveys as if her own kin. And although 70, she's still up for romance. June thinks she's struck gold when she meets salsa squeeze Harry. He has a big house and bigger pension – key factors when you've survived a winter using your dog as a hot water bottle. June is vaguely aware that she's attracted the attention of fellow dog walker Arnold, but her eyes are firmly on Harry as "the catch".

But then Cupid's arrow misfires causing madness and mayhem. Steph rekindles a childhood crush with Barry Hastings; Si unwittingly finds himself being seduced by barmaid Dawn; June discovers Harry is more than hot to trot; and Tom's latest strumpet impacts on all of them. Will Cupid's arrow strike again and, more importantly, strike correctly? There's only one way to find out....

AVAILABLE NOW AS E-BOOK AND PAPERBACK

ALSO BY DEBBIE VIGGIANO

Lipstick and Lies

41-year old Cassandra Mackerel is loved up and happily re-married to new husband Jamie. Together they have a ready-made family and a six month old baby boy. Juggling her own children with step-children and an infant is both hectic and stressful, especially with a mother-in-law who seems to have taken up permanent residence.

Cass has a strong support system in good friend and new mum Morag – who is the fourth Mrs Harding with more step-children she can keep up with – and also old neighbour and great pal Nell who has a baby girl.

Rising to the challenge of a second marriage and the emotional baggage that comes with it is tough. The last thing Cass needs is the reappearance of husband Jamie's ex-girlfriend Selina. Gorgeous and glamorous but utterly unstable, Selina once stalked Cass and contrived to split her and Jamie up. And now Selina is engaged to Jamie's business partner, Ethan Fareham. Seemingly it is appalling coincidence.

Cass can't shake the feeling that Selina is up to her old tricks. And she's right to be worried. For if Selina has her way, she'll split Cass and Jamie up permanently. Because this time it's murder...

AVAILABLE NOW AS EBOOK AND PAPERBACK

ALSO BY DEBBIE VIGGIANO

Mixed Emotions

Life is a funny old thing. There are times when we love it, relish every moment and can't get enough of it. Equally there are other times when life is jail sentence. Something comes along that knocks us right off our feet. The sun ceases to shine and our smiles vanish.

As we walk through life we fall in love, out of love, and in love again - sometimes many times over. We forge long and rewarding friendships - but sometimes are betrayed. We deal with tricky ex partners, and picky neighbours. We get pregnant, give birth and some of us experience stillbirth. And just when we think we can't take any more, something happens to cause our hearts to expand with love. We are left feeling warm and fuzzy inside.

Life is full of mixed emotions. And that's what this little book is about.

AVAILABLE NOW AS AN EBOOK AND PAPERBACK.

ALSO BY DEBBIE VIGGIANO

The Ex Factor

WARNING – CHANGE OF GENRE. DIVORCE DRAMA. CONTAINS SWEARING AND UPSET.

Sam Worthington is married to Annie. He's also a loving, hands-on dad to daughter Ruby. Then Sam discovers Annie is having an affair. Even worse, she wants a divorce. Devastated, Sam has to cope not just with the dismantling of a marriage, but being parted from the daughter he adores.

When Annie's new relationship breaks down, she wants Sam back. But Sam has now met teaching student Josie, and re-discovered love. Annie hatches a plan to seduce Sam and win him back, but her plan fails. Sam hadn't counted on his rejection of Annie backfiring on him so spectacularly – for Annie vows to use Ruby to destroy her ex-husband.

Hell hath no fury like a woman scorned. And for Sam Worthington, his journey to hell is just beginning...

AVAILABLE NOW AS AN EBOOK AND PAPERBACK.

ALSO BY DEBBIE VIGGIANO

The Perfect Marriage

Rosie Perfect is trapped in a loveless marriage to feckless husband Dave. Unlike her surname, the marriage is far from perfect but, as she's also mum to baby Luke, leaving isn't an easy option. When best friend Lucy announces she's getting married and having a hen night, Rosie relishes a night off from drudgery. Waking up the following morning in businessman Matt Palmer's bed wasn't on the agenda. But Matt is no marriage wrecker. Or is he?

Suddenly Rosie's life is turned upside down...from not recalling what took place between Matt Palmer's silk sheets to discovering her drunken husband is also a gambling addict...from having her home wagered away in a poker game to being pursued by a murderous loan shark. As Rosie lurches from one crisis to another, life is far from perfect. Indeed, will Rosie Perfect ever get her perfect happy-ever-after?

AVAILABLE NOW AS AN EBOOK AND PAPERBACK.

ALSO BY DEBBIE VIGGIANO

Secrets

Janey Richardson thought she had it all – the perfect job, a drop-dead gorgeous boyfriend, a cutesy cottage love nest, and a socking great diamond on her left hand. But things aren't always as they seem, as Janey is about to discover when an unexpected stranger turns up exposing a secret that shatters her world. There's only one thing for it. She's going to have to disappear.

Garth Davis thought he had it all too, until a secret is revealed that turns his world upside down. He is left with one burning question, but he's going to have to take a five-thousand-mile journey to find the answer.

When Janey's and Garth's worlds collide, a thaw takes place in Janey's heart. But is Garth 'The One'? Making the right decision isn't easy, especially when Janey's own past rushes back to meet her.

AVAILABLE NOW AS AN EBOOK AND PAPERBACK.

ABOUT THE AUTHOR

Prior to turning her attention to writing, Debbie Viggiano was, for more years than she cares to remember, a legal secretary. She lives with her Italian husband, a rescued puppy from Crete, and a very disgruntled cat. Occasionally her children return home from uni bringing her much joy - apart from their gifts of dirty laundry.

Tweet @DebbieViggiano or look her up on Facebook

www.debbieviggiano.com
http://debbieviggiano.blogspot.com/

###

20206028R00175

Printed in Great Britain
by Amazon